CONTENTS

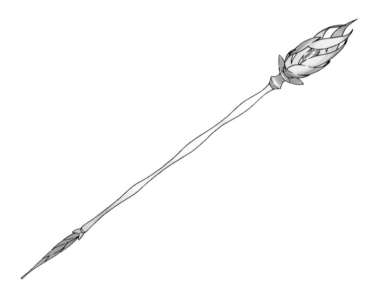

© Kiyotaka Haimura

"—Don't get cocky."

LEVIS:
Mysterious tamer who knows *something* about Aiz.

Silver and crimson blades crossed at breakneck speed.

Impact.

BETE LOGA:
Battle-hungry werewolf warrior.

"So you *can* talk, devious elf."

FILVIS CHALLIA:
Magic swordsman, member of *Dionysus Familia*.

"I, too, have no interest in becoming anything more than a reluctant acquaintance of yours, lowly werewolf."

"Um... We are a party after all, so try to get along..."

LEFIYA VIRIDIS:
An elven mage who deeply admires Aiz.

"So they made it this far..."

OLIVAS ACT:
Fanatic zealot scheming in the Dungeon to obtain a fetus seated within an orb.

VOLUME 3

FUJINO OMORI

ILLUSTRATION BY
KIYOTAKA HAIMURA

CHARACTER DESIGN BY
SUZUHITO YASUDA

NEW YORK

IS IT WRONG TO TRY TO PICK UP GIRLS IN A DUNGEON?
ON THE SIDE: SWORD ORATORIA, Volume 3
FUJINO OMORI

Translation by Andrew Gaippe
Cover art by Kiyotaka Haimura

DUNGEON NI DEAI WO MOTOMERU NO WA MACHIGATTEIRUDAROUKA GAIDEN
SWORD ORATORIA vol. 3
Copyright © 2014 Fujino Omori
Illustration copyright © Kiyotaka Haimura
Original Character Design © Suzuhito Yasuda
All rights reserved.
Original Japanese edition published in 2014 by SB Creative Corp.
This English edition is published by arrangement with SB Creative Corp., Tokyo, in care of Tuttle-Mori Agency, Inc., Tokyo.

English translation © 2017 by Yen Press, LLC

Yen On
1290 Avenue of the Americas
New York, NY 10104

Visit us at yenpress.com
facebook.com/yenpress
twitter.com/yenpress
yenpress.tumblr.com
instagram.com/yenpress

First Yen On Edition: June 2017

Yen On is an imprint of Yen Press, LLC.
The Yen On name and logo are trademarks of Yen Press, LLC.

The publisher is not responsible for websites (or their content) that are not owned by the publisher.

Library of Congress Cataloging-in-Publication Data
Names: Ōmori, Fujino, author. | Haimura, Kiyotaka, 1973– illustrator. | Yasuda, Suzuhito, designer.
Title: Is it wrong to try to pick up girls in a dungeon? on the side: sword oratoria / story by Fujino Omori ; illustration by Kiyotaka Haimura ; orginal design by Suzuhito Yasuda.
Other titles: Danjon ni deai o motomeru no wa machigatteirudarouka gaiden sword oratoria. English.
Description: New York, NY : Yen On, 2016– | Series: Is it wrong to try to pick up girls in a dungeon? on the side: sword oratoria
Identifiers: LCCN 2016023729 | ISBN 9780316315333 (v. 1 : paperback) | ISBN 9780316318167 (v. 2 : paperback) | ISBN 9780316318181 (v. 3 : paperback)
Subjects: | CYAC: Fantasy.
Classification: LCC PZ7.1.O54 Isg 2016 | DDC [Fic]—dc23
LC record available at https://lccn.loc.gov/2016023729

ISBNs: 978-0-316-31818-1 (paperback)
978-0-316-31821-1 (ebook)

1 3 5 7 9 10 8 6 4 2

LSC-C

Printed in the United States of America

VOLUME 3

FUJINO OMORI

ILLUSTRATION BY **KIYOTAKA HAIMURA**
CHARACTER DESIGN BY **SUZUHITO YASUDA**

PROLOGUE
ILL OMEN

Гэта казка іншага сям'і.

благое прадвесце

A cacophony of screams echoed through the air.

The deep, angry roars of men mixed with the high-pitched, shrill shrieks of women. The ferocious howls of countless monsters drowned out the overlapping sounds of metal and leather boots.

They were deep in a labyrinth that looked as if it had gone astray and wound up inside an incredibly massive tree. Patches of moss clung to the walls and hung from the ceiling, emitting blue and green light that made the surroundings seem like a fantastical, unspoiled frontier. Adventurers raced through the wide hallways of the giant tree dungeon with a frantic pace that didn't suit the idyllic scenery around them.

One could tell at a glance that their equipment showed their owners were experienced—the weapons and armor clearly belonged to upper-rank adventurers. Even streaked with the blood of their enemies, the weapons shone brilliant and sharp, as if to display their owners' valor. The armor protecting their bodies was much the same.

They possessed abilities that all lower-class adventurers strived to achieve. But now, they were tripping over themselves in a panicked rout.

These men and women turned tail and ran from an immense swarm of monsters that would make anyone shut their eyes tight in fear.

"Why are there so damn many?!"

"Shut the hell up and run!!"

The advancing monsters were so numerous that their procession filled the entire hallway.

Members of a variety of familias, swept up in this mess together, called for retreat with little regard for who belonged to which party. A token amount of resistance could be heard as blades slashed monster flesh and waves of arrows whistled through the air, but the innumerable multitude snuffed them out. The scarce few adventurers desperately trying to stem the inexorable tide dwindled, as one after the other showed their backs to the enemy and fled.

The horde pushed forward and fell upon a new party that happened to be in the way. Their screams quickly added to the pandemonium.

"What idiot drew all these monsters to us?!"

Deadly hornets, lizardmen, swordstags, dark fungi. One adventurer took a look at the terrifying host of middle-level monsters and snarled with certainty that it was a pass parade—someone had led the beasts to this location and left this party to deal with them. Everyone could tell from the overwhelming number of monsters alone that this could not be a natural occurrence.

The grotesque mass crashed through the halls like an oncoming tidal wave.

"This floor's been so out of whack…! The encounter rate's too damn high!"

This was the Dungeon—twenty-fourth floor, deep in the middle levels.

Even the parties accustomed to roaming this area couldn't contain their fear and screamed at the top of their lungs once they saw a new swarm of monsters approaching from another adjoining hallway. The two swarms merged, forming the world's most terrifying parade. The monsters' ghastly howls tore into the adventurers' ears, deafening them to their own screams in a matter of moments.

"They got my buddy!" "Anybody, please! Help me!!" "Damn it!"

Enveloped by the swarm, doomed adventurers called out to their allies as the myriad claws and fangs tore them apart. The survivors ran, the cries of their companions at their backs. The sight of all the monsters jostling one another to get their jaws closer to their prey drove them to coax every last bit of speed from their legs.

"What the hell's going on?!"

Still yelling in terror, the surviving adventurers barreled up the stairs to a higher floor.

"—Monsters have overrun the twenty-fourth floor!! Do something about it!!"

Wham!

A clenched fist slammed into the reception counter.

A bright, glistening moon lit up the night sky above Orario's northwest block. Guild Headquarters was almost deserted. The only exception was the area around the reception counter, where a human adventurer was aggressively posturing to get his point across.

His angry voice roared through the late-night air in the lobby, startling the receptionist behind the counter, Misha Frot.

"Run-of-the-mill upper-class adventurers can't do jack shit about this! At this rate, the casualties are only going to keep climbing!!"

"I-I'm so sorry!! I'll get on it right away!"

The intensity in the man's eyes made Misha squirm under his gaze.

The hour was quite late. It was her turn to cover the night shift, so most of her coworkers had already gone home. To have an adventurer issue a claim like this—luck was not on Misha's side. It was all she could do to hold back the tears welling up in her eyes.

Her 150-celch frame, dressed in the black uniform that all Guild employees wore on duty, bowed again and again.

"Do you have any idea how many died today and how many of them were my friends?! The hell with issuing quests, that takes too long! Declare a mission! Get exterminators down there NOW!!"

"Y-yes, sir!!"

As soon as the adventurer finished his rage-filled request, he slammed a completed document with the details onto the counter and turned on his heel.

"Uwaa…" Misha, completely exhausted, fell onto the counter as she watched the man shrink into the distance as he left the Guild.

Incapable of working for a while, she picked up the document and made her way to the office behind the reception counter. Asking someone else to cover her post, she went to her desk. After setting down the document, she stepped away, thinking a drink might help settle her nerves.

"Well, that was rough."

"Chiiiief."

Misha was halfway to the break room when one of her bosses came down the hall from the other direction. She looked up at him, unable to keep the tears back any longer. The section chief, a slender chienthrope, sympathetically handed her a wooden cup full of steaming-hot tea.

"Thank you, sir…Waahhh, I was so scared."

"So are the adventurers. They can't keep their cool when their lives are in danger."

Misha held the cup with both hands while she sipped the tea. Shrinking in on herself, she gave her boss a small nod to let him know she understood.

"I couldn't help but overhear, but is this another request for the twenty-fourth floor?"

"Yes. He says there are too many monsters…Do you know anything about it, Chief?"

"The Guild has issued several quests on that floor over the past few days, all of them concerning the unusual amount of monsters appearing on the main route through floor twenty-four…It hasn't even been a day yet, but it seems nothing has been reported on the upper levels."

Misha's superior explained that their information on adventurer activites mostly came from upper-class adventurers who ventured into the lower levels from the town of Rivira on the eighteenth floor.

The developments on the twenty-fourth floor were so recent that the Guild had not yet identified this as a bona-fide irregularity in the Dungeon, nor had they considered them significant.

The chienthrope adjusted his glasses, standing in front of the mostly empty office.

"Judging by the adventurer just now, the situation may be more serious than we previously thought. Yes, we should treat this matter with the utmost care."

"I-I think so, too. Everyone upstairs needs to know as soon as possible."

Misha quickly shuffled her feet back to her desk and pulled out a fresh sheet of paper to draft a document to present her superiors with the information she received from the adventurer. But she suddenly stopped.

"Huh? No way!"

The adventurer's document was nowhere to be found.

"Frot, don't tell me…You lost it?"

"O-of course not!!"

Misha started to panic as her stunned boss watched from beside her desk.

The surface of her workspace was poorly organized, with papers heaped in great mounds. She lifted several stacks and sifted through pile after pile but couldn't locate the wayward document. Even crawling around the desk on all fours to make sure it hadn't fallen off yielded no results.

Her pink hair swayed from side to side as she climbed back to her feet, a bead of sweat rolling down her cheek.

"…Th-this has to be the work of the ghost!! I definitely didn't lose it!"

She did her best to avoid the boss's eyes and tried to pin the blame on something else.

"What did you say…?"

"You mean you don't know, Chief? There's a *ghost* that appears at Guild Headquarters! There has been for a long time!"

Her boss regarded her with extreme suspicion, but Misha pressed on. "It's not just me! I heard other employees working security have seen it! Night after night, the mysterious shadow appears, wearing a pure-black robe that covers it from top to bottom! No matter how many times they try to chase it down, it always leads them to a dead end, disappearing without a trace!"

Misha used her small body to tell the story, wildly flinging her limbs about. "Some people say it might be an adventurer who was killed by a monster but came back to haunt the Guild…! That ghost must've taken the paperwork from my desk…!"

Even her voice adopted an otherworldly tone as the tale continued, but her boss only stared with a doubtful expression. He chose to not play her game and sighed softly.

"You know, your love of gossip has caused problems for Tulle before as well. Find that document—I don't care what you have to do."

"Ch-Chief, I told you I haven't lost it!!" Misha kept insisting that she had put the paper on the center of her desk.

He turned his back and walked toward the office, ignoring the girl chasing after him with a fresh wave of tears running down her face.

Amid the echoes of Misha's voice…

Far away from the office on the opposite side of the deserted hallway, something glided along.

The dark shape warped with a small noise, and a black robe dissolved into being, apparently from thin air.

"……"

The figure completely draped in the dark cloth—Fels—took a look at the piece of paper in his grasp. It was the document submitted by the adventurer that Misha "lost." Having taken the document completely unnoticed, the "ghost" Misha talked about was now reading everything written on it.

"This is…It can't be…"

Twenty-fourth floor, swarms of monsters sighted…As more and more details came to light, an androgynous voice mumbled in the darkness. Before long, the space beneath the hood lapsed into shocked silence.

Fels tucked the piece of paper into the robe's sleeve almost immediately.

"…We must play our hand." With that, the black robe once again dissolved into the shadows.

Ouranos's confidant disappeared into the darkness, and not a soul noticed.

Two days had passed since Udaeus fell at the hands of the Sword Princess.

CHAPTER
1

THE BLACK ROBE'S INVITATION

Гэта казка іншага сям і.

Запрашэнне ад Кокуй

"So that means the addiction period was relatively short?"

"Yep. Loads o' the children who tasted Soma became themselves again after they stopped drinkin' it, ya know?"

A conversation took place on the first floor of a manor as the sun started to slip under the western horizon. Evening had arrived.

What dim light came in from beyond the windows illuminated a half-elf woman and the goddess Loki during an exchange in a spacious room.

A guest had come to the home of *Loki Familia*, Twilight Manor.

Their meeting took place in a reception parlor just off one of the narrow hallways. The many round tables, sofas, and armchairs inside were dyed orange by the warm light. An old music box and several other antiques lined the spacious room, often used by the familia members for chatting.

There were four people present: Aiz, Loki, Riveria, and a half-elf woman.

Their guest was apparently an acquaintance of Riveria's, as well as a Guild employee. To Aiz, her glasses and full-black pantsuit gave her an air of intelligence and, most of all, graceful beauty. Most likely, the half-elf woman was a few years older than Aiz herself. At the moment, she was seated on a comfortable, plump sofa.

The woman seemed to have something to discuss with Aiz's goddess, Loki, while Riveria lent an ear as well. Three of the women were sitting around a table, conversing seriously.

—However, even though Aiz was present, she made no attempt to participate.

I couldn't apologize, again...

She was curled up in a ball atop an armchair and feeling rather downtrodden.

Aiz hid her face halfway behind her knees, which were wrapped in the pure-white one-piece she was wearing. Everything about her body language and demeanor signaled that she was depressed.

She kept replaying the night before in the back of her mind, unable to escape her gloomy state.

After defeating Udaeus on the thirty-seventh floor, Aiz had stumbled upon an adventurer who had collapsed in the Dungeon—the white rabbit she had been hoping to meet again. She had saved the white-haired boy from a Minotaur that she'd failed to catch sooner, and then hurt the same boy soon after at a bar.

Aiz had watched over his unconscious form while protecting him from monsters, all the while thinking she would be able to apologize once and for all. That was her best chance yet...but she had failed.

When the boy had dashed away as quickly as a startled rabbit, the cruel reality struck Aiz hard. It was exactly the same as after the Minotaur incident, like a repeat of that nightmare.

He...ran away from me!

After I finally found him, he did everything he could to get away!

The word *sadness* did not do justice to the anguish Aiz felt. She had hit rock bottom. She had returned to *Loki Familia*'s home with her head hung low. It wasn't surprising that other members of the familia couldn't approach Aiz after seeing her mood, but it was beyond even Tiona and Tione to call out to their friend.

Only Riveria, the person who had accompanied her until she discovered the unconscious boy, could get her to open up. Even then, Aiz's voice had been barely above a whisper.

"...away again."

"What?"

"He...ran away again..."

"...Keh!"

Riveria's shoulders had clearly been shaking. *Thump!* Aiz had pushed her away, thrusting both hands forward.

The high elf's face had flushed redder by the moment, until she couldn't contain the laughter any longer. Stunned, Lefiya and the other elves had watched the normally reserved and noble high elf laugh as though she couldn't help herself. It was likely the first time they had seen such a thing. It was a first for Aiz as well.

This is Riveria's fault...

Sniffle. Although Aiz didn't show it, she was on the verge of tears.

There was no doubt in her mind that the boy had fled because he had woken up with his head in her lap. It was the astonishment of waking up that way with a stranger that had sent the rabbit into a confused panic.

That was it. It has to be. It's all Riveria's fault. Those words repeated over and over inside her heart as Aiz's inner child threw her arms up and tearfully shouted. As she hugged her knees, Aiz regressed into that childlike state and pouted.

...Am I...scary?

*Maybe, just maybe...*Once that train of thought started, there was no stopping it. No matter how desperately she tried to avert her thoughts from that possibility, it always came back.

It was almost frightening how the public famously called her the "War Princess." Perhaps seeing her dismember a Minotaur right before his eyes had made the boy tremble with fear. She couldn't help but feel it was also her fault the boy had been drenched in blood during the incident.

Helplessly recalling the events, Aiz fell into a downward spiral. Deep in her heart, she painted the tragic mental picture of a charming, soft white rabbit fleeing from tiny child Aiz.

—He's...afraid of me!!

Aiz squeezed her body so hard the others could hear her shrivel up.

As the goddess Loki got to her feet, she called, "Hey, Aizuu. How long ya goin' to beat yerself up?"

Her conversation with the guest must have ended because the deity was making her way toward the armchair where Aiz pouted. "Must be serious," muttered Loki as she smiled drily at the girl whose golden hair had somehow lost its luster.

"'Kay, then, how 'bout updatin' yer Status? Haven't done it since ya been back, yeah?"

"…Understood."

It seemed like Loki made the suggestion because she couldn't leave the young girl in such a state, and Aiz sluggishly nodded. She climbed back up and resigned herself to go along with Loki's idea, heart still heavy.

"Heh-heh-heh, it's been too long since I had a chance to enjoy touchin' yer soft skin…!"

"I'll cut you if you do something weird."

"Y-ya serious?"

It had become a reflex for Aiz to warn the goddess about her antics due to her taste in women—but her monotone made Loki shrink back in fright. With that, Aiz left the reception room. She turned and gave Riveria and the half-elf a short bow on her way out.

They didn't have to go far to reach an unoccupied room. Unused tables and chairs filled the space; even spare weapons and items left over from their last expedition had been stuffed in there. That didn't leave much room for the two of them, but Loki managed to pull a seat out from this incredibly cramped makeshift storage unit.

Aiz turned her back to the goddess and took a seat while undoing the buttons on the back of her dress. She exposed her bare back to the deity a moment later.

"So, ain't in the mood fer jokes today, eh, Aizuu? Really, what happened?"

"…It's nothing…I'm…fine."

Loki set to work, spreading her ichor over Aiz's exposed white skin.

Aiz glanced slightly off to the side and dodged the question. Riveria had already had quite the laugh at her expense, and she wasn't in the mood to open up to anyone at the moment.

The boy—Bell…She couldn't get his face out of her head. All the skin from his neck to his ears had turned bright red so fast, it was almost as though he'd come down with an incurable disease. For his expression to change like that, the boy had to be incredibly wary of her...maybe.

Loki's fingers running up and down Aiz's spine might as well have been on the other side of the world. Her gloomy thoughts dragged through her mind.

"...?"

Aiz felt the fingers stop in the middle of her back. Glancing over her shoulder to see what was wrong, she saw Loki was trembling. She was on the verge of asking what the problem was—when the goddess suddenly raised her head and shouted at the top of her lungs.

"AIZUU'S LEVEL SIIIIIIIIIIIIIIIIIIIIIIIIIIIX!!"

Her excitement getting the best of her, Loki let out a great yell. As the goddess's cheers reached the other inhabitants, a confused noise began to rise from every corner of the mansion, as though a landmark had been reached.

As her deity let out a whoop and danced like a child, Aiz turned to face her.

She had been so caught up in thinking about the boy that she could only stare in puzzlement.

Aiz Wallenstein

LEVEL 5

Strength: D 555 -> 564 Defense: D 547 -> 553 Dexterity: A 825 -> 827 Agility: A 822 -> 824 Magic: A 899 -> S 900 Hunter: G Immunity: G Knight: I -> H

"Here ya are! Yer last Level Five Status!"

Loki quickly scribbled down the updated details in Koine onto a sheet of paper and held it out to Aiz with a flick of her wrist.

While all her Basic Abilities were well above average, her Magic stood out from the pack. When adventurers leveled up, their last Status update ordinarily showed Cs or Ds. If they were accomplished, it often settled at Bs. Virtually no one ever achieved the highest S rating, and it was indeed worth celebrating.

Aiz blankly stared at the information on the piece of paper in her hands.

"Would ya look at that! Ye're gettin' an Advanced Ability this time! Ain't that great, Aizuu? You didn't get a siiiingle one when you got to Level Five!"

"...What ability is it?"

"Regen! The one that only Riveria's got! There's nothin' else to choose from, so I can just go ahead an' give it to ya, can't I?!"

The excitement in Loki's voice was palpable. Aiz gazed at her with the same aloof expression before finally nodding her head.

As Aiz gave her goddess the go-ahead to raise her Status, ripples began to intermittently radiate from the center. The cinnabar-red characters—hieroglyphs—undulated in a steady rhythm and silently glowed with a strong light.

The Status awaited Loki's instructions, and she sent her fingers running across it in an instant. The goddess was almost bubbling over with joy at her follower's level-up, but it hadn't sunk in yet for Aiz.

Aiz Wallenstein

LEVEL 6

Strength: I o Defense: I o Dexterity: I o Agility: I o
Magic: I o Hunter: G Immunity: G Knight: H Regen: I

Barely a few moments had passed after her level-up was completed when Aiz looked toward a full-length mirror propped up in the corner of the room. Rather than wait for Loki to translate it for her, Aiz went ahead and peered over her shoulder to read her Status in her reflection. She quickly deciphered the reversed hieroglyphs.

Indeed, her Level had gone up by one, while the accumulated points had been added to her Basic Abilities and the counters reset again. Finally, she spotted the slot that held her new Skill.

The Advanced Ability Regen allowed her Mind to constantly recover. Even without taking an extensive rest, her magic energy would regenerate little by little after expending it. Basically, magic potions were now unnecessary for her as long as she had time. It was so rare an ability that magic users, who burned through Mind during battle, would cry tears of joy upon acquiring it. Aiz didn't know of anyone other than Riveria with the ability.

Most likely, it became available because she had constantly used Airiel over the years.

Her consistent efforts had borne fruit, including her Basic Abilities' performance as well as all the excelia she had accumulated.

"So ya took down Udaeus all by yer lonesome. Doin' that would level up just 'bout anyone."

Loki must not have known about Aiz's "great exploit." If Riveria had not told her directly, then it made sense for Loki not to know. Aiz hadn't been in the mood to talk since she returned.

"You're always so reckless," said Loki as she happily poked Aiz's cheeks. But soon after, she offered genuine praise. "Congratulations, Aiz."

After Aiz put her dress back on, she nodded as she responded with an "…Mhm." Even a stranger could tell her heart wasn't in it.

"…It ain't every day that ya level up, so why the long face?"

Loki tilted her head as she pointed that out. Only then did Aiz notice. She had finally advanced to the next level, but it didn't make her feel much of anything.

Even though it had been her greatest wish to become stronger. Even though she had waited eagerly all this time.

Now, her longing for it wavered. In this moment alone, Aiz had forgotten her obsession with strength.

Why? she thought curiously. But all she could see in the back of her mind was that boy running away from her in a terrified panic.

Her heart ached again.

"...There's somethin' more important to ya now, ain't there, Aiz?"

Loki smiled fondly as she watched the girl's dejected profile. Aiz looked up once at her smiling goddess and contemplated.

...I might not be able to deny it.

Ever since they had met, Aiz felt as though she had been think-ing of that boy every free moment she had. Even now, just coming into contact with him had made her happy one moment and abso-lutely depressed the next.

What's happening? She placed a hand over her beating heart. The question was born not from confusion but an innocent desire to understand.

"—Wha?!"

Loki had been watching Aiz with a happy gleam in her eyes when suddenly her shoulders lurched. "It c-c-can't be! You're love-sick?! Aizuu, is it a man?!"

"...?"

Aiz tilted her head. She had no idea what Loki was saying or why her expression had changed suddenly. Since she couldn't connect the dots, she arrived at the conclusion that this was one of her god-dess's "fits." The womanizing deity often said things Aiz could not understand. Loki's words flowed in one ear and out the other.

So...what do I do now?

Regardless, Aiz was still feeling very down.

Would there come a day when she would be able to properly apologize to the boy?

Aiz turned her back to the goddess, who continued to ramble one-sidedly. The white rabbit's face just before he took off popped back into her mind, and she grew despondent once more.

Word of Aiz reaching Level Six spread throughout *Loki Familia* with such speed that by the next morning, it was all anyone could talk about.

The familia's lower-ranking members were in awe of their captain's achievement, and many of them talked about it until they were blue in the face. Aiz herself was more distant than usual, wearing a blank expression all morning. At breakfast, she responded with as few words as possible and finished before anyone else, wandering off soon after. However, the fact that she was no longer in the dining room did nothing to change the topic of conversation. The lower-ranking members, mostly female, practically talked one another's ears off. Even the men couldn't contain their excitement. The Sword Princess's beauty and strength were fast becoming a greater source of pride for *Loki Familia* than ever before.

On the other hand, those closest to Aiz felt more frustration than anything else. A certain werewolf angrily sank his teeth into a slab of meat and sent Raul flying when the young man came to speak with him. The younger Amazonian twin wailed in frustration, "She's gone ahead without me!" and her older sister wearily told her to hush. Their elf junior stood next to them, her ultramarine eyes trembling as mixed emotions swirled inside her.

The heads of the familia paid little attention to the morning's unending commotion. Instead, they gathered at the general's private quarters, which doubled as his office.

"So then, Aiz is Level Six now, eh?"

"With that as motivation, Tiona and Tione will catch up to her soon, no doubt…One can only hope they do not attempt something as reckless as Aiz did."

"Ha-ha, true. But everyone's morale is through the roof now, and that's a good thing."

The dwarf Gareth, the elf Riveria, and the prum Finn all voiced their respective thoughts.

Loki Familia made their home in a collection of towering spires, with Finn's office located in the northernmost one. The room was lined with bookshelves and a large fireplace in the corner. The prum sat behind his desk, while Riveria situated herself near the wall and Gareth sat on a round wooden stool.

"Looks like y'all need to stay on yer toes. Wouldn't want the senior adventurers to lose face, now would we?"

And there was one more in the room.

The goddess glanced around the room with her vermilion-red eyes with a playful grin on her lips. Ignoring common etiquette, Loki sat on top of Finn's ebony desk, taking in the exasperated reactions of her followers. She wore the smile of the fool, matching the emblem of the trickster that adorned the wall directly behind her.

"Now then, how 'bout gettin' down to business and talkin' 'bout those extra-colorful magic stones? They're causin' quite a ruckus recently, so gimme all the details," Loki instructed, still positioned on the desk in a rather unladylike way.

Just as she said, the purpose of the meeting was to discuss the incidents their familia had found themselves involved in over the past few weeks—specifically to share information about the carnivorous plant monsters. As the events continued to cast larger shadows over Orario, it was becoming more difficult to dismiss them as isolated incidents.

Considering how members of her familia had been directly affected by the sudden appearance of these unusual monsters, Loki started to take them more seriously.

"Magic stones with an intense color…That'd be the new species on floor fifty an' the ones that popped outta the ground at the Monsterphilia—those man-eatin' flowers, yeah?"

"Putting that connection aside for a moment…What happened in the sewers, Loki? You went there with Bete, no?"

Finn followed up Gareth's comment with his question.

Loki leaned back to look over her shoulder at the prum sitting behind her and answered. "Monsters showed up and everythin', but there wasn't even a scrap of a clue. Then this shady god pushed his pain-in-the-butt job on me…"

She went on about the evidence they found in the old network of sewer tunnels, the massive reservoir where the monsters appeared, and then about the encounter with Dionysus, who was following up on his own investigation, as well as the information he had shared.

This journey into the sewers with Bete had transpired ten days ago.

She recounted that, in the end, she broke into the Guild to speak with Ouranos directly.

"Is it wise to believe the Guild is innocent?"

Someone was bringing these new monsters to the surface, including the ones that had turned up at the Monsterphilia. While she could not conceive how this was being done, Riveria questioned if Loki really thought the Guild was completely uninvolved.

"Pretty sure they're hidin' somethin', but I got a feelin' they're not directly connected to this mess…"

She added that it was just a baseless hunch, her divine intuition.

"If Loki thinks so, then it's probably true." The goddess's three subordinates had been with her a long time. The confidence born of that relationship made itself evident as they acknowledged her assessment.

"How was your little jaunt with the others, Finn?"

Now it was Finn and Riveria's turn to share their story—specifically, the murder that had taken place in the eighteenth-floor town of Rivira and the ensuing swarm of carnivorous flowers that had descended on the town.

They had determined that the mastermind behind both incidents was a red-haired female tamer. Her strength was well in the league of top-class adventurers, evident from Hashana's murder and Aiz's defeat. She was also the one who had led the monsters into Rivira.

She had been after an orb containing an eerie "fetus" that a mysterious client had hired Hashana to carry out of the Dungeon.

Gareth stroked his beard. "Makin' monsters mutate, ya say… Kinda hard to believe. That means one o' them orbs made that woman-lookin' monster on the fiftieth floor, too?"

"Most likely, though only Aiz and Lefiya have seen the orb with their own eyes…" Riveria responded.

"That lady tamer's kinda botherin' me. Holdin' her own against Finn an' Riveria at the same time an' barely losin'…? This ain't Freya's Ottar we're dealin' with. Think ya could win if ya gave it your all, Finn?" asked Loki.

"I have no intention of losing…is what I'd like to say, but honestly, she's someone I'd rather avoid fighting one-on-one."

Several of the flower monsters hosting the parasite had mutated into behemoths nearly identical to the spore-producing, corrosive-liquid-spewing, woman-shaped abomination they had encountered on the fiftieth floor. The only information they possessed about the orb was that Hashana had acquired it on the thirtieth floor before being killed.

Loki frowned as she listened to Finn describe the appearance of the attacker. The unknown woman could fight on par with Finn and Riveria, both Level Six. There was a high possibility that the tamer was also one of Orario's elite Level Six adventurers.

Loki mumbled under her breath, wondering about the completely unknown woman and to what familia she belonged.

Riveria broke the heavy silence. "…I heard this from Aiz just the other day, but…" The high elf began by explaining that Aiz had told her this only after defeating Udaeus, then said, "Apparently, the tamer woman referred to that child as 'Aria.'"

Every face in the room became deadly serious.

"Riveria, are you certain?"

"I am. The first time was immediately after she saw Aiz's Airiel. It happened repeatedly after that." Riveria added that the woman had acted as if her search had come to an end.

Loki and Finn closed their mouths, gulping in reaction to the news that "Airiel" had triggered the name "Aria."

—Was Aiz one of the enemy's targets?

Everyone in the room had the same thought.

"...Can't think of anyone other than us who knows 'bout Aiz's past."

"Then how could it be that a stranger knows her mother's name?"

Gareth frowned as Riveria countered his assertion. Finn watched their exchange from the corner of his eye before facing Loki.

"Loki, are any other deities familiar with Aiz's situation?"

"...Ouranos is probably the only one who's noticed."

The three mortals looked sharply at their goddess after hearing that. The Guild was suddenly back on the list of suspects, and their expressions said as much.

Beads of sweat rolled down Loki's face under the pressure of their stares. "Wait, hold up," she said with her hands raised.

They decided to leave coming to a verdict on the Guild's possible involvement for another time.

"But still, she called Aiz 'Aria'...Maybe she confused her for her mother?" Finn thought the mysterious tamer might not know all the details of Aiz's past. "Any thoughts?" He glanced at his allies in turn to see if his guess held any merit.

Riveria had a new question. "...On the other hand, even if the enemy knows who Aiz is, what are they trying to achieve?"

No one had an answer. They had only bits and pieces of information, making it impossible to draw connections between anything. Since they also had Aiz's circumstances to consider, they couldn't afford to rush to conclusions.

Silence descended upon the room.

"The tamer didn't seem to know who we were."

"What do ya mean by that?"

At Gareth's question, Finn turned his attention to Riveria.

"Do you remember, Riveria? What she said when our fight came to a standstill."

"...Ah, I believe so."

Riveria searched her memories of the battle more than ten days ago.

"*First tier...Level Five—no, Six.*"

After holding off Riveria and Finn's tandem attack, the tamer had said that. She was certain.

Judging by that statement, the tamer woman had assessed from their clash that Finn and Riveria were Level Six—and by extension, she had no knowledge of their abilities or identities before exchanging blows.

She had never heard of the two top-class adventurers who were known throughout the city.

"Ahh, I gotcha now. My familia's famous far an' wide, over mountains and seas, around the world. Especially Finn."

"Yes. I'm not trying to brag, but we're household names both inside and outside this city's walls. You'd be hard-pressed to find someone who *didn't* know us."

Loki and Finn nodded.

Information about Orario, often referred to as the "center of the world," quickly traveled all over the globe. The name of a famous adventurer in Orario, especially a Level Six—the highest position with the exception of the "apex"—would be known the world over.

"Braver" Finn Deimne. "Nine Hell" Riveria Ljos Alf. The fact that anyone didn't know their names was unbelievable, especially an adventurer. The explanation that she had no interest in what was going on in the world would have been painfully inadequate.

"Able to bend hordes of monsters to her will and lacking even the most common sense about adventurers...It's as if—"

Finn voiced his train of thought to that point and suddenly stopped.

"As if what?"

"...Nothing. Please forget it."

Riveria pressed him to finish the thought, but Finn shook his head. He said it was nothing more than his imagination and seemed to discard the idea entirely. Sighing lightly to himself, Finn leaned back into his chair.

"...Even with Loki's trip underground, we can't make out anythin' 'bout this enemy."

"True."

The wooden stool creaked as Gareth shifted his weight while Finn nodded in acknowledgment. "Hmmm," mumbled Loki, scratching her chin.

The meeting paused. Some time passed before Finn spoke up.

"...I'd like to hear what Aiz has to say."

He opened one of the drawers in his desk and took out a small handbell.

A large, gaudy bow was tied around its red handle. Finn held the bell in his right hand and gave it a quick shake. *Ding-ding-ding.* The high-pitched metallic sound rang through the air. After a few moments...

Thump, thump, thump, thump, thump!

A crescendo of hurried footsteps approached until they halted in front of the office and the double doors loudly swung open.

"—You called, General?"

Tione stood in the doorframe, her face aglow.

She had given the bell to Finn—rather aggressively—as a way to summon her. The prum wasted no time making his request.

"Would you find Aiz for me? I'd like you to ask Lefiya and your sister for help to bring her here."

"Leave it to me!!"

The four inside the office caught a glimpse of the joy on Tione's face before she rushed off at a dead sprint. The doors were still wide open. Riveria quietly walked over and closed them.

"Ain't that convenient..." muttered Gareth as he eyed the bell with the power to call an Amazonian warrior to Finn's side at any time.

"It can be..." the prum quipped with a dry smile.

"Looks like we got some time to kill before Aiz gets here. How 'bout updatin' me on the next expedition?"

Loki grunted as she hopped off the desk and onto the floor.

The planned departure date for the expedition—*Loki Familia's* next trip into the unexplored Deep Levels of the Dungeon—was already less than two weeks away. Eleven days, to be exact.

No one objected to their goddess's suggestion to discuss the arrangements.

While confirming what equipment to take on the expedition, Finn posed a question to his goddess. "Loki, have terms been reached with Goddess Hephaistos?"

"Ah, right, ya wanted to take smiths with ya this time. Yer all good to go. She wouldn't agree to it unless her kids had first dibs on drop items in the Deep Levels, but she got on board in the end." The goddess made a circle with her thumb and forefinger to signal there was no problem.

On their previous excursion, they had encountered caterpillar monsters that spat acid, and a great deal of their weapons, armor, and spares ended up melting. Although they managed to defeat them in the end, their losses were so great that continuing the expedition was impossible and they were forced to return to the surface.

Finn wanted to use that experience to avoid making the same mistake. His solution was to bring smiths capable of repairing their equipment into the Dungeon as part of the group, though he had needed Loki's help to recruit them from another familia.

Thus he had requested the assistance of *Hephaistos Familia*, the largest group of smiths and artisans.

It went without saying that *Hephaistos Familia's* High Smiths were masters of their craft, but they were also stronger in battle than most high-level adventurers. Should members of that familia agree to accompany them on the expedition, Finn was confident they could take care of themselves even if one or two unforeseen challenges occurred during their journey through the Deep Levels.

"We can use the same weapons the entire time if we have smiths there to repair them...The need for spares all but disappears."

"Yes, and all that free space will be used to carry magic swords. Gareth, how is that coming along?"

"Done. We're all good to go. I made the rounds to different weapon shops in the city an' got us thirty, all top o' the line. Pickin' 'em up today."

The magic swords were a safeguard against the corrosive attacks of the caterpillars, allowing the adventurers to avoid risking their regular equipment in a direct assault. These specialized weapons could produce the same effect as spells, allowing their users to engage enemies at a safe distance.

There was no guarantee they would encounter the caterpillar monsters again this time around, but Finn prepared for the worst. The plan was to equip the lower-ranking members with magic swords and put them to work guarding the base camp.

"Lastly...Durandal weapons must be prepared for our core fighters, apart from Riveria and Aiz."

The only weapon that could stay whole after coming in contact with the acid-spewing monsters during their previous expedition had been Aiz's Desperate, which contained the Durandal trait. Finn wanted every high-level adventurer besides the magic user Riveria to have a Superior weapon that shared this trait.

This was another tactic to counter the new breed of monsters. Finn believed it was impossible to press into uncharted territory if they were unable to slay those strange creatures in close combat.

"Magic swords and Superiors fer everybody...Hee-hee, I knew the cost was gonna be up there, but valis are flyin' right out the door."

Magic swords didn't come cheap, and Superiors were some of the most expensive weapons an adventurer could buy.

Even with Riveria and Aiz taken care of, that still left Finn, Gareth, Bete, Tiona, and Tione. Ordering those five weapons alone would burn through all the profits from the last expedition entirely. If they bought magic swords on top of that, the familia's savings would be in jeopardy.

"Sorry about this, Loki."

"I'm leavin' everythin' up to you, so do what ya feel…Plus, I'm a bit of a gambler, so high stakes are more fun."

One of the perks of being a Dungeon-crawling familia was the "high risk, high reward" nature of the job. The dangers that came with an expedition were part of the thrill for Loki. Finn oversaw all the familia's activities concerning the Dungeon and felt guilty for putting their livelihoods at risk. But his goddess just grinned, laughing off his concern.

"However…the looming presence of that tamer concerns me."

Riveria entered the conversation.

Their mysterious enemy had shown interest in Aiz, which meant her involvement in the expedition could draw unwanted attention.

All the high elf's worries boiled down to a single fact—if their party was ambushed by the tamer and a swarm of hungry plant monsters during the journey, it would be impossible to protect everyone.

"Hmm…The option of canceling this expedition is still on the table."

"Callin' it off now after all this prep? Bete an' Tiona would be groanin' for weeks…"

Immediately after Gareth, Finn added that Aiz had just leveled up as well. The dwarf sighed.

"There's one other thing. We might be able to learn more about the monsters with those colorful magic stones during this expedition."

"Mm-hmm…"

"For now, let's continue with the preparations as planned. Agreed?"

While the origin of the man-eating plants was still a mystery, they knew the caterpillars resided around floor fifty. Even Riveria had to agree that launching an expedition right now would be worth it even if only to collect new information.

Then, just as they'd reached that conclusion, there came a knock at the door.

"General, it's Tione. Is now a good time?"

"Oh? Looks like they're here."

A muffled voice came from the other side, and Finn granted his permission.

The heavy office doors creaked open to reveal Tione, Tiona, and Lefiya.

However, the all-important Aiz wasn't among them.

"Eh? Where'd Aizuu get to?"

"Well, um..."

Tiona broke off eye contact as she started to answer Loki's question.

The three girls had searched the manor top to bottom, but guilt still shadowed their expressions.

It wasn't until Lefiya spoke for the three of them that the truth came out.

"From what we can tell, she went to the Dungeon...alone."

"......"

The young elf sounded extremely apologetic after bringing the heavy silence to an end. Finn and the other leaders stayed quiet.

After sharing a few glances, the four of them let out a long sigh.

"But we just got home after spending all that time in the Dungeon..."

"She seemed kinda down in the dumps since we got back. Maybe she went to cheer herself up?"

Less than a day had passed since Aiz defeated Udaeus and returned from her long sojourn in the Dungeon.

Riveria looked at the floor, clearly disappointed by the news. Gareth was tired of hearing the same thing over and over. Finn smiled wanly, knowing there was nothing they could do.

"It might just be because of what we were talking about, but I'm a little worried."

"Ye're worryin' 'bout nothin'...She's Level Six now."

"Even if we did pursue her, there's no guarantee we'll be able to find her in the vast Dungeon. This is Aiz we are talking about. She has no qualms about going to the middle levels on her own…I cannot believe that girl."

The tamer was still on everyone's minds due to their earlier conversation. They were well aware they were especially on edge right now, but even so, the leaders were slightly worried about her.

"Well, if y'all are gettin' bent out of shape, Bete could track her down pretty easily. He was plannin' on goin' to the Dungeon an' hates losin' just as much as she does." Loki offered her advice from her spot off to the side.

Bete hadn't been able to stand still ever since he heard about Aiz's level-up. The leaders seriously considered Loki's suggestion as a viable option. Being a werewolf, Bete had an extraordinary sense of smell. It might be difficult in the Dungeon, where the stench of all kinds of monsters pervaded, but it was possible he could follow Aiz's faint scent.

"Ah, one more thing, Finn. Can I ask ya to have a look through the sewer system without the Guild noticin'?"

"By that do you mean the place you mentioned earlier?"

"Yep. Couldn't exactly check every nook an' cranny last time." Finn glanced up at the goddess as she continued. "It's no fun to go lookin' fer clues when they fall right in yer lap, right? Plus, I'd get in yer way if I joined in, so can I leave this to you?"

"Hmm, I can do that. Shouldn't take long, so I'll head out now."

"Sorry. There's a lotta ground to cover, so go ahead an' take some folks with ya. But maybe leave the magic users behind."

She warned him of the very real possibility of encountering the carnivorous plants, which responded to magic energy. Finn nodded and thanked her for the tip.

He hopped down from his chair and addressed the three girls who had been waiting quietly in the doorway the whole time.

"Tiona, Tione. The investigation of the network of tunnels beneath the city starts now. I'm counting on the two of you."

"Of course! Leave it to me!" "No idea what's going on, but sure!"

He instructed the twins to gather up anyone who wasn't busy and wasn't a magic user. The girls raced off in an instant.

"We should proceed with the expedition preparations."

"Aye. I'll round up some rookies to help carry my order of magic swords."

People exited the office left and right. Soon, Loki and Lefiya were the only ones remaining.

"Huh, what? Well, I, um…"

"Ohh? Why don'tcha keep me company while everybody's out, Lefiya?" A playful grin appeared on Loki's lips.

"Oouuhh…" groaned the elf, head drooping at being left behind.

At a glance, the high, sturdy wall surrounding Orario resembled a cage.

In fact, the wall had been in place since the Ancient Times, over a thousand years ago. It was built to stem the seething tide of monsters that constantly emerged from the Dungeon. Anyone standing in the middle of the thriving city with her back to the tall white tower in its center would see it encompassing the whole metropolis, creating a barrier that separated outside from in. Under the gaze of those imposing ramparts, first-time visitors often said it felt as if everyone was trapped inside an enormous prison.

In truth, Orario prospered more than other countries and cities around the world despite the thick wall isolating it. With the sea close by, a massive lake to the southwest, and countless paved roads crossing the wide plains beyond the walls, there were many ways to export the Labyrinth City's magic-stone products and to receive foreign imports. Orario possessed the ultimate resource—the Dungeon. People came from far and wide to reap its benefits.

A way station located in the southwestern outskirts functioned as a foreign market. Goods from many countries entered the city every day. Boxes containing myriad ingredients, expensive decorations and jewelry, as well as weapons and armor reached shops all over Orario by horse-drawn carriages. Townspeople unloaded the goods one box at a time amid the constant activity on city streets.

The large wall loomed in the background as the metropolis's residents went about their daily lives.

"..."

Aiz made her way through the crowd by herself, shoulders slouching.

Desperate hung at her waist, listlessly swinging from side to side with her heavy gait. Her footsteps were but one set of many that filled the main street. Aiz was on her way to the Dungeon.

She had depleted her items during her prolonged stay last time, so she thought about visiting the many shops located within Babel Tower to replenish her supply before going back in. She didn't feel any better than she did yesterday, but she knew in the back of her mind that moping around at home would do her no good. It took what little willpower she had at the time to convince herself to leave home and trudge toward her destination.

She had leveled up. Now was the time to focus on reaching an even higher point...Her mind and body were ready, but for some reason her spirit wasn't in it.

She was already a good distance away from Twilight Manor, and her allies were only now realizing she was gone. The dignified face of the Sword Princess was nowhere to be seen. In its place was the lost, confused expression of a child who just happened to carry a saber and wear body armor.

...*Why? Why am I so depressed?*

Because it was the second time. The boy had run away from her twice.

She had never cared about what other people thought of her before, nor what rumors said...but for some reason, thinking the white rabbit was afraid of her made Aiz immeasurably sad. It pained her.

Her state of mind resembled that of a child who wanted to pet a cute little animal, only to have it run away.

Did the white rabbit's rubellite eyes see her as more monstrous than that Minotaur? The thought made her even gloomier.

...The sun...is too bright, she quietly thought.

An ultramarine sky spread out overhead, the warmth of the sun bathing her face as she walked in the crowds traversing the main street.

She wasn't the only one in armor. The sight of her fellow adventurers sporting bulky plates of metal and large blades was far from uncommon. Yet, without realizing it, Aiz had become the center of attention. She received envious and admiring stares alike from all directions, but she didn't even glance up as she joined the wave of people commuting south.

The street widened once it reached Central Park, the point where all eight main streets converged. Adventurers streamed into the circular park from every direction.

Aiz was among those entering from North Main Street. She entered Central Park and cast her gaze up at the soaring white tower, Babel.

Setting off for its base, she walked for several moments before...

"Ah!"

"......?"

It was the woman she had met last night—the half-elf who had visited Aiz's home was now purposefully marching toward her.

Beneath Babel Tower...

A ten-meder-wide hole breached the spacious chamber's floor. This was the one and only entrance to the Dungeon.

The room was shaped like a round tube with tall pillars lined up along its edges. The ceiling was a beautiful, deep sky-blue that was detailed enough to be mistaken for the real thing.

This place served as the buffer between the city above and the labyrinth beneath. Adventurers passed through this chamber daily in order to enter the expansive Dungeon and begin their journeys. There were too many demi-humans crossing the threshold to count, many accompanied by supporters.

A blond, golden-eyed female swordsman made her way down the spiral stairwell into the always-open hole under the tower. Weaving her way among the throngs of adventurers, Aiz disappeared into the massive opening.

Amid all that, a sparkle.

A tiny blue orb built into the ceiling, camouflaged in the color, twinkled as it followed her movements.

"—Now's my chance."

In a room shrouded by darkness, a figure wearing a hooded black robe—Fels—stared down at a crystal sphere atop a pedestal and whispered.

The crystal glowed the same hue as the orb concealed in the ceiling of Babel Tower's basement floor. An image of a spiral staircase descending into the yawning hole floated beneath its clear surface. A flash of blond hair appeared at the lower part of the stairs—Aiz.

Fels watched her enter the Dungeon by herself for only a moment before making a move.

"Ouranos, I'm going."

The jet-black robe fluttered as the figure vanished into the darkness.

Aiz had agreed to a request.

While it wasn't a formal quest by any means and no reward was involved, she had a purpose in accepting it.

The "client" was the half-elf she had met the previous night.

The Guild employee she had met in Central Park—Eina Tulle—made the request without going through the official channels. Her request was simple: please save Bell Cranell.

Apparently even as they spoke, he was in a precarious situation. Eina was the boy's adviser and had decided to ignore the proprieties to ask someone she had only just met for help.

Aiz had listened to her plea. She had her own reasons for wanting to save him, and there were some words that needed to be said.

Eina had informed her the boy was already in the Dungeon, but she didn't know where. It was up to Aiz to find him, and now she called on every leg muscle to cover as much ground as possible.

"—Excuse me, but have you seen a boy with white hair?"

"Holy shit!"

"You! You're th-the Sword Princess!"

Not only did the animal person Aiz addressed come to a complete stop, but the entire party froze like statues when she suddenly appeared.

She went into further detail, describing a boy with "white hair and rubellite eyes." As soon as someone answered in the negative, Aiz took off in a flash. The adventurers were left behind, standing in awe of the elite adventurer, the flower at the top of the mountain, who had said something to *them*.

Of course, the search for Bell Cranell would take place in the upper levels.

Only elite adventurers were able to venture into the middle levels, so the ones prowling the levels closer to the surface were for the most part lower class. Luckily, there were many people in the upper levels, and the size of each floor was relatively small compared to the ones farther down. Collecting information was a cinch.

Aiz approached every party she could find and immediately asked if they had seen the boy. She traversed the entire floor, gathering clues along the way.

"A white-haired human…Now that you mention it, yeah, pretty sure I saw that guy."

"You did?"

"Ah, yeah…Passed through earlier this morning, and I think he had a supporter with him…They were headed for the eighth floor."

Her Level Six speed allowed her to zip through every hallway of every floor in the blink of an eye, questioning dozens of adventurers along the way.

Several of them had seen the boy at some point or another, and Aiz was hot on his trail. As the hunt for new information continued, she descended farther and farther into the Dungeon.

Aiz reached the ninth floor before realizing how deep she was.

The next person she spoke to provided her with the most pivotal piece of information yet: Her target had been seen descending stairs that led to the next floor. She immediately set her course.

—The tenth floor?

Aiz, who had been so focused on tracking him down, suddenly paused.

It was the same strange feeling she had experienced after hearing the boy had taken down one of the monsters that escaped on the day of the Monsterphilia.

The boy Aiz knew was a greenhorn. After he had been nearly killed by a Minotaur twenty days ago, she could tell from his movements and overall fighting ability that he was firmly among the lowest of the low, even for the newest adventurers.

Despite all that, for some reason, he was able to journey deep into the twelve-floor range known as the upper levels—already on floor ten. According to Eina, the boy didn't have any party members for protection and support. He would have gone solo.

...Did he...improve?

In that short amount of time?

It had taken Aiz more than six months to set foot on the tenth floor back when she was a lower-class adventurer. But he pulled it off in twenty days?

It was...unbelievable.

Much too fast...

Absurd no matter how she thought about it.

After all, she'd never even heard of an adventurer like that.

But even so, why go so deep in the first place? She shook her head, returning to the present. She scolded herself that now was not the time for stray thoughts.

Descending to the next floor, Aiz did her best to push aside questions that couldn't be answered as well as her renewed interest in the boy.

At last, she arrived at the tenth floor.

Crossing the open space with a few quick strides, the first thing she saw in the next zone was thick white fog, dense enough to obscure vision and one of the unique characteristics of the tenth floor. A phenomenon like this was called a Dungeon gimmick. This "veil" prevented lower-level adventurers from accurately locating monsters and was detrimental to situational awareness. In short, it caused a lot of problems, including making Aiz's search for the boy much more difficult. She raced across the tall grasses that covered the Dungeon floor, shredding them in her wake.

All the imps that barred her path or just happened to be in the way were eviscerated as she flew by, slowing her pace by only a fraction of a step. Noting every disturbance in the fog, she proceeded down the main route through the tenth floor by memory.

And as she relied on her ears rather than her eyes—she heard it.

"!"

Ferocious monster roars, quickened footfalls of battle, and human screams sounded in the distance.

The yells didn't belong to a battle-hardened warrior or a reckless fighter. They were pitched higher, in the voice of someone much younger.

Aiz changed course. She followed the echoes through a long tunnel toward their source, a cavernous room.

Leafless, dead-looking trees protruded from the ground all around the wide room. She could see about as far as the middle of the chamber, which was enough to make several bulky shadows visible in the gloom. She could tell they were large-category monsters—orcs.

The beasts were engaged in battle with a lone human figure.

"—Firebolt!!"

She heard another shout before a flaming missile parted the heavy mist.

Aiz's eyes widened as she took in the scene of a smoldering orc corpse and a white-haired adventurer thrusting his right arm forward.

—That's him!

The burst of magic had created a momentary clearing in the murk. The boy was fighting on the other side.

He used a shortsword to counterattack while dodging the swinging limbs of the monster swarm. Although he struggled to keep pace with all the orcs and imps surrounding him, his rabbit-like agility prevented him from being overwhelmed by their numbers.

So it is true. He has grown. She was witnessing proof that the boy was more than able to hold his own on the tenth floor.

Seeing him use magic, likely a very short-trigger spell, Aiz was sure the boy could break free of the ring of monsters on his own with enough time.

She rushed toward him, genuinely surprised.

Suddenly, the boy miscalculated and dodged an attack too late. An orc wielding a dead tree like a club pressed its advantage, forcing the boy to parry with the armor on his left arm. *Thwak, thwak, thwak!* The plate came up to meet the impromptu cudgel's rough bark several times, taking the brunt of the impact but also knocking the boy off balance.

Imps charged his exposed back, practically licking their lips—but Aiz didn't let them.

"Gweee—!"

"!"

A flash of silver light and three imps came apart.

Her saber's slash behind the boy lasted only an instant. Aiz sensed the boy's surprise at something happening outside his field of vision, but reducing the monster battle line took priority.

Obscured in the haze, a flurry of fierce slashes shook the air as monsters howled their death cries.

No one on this battlefield could keep up with her. It seemed as though her afterimages delivered the final blows. Desperate cleaved imps one after another as her hair whipped about with her movements. The lumbering orcs had no time to react. By the time they noticed her, their bodies were already neatly segmented.

After a short while, the enemy numbers were severely reduced.

"S-sorry!!"

"Wha—?"

The boy beat a hasty retreat through the broken ring of monsters.

Aiz was left behind, the panicked apology ringing in her ears. He hadn't even glanced over his shoulder as he barreled toward the exit. She turned in the direction he had gone, but his form had already vanished in the mist.

She froze, completely bewildered. However, there were still threats around that she needed to tackle.

It was her responsibility to ensure nothing chased after him. A heartbeat later, piles of ash and monster corpses littered the ground.

"He's gone..."

The words quietly slipped from Aiz's lips. She hadn't gotten a chance to say anything.

A silence fell over the savanna-like area, the scuffle from just moments ago feeling like a distant dream.

Their reunion had turned into a back-to-back battle that lasted but an instant.

They never even saw each other's faces because of the low visibility. Most likely, the boy had no clue it had been Aiz. She had come here to save him...but she had missed him yet again.

"......"

Then a new thought entered her mind.

Perhaps she had done him a favor.

The boy was in a rush. Although he had been cornered, he had passed up opportunities to attack in his desperation to escape. It was as if he was hurrying to someone's aid.

It was only a guess, but a part of her felt that was it.

He was supposedly a solo adventurer, and yet many she'd talked to had described a supporter accompanying him.

What should I do now...?

According to Eina's information, there was reason to believe the young boy was caught up in his supporter's familia problems, but...it was probably all right.

It would look suspicious if she started tracking him again. And... he could use magic. Lower-level troublemakers wouldn't stand a chance against him now. Thinking back on what she had seen, Aiz was confident the boy stood among the strongest lower-level adventurers. There was no reason to worry.

A few moments passed as she thought it over, when suddenly she saw a flash, a slight glimmer, from the corner of her eye.

"...What's this?"

She crossed the tall grasses toward the source of the glimmer— and found a piece of armor.

It was an emerald-green vambrace. The light had come from this arm covering.

The damage to the once-smooth surface hinted at how much battle it had seen. In fact, it was in rough shape.

Was this a rare piece of equipment dropped by an adventurer in the Dungeon? Aiz tilted her head as she regarded the vambrace, when suddenly she exclaimed, "Oh!"

"Could it be..."

...what the boy was wearing?

It had probably come loose when that orc hit him with the club. The visibility had been extremely poor, but Aiz was positive she had seen a faint green glint on his arm at some point.

Bending over, she carefully picked up the piece of armor and held it like a valuable treasure. Upon closer inspection, she noticed the securing straps had been violently ripped off. She was convinced—it belonged to the boy.

She stood quietly for a moment, looking at the emerald-green vambrace in her grasp.

"......?"

Aiz looked up.

The sound of parting grass caught her attention.

A needle rabbit jumped out of the grass behind her. It had likely come up from a lower floor and gotten lost in the fog. The horned rabbit made eye contact with Aiz for a moment before bounding away in alarm. All the monster corpses littering the ground around her had tipped off the creature about their difference in strength.

Was it just a monster...?

Aiz wasn't so sure. She felt a presence *spying on her.*

Was it just her imagination?

"......"

No.

She focused her gaze into the fog in front of her.

Gripping the vambrace firmly in her right hand, she grasped her saber's hilt and slid it from her sheath.

There was *something* hidden out there.

"...Noticed, did you? I underestimated your ability."

Ripples passed through the heavy mist.

Moments later, a black shadow emerged.

The mysterious figure was draped in cloth the color of night, and the space beneath its hood was so dark it erased any facial features. Black gloves decorated with intricate patterns completely encased its hands. Not a single strip of skin was exposed.

The indescribable atmosphere surrounding the figure made Aiz question whether this mysterious person was human or not. Suspicious of the robed visitor, Aiz stood ready to attack but opened with a question. The voice that responded had a timbre somewhere between male and female; she wasn't sure which.

© Kiyotaka Haimura

"Do you…have business with me?"

"That I do. However, before stating my purpose, I would like you to lower that sword. I mean you no harm."

The unidentified black-robed figure came to a halt.

Indeed, it appeared to be perfectly benign. Well within her reach, whoever it was, its life was in Aiz's hands. She could carve anyone in half instantly at this range.

"I only wish to talk." The voice from beneath the hood claimed to have no ulterior motive. Aiz kept her gaze fixed on the shady person but pointed the tip of her blade to the ground.

"…Who…are you?"

"Me? I'm just a washed-up old mage…Perhaps you would understand if I told you I'm the one who contacted Lulune Louie?"

Those words sent a chill down Aiz's spine.

Lulune Louie was the young chienthrope who had received the murdered Hashana's "cargo" in Rivira. She said a mysterious client had hired her to take on a delivery.

"They had on a thick black robe. I couldn't tell if it was a man or woman." Lulune's description matched the individual before her to the letter.

"Aiz Wallenstein…I would like to entrust a quest to you."

The robed silhouette got right to the point before Aiz could recover from her astonishment.

"An abnormally large number of monsters have appeared on the twenty-fourth floor. An Irregular has appeared. I would like you to investigate or eliminate the cause."

The shadowy figure added that there would, of course, be a handsome reward.

"The origin of the Irregular has been traced to the deepest part of the floor, most likely…a pantry."

Aiz said nothing, but her thoughts raced.

An Irregular that she knew nothing about on floor twenty-four… why was *she* being asked to look into it? Judging from how she'd received this invitation, this mysterious character had sought an opportunity to speak with her specifically.

She still hadn't the slightest clue about the identity of her "client." If Aiz believed this person's claim about being a mage, that meant it was a member of a familia and receiving a Blessing from a deity. Why would it be so involved in looking for help from another familia?

The blond knight studied her guest, searching for an indication of its true motive.

"Another Irregular appeared on the thirtieth floor—the same place that Hashana was sent not too long ago. The similarities between the two events are uncanny."

"!"

Aiz's shoulders trembled, and her expression changed.

The figure shifted its balance, as if to say, *Need I go on?* The robe's hem swished as the strange voice reached the heart of the offer.

"The woman who led the attack on Rivira…The possibility she is connected with the orb is rather high."

Aiz gulped.

This was clearly bait to seize her interest. She knew but was still shaken.

The orb—the strange crystal object whose contents had made her feel physically sick…And the red-haired woman who had called her Aria…

Memories of those moments played across her mind.

"The situation is grave, Sword Princess. Please lend your strength."

Aiz was troubled.

The content of the black figure's request stirred many thoughts within her…After a few heavy moments, she raised her thin chin.

"Understood…"

She agreed to take on the quest.

Whatever this person's scheme was, luring her into a trap wasn't part of it. After considering all the details and possibilities, Aiz relied on her gut feeling and reached a decision.

Above all else, she wanted to know more about the red-haired woman and the orb.

"You have my gratitude," said the black-hooded figure. "If at all possible, I would like you to set off immediately. Is that all right?"

Aiz wasn't sure how to respond.

That would mean she would be proceeding all by herself...There was nothing to lose, so she decided to make a request of her own to this incredibly suspicious character.

"Um, may I send a message? To my familia..."

"Hmm? Oh...I see. No problem. You can leave it with me."

The hooded figure must have understood Aiz's concern about making her companions worry and agreed, unlikely as it had seemed.

While a little surprised, Aiz immediately thanked it and began writing a letter. She reached into her belt pouch to retrieve a small feathered pen—a slightly expensive magic item that could turn a small amount of blood into ink—and a piece of paper. Addressing her message to Loki, she wrote down a few details and signed her name using hieroglyphics to prove authenticity. The hooded figure held out its hand, and she set her dispatch directly into the glove.

If there was one loose end bothering her, it was concern for the white rabbit. However, she chose to trust in what she had witnessed. The adventurer had grown so strong, he seemed a completely different person.

"First, go to Rivira. Allies are already there."

"Understood."

Then he gave Aiz directions to a specific bar as well as a password. She nodded.

After saying all that needed to be said, the hooded figure didn't waste any time on small talk and promptly disappeared back into the fog.

Aiz watched it go. Then she faced the other direction and set off, her boots thudding against the ground.

Her first destination was the eighteenth floor. Once she met up with the "allies" the mysterious client had mentioned, they would all journey to the twenty-fourth floor.

Thoughts of the redheaded tamer and the orb circling in her mind, Aiz sped off.

CHAPTER

2

LET'S PARTY?

Гэта казка іншага сям'і.

Давайце святкаваць?

The sun was high in the sky. Clocks all around the city read just past ten.

The adventurers who had stopped by the Guild on their way to the Dungeon were long gone, and the lobby was mostly idle.

Passing by a fully equipped party off to a late start, the remaining adventurers crowded in front of a large bulletin board to find a quest they could manage. In the meantime, many shared their best Dungeon stories, though their audiences were unsure how far they could trust the narrators.

Amid all that, one young woman walked straight up to the bulletin board without so much as a glance at the others.

She was a beautiful elf with long, silky black hair and stark white skin. Her combat gear resembled what priestesses wore in isolated temples, mostly white with very few accents. A high collar around her neck hid all the skin beneath her chin from view. She was a walking example of how elves should look and dress.

Her red eyes swept across the bulletin board, checking each posting individually.

After a thorough examination of each quest on the board, she frowned slightly. She was after specific information—as soon as she realized that none of the available quests involved the twenty-fourth floor, she stepped away from the bulletin board.

She continued on to the reception counter.

"May I have a word? The quest to investigate floor twenty-four isn't on the board. About the alarming number of monsters?"

She chose her words carefully, implying she had made such a request in an attempt to trick the receptionist into confirming her suspicions. The animal person behind the counter froze on the spot.

The floppy ears on top of her head twitched. "Please wait a moment." With that, she disappeared into the office behind the counter. The Guild worker cautiously emerged after a few minutes and meekly returned to her spot.

"That's under deliberation as we speak...I apologize for the inconvenience."

The young elf turned on her heel after that and left without another word.

As she made her way through the white marble lobby, the elf cast a subtle glance over her shoulder and saw that the receptionist appeared to be confused, muttering the words *under deliberation* to herself.

"The Guild is purposely withholding information concerning the twenty-fourth floor...?"

The elf tried to guess the Guild leadership's intentions based on the employee's reaction.

An irregularity in the Dungeon—there were some who wanted that information to stay under wraps. She quietly whispered to herself, "...Lord Dionysus must be informed."

A member of *Dionysus Familia*, the elf Filvis exited Guild Headquarters.

In a block off North Main Street in Orario's first district...

On the street was a flower shop with a decent amount of traffic, run by a group of demi-human girls who weren't members of any familia. A cute wooden sign hung above the door that read DIA FLORAL.

The store was currently filled with adventurers—unshaven and rugged—who didn't seem the type to have much interest in the rows and rows of beautiful blossoms. Their true motives were transparent, but it was good for business either way.

A certain deity happened to be visiting the flower shop.

"Sorry to bother you, but would you pick some good ones for me?"

"Ah...Y-y-yes! Right away!"

A young prum girl found herself lost in the deity's dazzling eyes for a moment, turning bright red before finally blurting a response. As she frantically waved to her coworkers, several of the girls cooperated to assemble a bouquet.

All the while, each of the staff members tried to steal glances at the golden-haired god standing at the front of the store. Dionysus had the presence of a prince from a far-off kingdom, and it made their hearts skip a beat.

He wasn't like the other gods with their sick sense of humor. The balance of his perfect facial features was enough to indicate that Dionysus possessed exceptional dignity and grace. A mere mortal could never rival him.

In front of the shop overflowing with beautiful flowers, the deity's every move caught everyone's attention.

His bouquet complete, Dionysus paid in full and thanked the girls for their hard work. It wasn't long before the staff surrounded him and worked up the courage to talk to him.

"Is this a gift for a lady?"

"I would loooove for a god to give me flowers."

"Oh-ho? But you are more beautiful than any flower. In that case, why don't I treat each of you to a bouquet of your own?"

The girls had only been joking, but the deity's response sounded sincere. Their expressions lit up, as if their wishes had come true.

Dionysus narrowed his glass-colored eyes and leaned in closer to the group of excited girls.

"Making faces like that—I might just help myself right now."

The girls squealed with delight at Dionysus's soft voice, like honey, but then—

They looked behind the deity, and everything stopped.

"..............."

A beautiful elf, appearing out of nowhere, stared at them with a perfectly blank, emotionless face.

Crick! Crick! Crick! An unnatural sound came from her tightening fists.

© Kiyotaka Haimura

The girls came to their senses and scattered back to the safety of their shop. Dionysus was alone, the charming mask fading with each heartbeat. Slowly but surely, he turned to the member of his familia behind him.

"Th-that was fast, Filvis..."

"Yes. I acquired some valuable information for you, Lord Dionysus. So I returned as quickly as possible, Lord Dionysus."

Dionysus tried to keep his voice from trembling as a point of pride as a god, and Filvis responded in a cool, even tone.

A dark emotion swirled quietly deep within her crimson eyes. Her heavy silence surging over him, Dionysus grew tense...But the moment passed. The deity let his shoulders relax and smiled at her.

He removed a single flower from inside his vest, completely separate from the bouquet in his left hand.

"While I don't know how long you've been standing there...everything that transpired is what we deities refer to as 'lip service.' They helped me pick out this flower for you as well."

Filvis's eyes widened as Dionysus presented her with the blossom.

In a complete turnaround, the elf became so docile that she seemed a completely different person from the girl who had arrived just moments earlier.

A faint dusting of pink appeared on the elf's cheeks as she looked at the white gift in her hands.

"You may be a deity, but using misleading words...Such superfluous requests for affection are unbecoming."

"What's this? Are you jealous?"

"...Lord Dionysus is the only person to show affection for someone like myself."

Filvis seemed to shrink as she mumbled quietly. Dionysus smiled again and spoke up.

"Ha-ha-ha, how cute."

"......"

The elf turned even redder as the deity caressed her bangs. His touch practically melted her from the inside out.

Flashing another grin, Dionysus looked up.

"Now then, shall we get going? I'll listen to whatever information you brought me, as well as anything else on your mind once we arrive."

Dionysus flagged down a horse-drawn taxi with the bouquet of flowers cradled in his arm. He and Filvis climbed in a moment later.

There was a graveyard filled with countless headstones located in the southeastern part of the city.

Officially dubbed the First Graveyard, it was commonly referred to as the Adventurers Graveyard, devoted to those who lost their lives every day in the Dungeon. With more stones being added constantly, two more graveyards, the Second and Third, were constructed on top of a small hill to the north outside the city wall to accommodate them all.

Adventurers who had left their mark on history—those known as heroes, dating back to the Ancient Times—were given more grandiose memorials in front of Guild Headquarters. Large monuments built in their honor decorated the grounds. People of all races and familias gathered here to pay respects to their forebears by leaving bouquets of flowers.

Dionysus and Filvis made their way down the stairwell and walked among the graves.

"……"

They arrived at a plot of land the familia had purchased in a corner of the graveyard. There were already many headstones within. Dionysus took a step toward three of the most recent markers and placed the bouquet of flowers in front of them with his own hands.

In reality, there were very few bodies resting beneath the surface. It was rare that conditions in the monster-filled Dungeon allowed for the bodies of slain adventurers to be returned to the surface.

Therefore, most of the graves were nothing more than symbols of the adventurers they represented. That wasn't the case for Dionysus's former children, who had met their fate aboveground not too long ago. Their bodies had been placed into coffins and laid to rest in a relatively unoccupied area of the plot.

As a deity, Dionysus knew that the act of placing flowers at a grave was ultimately pointless. The only things beneath the ground here were lifeless amalgams of flesh and bone. There were no regrets that needed to be soothed, no spirits fearing retribution. Their prayers should have been for the mercy of the deities in Tenkai. He made offerings mainly out of respect for the customs of this world.

But it was also Dionysus's way of expressing his gratitude for his followers.

"Restricting information about the twenty-fourth floor, are they...?"

"Yes. Not a single relevant quest has been made available."

After placing the bouquet in front of the gravestone, Dionysus stood still for a moment and asked Filvis to give the details behind his shoulder.

They were completely alone in the graveyard as the conversation continued.

"During my recent trip to Rivira, many were concerned with the alarming rate of monster sightings. They were of the opinion that it would be wise to avoid traveling below the twentieth floor until the Guild has proposed a plan to rectify the situation." The reason that *Dionysus Familia* was aware of the events occurring on the twenty-fourth floor was because Filvis had journeyed to the eighteenth floor, a safe point, to acquire information.

The deity considered everything his follower had to say.

"I agree. It's bizarre that the Guild hasn't issued a mission under these circumstances..."

Muttering to himself, Dionysus added that it would be common sense for the Guild to investigate an Irregular of this nature.

The Guild was the closest thing Orario had to a governing body, and it held the authority to requisition the power and resources of every familia by issuing a "mission"—an urgent quest.

"The highest-ranking members of the Guild…no, perhaps Ouranos is behind it?"

Is this a way to prevent widespread panic? Or a plan to quickly solve this problem involving as few people as possible?

Dionysus frowned at the possibility that the god in command of the Guild, Ouranos, could have his own private army and that it might be mobilizing at this very moment.

"What shall we do, Lord Dionysus?"

Dionysus remained silent even after his follower asked the question. At last, he turned to face her.

"Why don't we see what Loki can do?"

"Here we are again…"

Loki's lips twitched as she forced herself to greet Dionysus.

Their reunion took place outside her familia's home, Twilight Manor. Loki's guards had informed her that the deity wished to speak with her. When she stepped outside, sure enough, the god stood with Filvis on the opposite side of the gate.

Dionysus grinned from ear to ear, his perfect white teeth sparkling.

"I have acquired relevant information—a great deal of it, at that—so why don't we find some place to sit down?"

While he hadn't come out and said it directly, Dionysus was attempting to invite himself into Loki's home. The goddess humorlessly cocked an eyebrow and said, "Skedaddle, why don't ya?" It wasn't until she caught a glimpse of the bottle of grape wine Filvis was carrying that she reluctantly let them pass. The guards rolled their eyes at her apparent priorities.

However, she wasn't about to let them inside the actual building.

Instead, a table and a few chairs were hastily set up in a secluded area of the garden.

"'Kay, then, spill the beans. What's this 'relevant information' that's so important?"

Loki had already removed the cork from the wine bottle as Dionysus started recounting the Guild's suspicious behavior and its possible connection to the situation on the twenty-fourth floor. Then he shifted to discussing the unusual amount of monsters present in that area and everything else he had learned.

"Although very few people are aware, there was another occurrence much like this one not too long ago. On the thirtieth floor."

That caught Loki's attention, her eyebrows rising.

Thanks to her meeting with Finn and the other leaders, she knew that Hashana had picked up the mysterious orb on that floor before he was killed.

"So, when did that go down?"

"Three weeks ago…if memory serves me right. Due to its location in the lower levels, only the strongest upper-class adventurers caught wind of it."

The lower levels were much more dangerous than the Dungeon's middle levels, and only a select few adventurers ever made it that far down. Dionysus explained that there hadn't been enough witnesses for rumors to spread.

Loki listened quietly as she sipped on her wine. Dionysus proceeded to talk about how the Guild was trying to prevent the dissemination of information.

"It's my belief that the Guild is attempting to cover up the very existence of this incident."

"So ya can't trust the Guild after all, can ya?"

"…You are the one who spoke to Ouranos personally, so if you say they're innocent, I have no right to object…But there's something about them."

"Can't blame ya," muttered Loki, acknowledging that something suspicious was happening with the Guild. "So, what is it ya came here to ask me to do?"

"Ha-ha-ha, I only came here to pass along information, just as I said I would. I have no ulterior motive."

Dionysus answered Loki's doubtful stare with another of his friendly smiles.

Loki's followers and Filvis watched the two deities converse, one wanting to pass on a burden while the other tried to avoid it.

"My kids are busy, so investigatin' the twenty-fourth floor ain't possible right now."

"Might they be looking around a certain sewer system?"

"Damn that intuition of his," Loki grumbled to herself and nodded. She informed Dionysus that Finn had led a group of her strongest followers into the sewer, leaving the magic users behind.

"The others are out an' about, gettin' ready for the next expedition," she said before sticking out her tongue.

"What about the Sword Princess? Having her would be more than worth a hundred warriors."

"Aizuu? She's—" Loki began, but then something plopped onto the table.

A rolled-up piece of paper had dropped from above.

"Whazzat?" Loki looked overhead in time to catch a glimpse of an owl in flight.

A messenger bird…or maybe some kinda magic? she speculated as the owl soared away.

"A letter?"

"Sure looks like it."

Loki picked it up to have a read.

Dionysus took a sip of tea that had been prepared for him as Loki pored over the script flowing across the parchment. She stared blankly at the sky a moment later.

There was a loud slap as she brought the palm of her hand to her cheek.

"Aiz went to the twenty-fourth floor…"

"*PFFF!*" Tea sprayed from Dionysus's lips.

The deity coughed a few times as Filvis watched from behind, also in shock.

"She accepted a quest on the twenty-fourth floor...The timin's too perfect. 'Don't worry 'bout me'—'course I'm worried. Why ya gotta be an airhead, Aizuu?"

Loki knew the moment she saw Aiz's signature in hieroglyphics that the girl had dived into the belly of the beast. She leaned to one of her followers standing directly behind her and said, "Bring Bete...and Lefiya out here right away."

"What are you planning?"

"Sendin' the two of 'em after Aiz. I'd be surprised if this had nothing to do with the attack on Rivira."

Loki immediately connected the information she had from Finn to Dionysus's new input and decided to dispatch a team to assist Aiz right away.

Filvis handed a handkerchief to Dionysus, which he used to wipe his mouth before frowning.

"You believe those two are enough? Of course it's up to you, but the twenty-fourth floor seems exceptionally dangerous right now."

"Can't do a damn thing 'bout it. I ain't got no one else. Bete and Lefiya are the only ones here I can send to help her."

It might have just been his divine intuition, but Dionysus emphasized the need for caution. Of course, Loki wasn't thrilled with the situation, either, frowning as she brought her hands together behind her head. He considered the goddess's position, understanding she lacked enough manpower at her disposal...and turned to his follower.

"Filvis. Accompany Loki's children to the twenty-fourth floor."

The elf jumped back in surprise. Even Loki's eyes opened wide.

Filvis struggled to keep her voice calm under her god's serious gaze.

"Lord Dionysus, what is the meaning of this?! Who will protect you?!"

"Listen well, Filvis. I'm the one who got Loki involved, under my terms no less. Therefore, I cannot leave everything to her and simply watch from the sidelines." Dionysus continued to his main point. "I want Loki's trust above all else." Finally, he laid out his true motivation. "Trust is earned through action...I'm sure you understand, Filvis."

"......!"

Dionysus was reiterating the fact that Loki still didn't completely trust him.

"This ain't somethin' folks usually say so openly, ya know?" said an exasperated Loki.

"But I..."

Filvis was about to start her counterargument when Dionysus stood up from his chair.

His glass-colored irises met her crimson ones, and the two of them came to a mutual understanding.

"Filvis. Please."

"...As you wish."

The elf reluctantly agreed. She turned to face Loki and straightened her posture. "Goddess Loki. With your permission, I shall join the party."

"Hmm. Can't say I don't appreciate it...Think ya can keep up?"

"Filvis is my familia's only Level Three adventurer. At the very least, she won't hold your children back on the twenty-fourth floor."

Dionysus provided his vote of confidence from his spot off to the side, and Loki tilted her head.

"She's Level Three? News to me."

"...I called in some favors, and used quite a bit of money, to keep her level-up a secret at the last Denatus. This girl has enough *negative attention* as it is," Dionysus explained. "I'm just an overprotective parent. Everything I've done has been to keep her out of the spotlight."

He revealed that he personally had ensured his follower's name wouldn't come up at the previous gathering of the gods.

He did, however, make sure that her correct Level was documented in the Guild's records. "Hmm," muttered Loki as her gaze shifted between the two of them.

The elf with long black hair averted her eyes, unable to say anything as she stood between the two deities.

"Ah well, that don't matter. We're hurtin' for folks as is, so I'll let Bete know."

"Thank you, Goddess Loki."

Filvis gave a small bow when Loki granted her permission.

That was when they heard a chorus of noises and echoes from inside the building. The werewolf warrior had already begun his preparations to pursue Aiz while the younger elvish magic user gathered supplies as fast as she could. The two of them made ready to find and help their comrade in record time.

Soon after, Loki and Dionysus saw off the newly formed party of Bete, Lefiya, and Filvis at the front gate.

"You again…"

"L-looking forward to working together!"

Bete, who had met Filvis once before, didn't hide his misgivings about having to work with the elf. Lefiya held her tube backpack in place and clutched her staff as she introduced herself.

Filvis's only response to her new party members was heavy silence.

"I'll send your sorry ass flying with a good kick if you're in our way. Get lost before you get yourself killed."

"…Spare me the lecture, werewolf."

"U-uuoohh…"

The tension between Bete and Filvis crackled from the very beginning. Werewolves often didn't get along with the famously prideful elves. Lefiya could sense the storm brewing in their new party; it made her stomach churn.

She was concerned for what lay ahead.

Caught between loyalty to her familia and a bond to her kin, Lefiya joined the other two as they passed through the front gate.

After leaving the tenth floor, Aiz headed for the eighteenth.

Beneath a ceiling comprised of innumerable blue and white crystals that resembled the real sky aboveground, she passed the safe floor's expansive forests and vast plains on her way to an island in the middle of a massive lake. Following the black-robed person's instructions, Aiz entered the Rivira settlement, which was located on top of the island.

Even though the town had been utterly devastated by the plant-monster attack that took place ten days ago, many of the shops in the rogue town were already up and running again. The Dungeon's natural healing power had even restored the damaged cliff face and crystals. Aiz looked around this town, completely populated by upper-class adventurers.

Many carried materials to rebuild the shops that still lay in pieces or to fix the many broken ladders and stairwells. She wasted no time searching for the bar that was the designated meeting place.

Walking along a narrow path away from the sounds of the main square, she followed the directions she'd received. She arrived at the northern edge of town via a backstreet formed from rows of giant mineral formations, near Cluster Street.

Gemlike fragments crunched underfoot as she made her way into the mouth of the cave.

"There's a bar all the way back here...?"

The light from overhead couldn't reach this isolated cul-de-sac. Aiz advanced cautiously down the path as she mumbled, unable to sense anyone else's presence. She'd been to Rivira numerous times but never knew about any establishments in this location.

The stranger in the black robe had instructed her to visit a bar called The Golden Cellar.

A sign in front of the cave entrance pointed the way with a red arrow. A wooden staircase stood just inside. It lightly creaked as Aiz descended, and she discovered a door at the foot of the stairs. After slowly swinging it open, she noticed several adventurers were already inside and enjoying themselves.

The first thing she saw was a crystalline pillar in the middle of the cave that emanated golden light. White and blue crystals were a common sight on the eighteenth floor, but this was the first time she'd seen one like this. In fact, she was fairly certain this was the only one of its kind.

A feeling of wonder swelled in her chest as she took a closer look at her surroundings. The bar itself was decently large, each of its walls composed of exposed black rock. Several tables were set up, each with their own matching chairs. The adventurers played card games by the light of magic-stone lamps affixed to the ceiling and walls, which added to the yellow glow of the pillar. They used magic stones as playing chips.

All five tables were completely full, catching Aiz by surprise. The only open seats in the entire bar were by the counter. *Someone might be watching*...she thought as she walked through the tavern toward the open seat.

She caught sight of a long shelf filled with bottles in every color imaginable behind the counter as well as a grumpy-looking dwarf, who was the bartender.

Only one person sat at the bar—a female chienthrope.

"Oh? Well, if it isn't the Sword Princess! Fancy meeting you in a place like this!"

"...Lulu...ne?"

The chienthrope girl Aiz had noticed—Lulune—was surprised at first but soon wore an open smile.

Lulune was the adventurer belonging to *Hermes Familia* who

had accompanied Aiz and Lefiya for a short time because of the orb. She became involved when, just like with Aiz now, the mysterious black-robed character had hired her for a delivery.

She had dark hair, wheat-colored skin, and lithe limbs; minimal armor and light gear covered her thin, streamlined body. She fit the description of a thief through and through.

Aiz sensed a connection between the two of them, albeit difficult to describe, as the chienthrope casually struck up a conversation.

"Thanks for last time. I got out of there in one piece, thanks to you. Mind if I say thank you again?"

"You don't have to…Have your injuries…healed?"

"Eh-heh-heh, healthy as a horse! Now let me buy you a drink!" she added with a big smile.

Aiz's mind raced to find a polite way to decline as she walked to the seat described in her instructions, the second from the corner—next to Lulune. The girl watched her in confusion for a moment, but her smile came right back.

"Prowling by yourself today? I can't believe the Sword Princess knows about this place! You're really in the know, aren't you?"

Aiz casually responded to the verbal deluge with the occasional nod and a short "Yes" or two as she examined the other side of the counter.

The dwarf bartender grumpily trudged over to her and questioned her.

"Whaddaya havin'?"

Now was the time to use the password the darkly dressed client had given her.

"Green tea–flavored Jyaga Maru Kun."

The moment the password left Aiz's lips, a loud crash rang out. The seat next to her had pitched over.

Head snapping to the side in surprise, Aiz saw an utterly dumbfounded Lulune on the floor gazing up at her in disbelief.

"…Y-*you're* our reinforcements?"

—*No way*, Aiz thought as she noticed movement around her.

The human who had been happily downing his ale, the animal people who had been arguing over the last round of their card game—every single bar patron was on their feet and staring right at her. Aiz leaped away from the counter and took a defensive stance in the middle of the floor.

The vibrant atmosphere had evaporated. The patrons' eyes were different, their gazes far more intense. Then Aiz figured it out.

All the customers in this bar, including Lulune, were the "allies" the robed figure had mentioned.

"Are you sure it's her, Lulune?"

"A-Asfi..."

A woman stepped in front of the crowd around Aiz.

Her aqua-blue hair, one lock dyed white, shifted from side to side as she walked. Her eyes were pure blue, like her hair. Everything about her seemed perfectly in place, right down to her silver-frame glasses, giving her a very intellectual impression.

She wore a narrow white cloak and sandals decorated with golden wings. The portion of her belt visible beneath the cloak held a weapon; there were also several holsters hanging from it.

Their eyes met. Exchanging looks of surprise, Aiz became aware of the identity of the beautiful young woman.

Asfi Al Andromeda...

One of only five adventurers with the Advanced Ability Enigma in Orario, she was also the head of *Hermes Familia*.

Known by the title Perseus, she was an item maker with unparalleled skills.

Utilizing the rare ability Enigma, she had created various serums and unique items too numerous to describe. Herbs that could protect someone from the effects of curses and status magic. A harp that could attract specific monsters based on sound frequency. Even the feathered pen that didn't require ink in Aiz's waist pouch was her invention. Her reputation preceded her far and wide as one of Orario's top-class adventurers—like Aiz, only in a different field.

"Looks like it..." conceded Lulune as she climbed to her feet beside Aiz and Asfi's momentary staring contest.

"...Were all of you...asked to do a quest as well?"

Aiz posed her question as her gaze shifted from Asfi to Lulune, and then to the other adventurers.

Judging by their familiarity with one another, as well as their shared mood, Aiz was positive they belonged to the same familia. Asfi, Aiz's senior by at least a few years, acknowledged with a yes and let out a long sigh.

"Thanks to this mutt who can't say no to money, our entire familia has a mess to clean up."

"A-Asfiiii..."

Lulune whimpered at the harsh assessment.

The human cast her blue gaze in Aiz's direction, looking ashamed as she explained the situation.

"I believe you have experienced this yourself, Sword Princess... but a person in a black robe appeared to her a few days ago and simply said our 'cooperation' was required. She said she'd had enough right away, or so I'm told..."

The black-robed figure hadn't been seen since the attack on Rivira until it recently paid Lulune a visit. Asfi explained how the enigmatic being bided its time for a chance to speak with the chienthrope alone. Considering how much danger she had been involved in the last time she accepted a quest from that person, the girl had staunchly rejected the offer at first...

Lulune tried to defend herself, though her mumblings were inaudible as Asfi continued.

"From what I've been told, 'Black Robe' threatened to expose her true Level."

"......"

"With that, we had no choice but to get involved..."

Aiz understood their predicament but was unsure how to respond.

She had already heard about *Hermes Familia*'s situation from

Lulune, specifically that the god was reporting false information about his followers' Levels. Should their true strengths be revealed, he would lose his ability to remain "in the middle of the pack," his preferred place in the hierarchy.

Certainly, there would be many consequences if the truth came to light; the first would be a higher familia rank. The Guild levied a tax on each familia based on their rank, meaning the amount they had to pay would dramatically increase. Since they were most definitely committing fraud, there would also be a hefty penalty levied against them if the Guild ever caught wind of it.

The blackmail effectively left Lulune no choice. Unable to protect herself or her familia, it became a necessity to accept the quest.

"This idiot, this absolute imbecile, should have claimed ignorance until the very end. What thief worthy of the name can't spin a good story?!"

"Waaah! Forgive meeee!"

Lulune tucked her tail between her legs as Asfi unleashed her anger and indignation. The other adventurers said nothing but all wore the same expression of loosely veiled irritation over being dragged into this.

"It's hard enough being at the mercy of Lord Hermes's every whim, but now this...?!"

A kind of fatigue unique to mortals constantly on edge due to their patron deity's selfishness revealed itself on Asfi's face as she rambled under her breath.

"Um...What...do we do from here?"

"...My apologies. You shouldn't have had to see that."

Aiz worked up the courage to try and get the leader's attention. Asfi's eyes popped open, and she readjusted her glasses. Her expression returning to normal, she focused on the task at hand.

"To confirm, the aim of this quest lies in the pantry on the twenty-fourth floor. Our jobs are to locate the cause of the monster outbreak and eliminate it. Is that correct?"

"Yes."

"Then allow me to detail our manpower. Including myself, there are fifteen of us, all from *Hermes Familia*. More than half of us are Level Three."

The group went over the contents of the quest as well as their combat strength.

Their stock of weapons and items, the composition of the formation's front and rear lines, and basic strategies were all discussed. This might be a one-time-only affair, but Aiz was still counting on these adventurers to watch her back.

The men and women of the party introduced themselves to Aiz, and she did the same.

"We no longer have any choice. All of you, hold nothing back until this quest is complete—especially you, Lulune. I expect you to work yourself to the brink of death."

"I will, I wiiiiill…"

Every member of the party nodded in response to Asfi's call, though Lulune's reply was almost inaudible.

Lastly, Asfi turned to face Aiz.

"Having you fight alongside us is a great honor, Sword Princess. It might only be for a short while, but we're glad you're with us."

"Happy…to be here."

Asfi flashed a grin; Aiz, too, showed the hint of a smile.

They shook hands. Now they were allies who had come together to complete a quest—members of two familias with the same goal.

Aiz was now officially part of *Hermes Familia*'s party.

"But please don't tell anyone about our circumstances."

"Ah…I won't."

Asfi issued a quick warning before leading the group out from The Golden Cellar.

After briefly visiting a few shops in Rivira, they set off for the twenty-fourth floor.

"Fels."

A booming voice echoed through the chamber.

The space embodied the image of the inner sanctum of a holy site built during the Ancient Times. Four torches ablaze with bright-red flames provided the only light in the stifling darkness.

Located directly beneath Guild Headquarters, this was the Temple of Ouranos.

The physically imposing deity, clad in a hooded robe, sat on his throne that doubled as the altar. Four torches ringed him as he directed his piercing blue gaze at the figure below—Fels.

"Why did you involve the Sword Princess?"

Several hours had passed since Aiz was brought into the quest. As soon as all the arrangements had been made, Fels had returned to the temple and did not so much as flinch under the questioning.

The god's somber and unyielding tone made their meeting feel more like an interrogation. The deity presented a strong case, recalling Fels's statement that it would be wise to avoid *Loki Familia* after the goddess had personally paid them an unexpected visit.

Ouranos asked if directly contacting Aiz was worth the risk.

The robed individual standing in front of the altar replied evenly, "I have been told that the Sword Princess displayed an unusual reaction to the orb."

Fels passed along the information acquired from Lulune during their brief conversation before the newest quest had been issued. In fact, Aiz had nearly keeled over after encountering the fetus-like organism in the orb.

Hearing that, Ouranos raised his eyebrows.

"I've come to the conclusion that there is a yet-undiscovered connection between the orb and Aiz Wallenstein. This might be the only opportunity to bring that connection to light."

Ouranos kept silent as Fels finished explaining. However, the deity's mind was hard at work, and he passed the time in contemplation.

Fels broke the silence with an "Also…," drawing the deity's gaze. "While we did manage to contain the incident in the thirtieth-floor pantry, Lido and many of our allies suffered heavy casualties. They cannot shoulder any more duties at this time."

The thirtieth floor—the place where Hashana had first retrieved the orb.

The voice continued from beneath the hood masking the figure's face in darkness.

"There were no 'guards' present on the thirtieth floor, but the enemy is sure to take more precautions this time. Examining all the gathered information, I assembled a team able to contend with that danger by including the Sword Princess."

"Guards, you say…So that tamer might appear again."

"Most likely," answered Fels as Ouranos closed his eyes.

"I shall speak to Hermes myself."

"My apologies, Ouranos."

Like Aiz, *Hermes Familia* was at risk of sustaining serious damage while carrying out this quest. Ouranos would handle the follow-up. Fels sounded sincere as the darkness beneath the hood rose to face the deity.

"I have sympathy for the Sword Princess, but we cannot allow this situation to continue unabated."

The voice was thick with determination.

It was a spacious cavern deep in the Dungeon, far from the surface, on a lower floor in the middle levels.

A stench hung in the moist air.

It wasn't a natural result of nearby monsters, nor was it blood. Even the putrid odor of a dragon's intestinal tract couldn't hold a candle to this foul aroma—the kind that drew in maggots and insects from far and wide. The scent of rotting flesh.

No adventurers came close to this corner of the Dungeon,

inundated with the smell of death. Even the howls of monsters were nowhere to be heard. It was almost as if this cavern were completely isolated from other events in the labyrinth.

Amid the eerie stillness drifted the sounds of many people walking about, mixed with the echoes of mysterious squirming and far-off howls that sounded like the ring of broken bells.

Bloodred light illuminated the interior of the dim cavern.

"......"

Crunch. A mouth tinted crimson took a bite out of an oddly colored fruit.

A long shadow spread across the floor. There was no doubt from the curvy form and ample breasts that it belonged to an enticing woman.

Sharp green eyes peered out from beneath bangs that reached her cheeks; hair the same color as the red light swished from side to side.

There was no mistake. She was the one Aiz had referred to as the red-haired tamer.

Sitting on the ground with one knee up, she showed no signs of moving anytime soon.

"—Oi! Adventurers figured out something's up with all the monsters romping through the Dungeon! You okay with that?"

Another person ran up to the woman.

It was a man wearing a large robe that completely hid his upper body from view, as well as a mask over the top half of his face, concealing his identity.

He raised his voice, but the woman's tone was simply cold.

"Shut up. Stop flipping out."

She spat out the unchewed fruit and crushed the other half between her fingers. The flesh of the mysterious fruit shot out in all directions, scattering like a brain stomped underfoot.

"I'll lend you some violas," she said, referring to the carnivorous plant monsters. "You all should handle the rabble." She never even glanced up.

© Kiyotaka Haimura

"Tsk!" Angrily turning on his heel, the masked man started off. Just as he disappeared into the reddish darkness, another figure emerged to take his place.

It was another man, the stark-white cloth covering his body tinted crimson by the light.

"Discovered by adventurers...Luck is not with us."

The newcomer was also wearing a mask, except this one was an unaltered white skull of a monster, a drop item used as a helmet. The man's features were hard to discern, and it gave him an ominous aura. There were no weapons anywhere on his tall frame.

The red-haired woman shifted her gaze in his direction for only an instant as the man stopped near her.

"Can we afford to leave this alone, Levis?"

The red-haired woman—Levis—looked back out over the cavern.

"I don't give a damn how many adventurers know we're here."

"So you're making the Evils do the dirty work?"

"Yeah. I ain't lifting a finger."

Levis's gaze followed the numerous people moving in the dim light with absolutely no interest.

The masked man looked down at her and strengthened his tone to get his point across.

"What if they've come for *her* again, like on the thirtieth floor?"

Thud! The light source swayed, casting its red glare back and forth.

"There's reason to believe a faction of surface dwellers is watching our every move."

Levis answered the man's warning of a possible incoming attack bluntly.

"Just crush them."

A HIDEOUS BEAUTY

Гэта казка іншага сям'і.

Прыгажосць або пачварнасць дзяўчыны

This could very well be the most uncomfortable party of all time.

Lefiya thought. Aloud, she said, "…Wh-what wonderful weather we're having today."

"You ever see the weather on the eighteenth floor change?"

"……"

With a strained smile, the elf forced herself to make small talk, but Bete shot it down instantly. Even Filvis, a mere step away, didn't even dignify it with a response.

"Ugh…" The tension in the air made Lefiya moan and clench her stomach.

They had reached the safe zone on floor eighteen. The group had departed from Twilight Manor in order to catch up with Aiz. Thanks to their incredibly rapid pace, they had reached this point in only a matter of hours.

After dashing out of the tunnel that connected the seventeenth and eighteenth floors, they were already well into the forest that covered the southern area. Their gait slowed to a power walk with a few breaks here and there. With a top-class adventurer like Bete leading the party, it took a great deal of pleading from Lefiya to slow down at all—earning her one hell of a snarl from the werewolf at the same time.

Surrounded by the cooling presence of trees, the gentle sound of running water, and the soft blue light shining through the canopy overhead, Lefiya was reminded of her elven homeland every time she visited the eighteenth floor. However, even the memories of that pristine forest couldn't sooth her current discomfort.

Lefiya was extremely aware that she wasn't very good in these kinds of situations. The trip had been unforgiving on many levels— Bete hadn't displayed even the slightest sign of friendliness, and

Filvis's stone-cold silence showed no signs of cracking. And she was stuck right between them, utterly useless.

The party had been suffocating in this unbearable atmosphere from the very start.

Although it could all just be in my head…

She had no idea that lack of conversation could make her feel so lonely. Lefiya was so used to Tiona constantly talking to everyone about anything at all that she felt like something was missing without her around. What she wouldn't give to hear that Amazon's carefree voice right about now!

Her heart heavy, she glanced over to the side.

She saw silky black hair and eyes like scarlet gems—elegant and dignified, the beautiful elf was most likely older than Lefiya. Her long, pointed ears were proof of her heritage.

Miss Filvis, was it…?

The elven adventurer who came with them on their journey to find Aiz had maintained a stout wall between herself and the other party members…although that could be considered normal behavior, since she belonged to another familia.

Filvis never initiated any interaction, maintaining her distance and shunning any attempts at conversation. Lefiya had tried to call out to her many times but was met with no success, as Filvis ignored her completely. At this point, she was afraid the other elf despised her.

Elves tended to give off the impression of being cold and aloof.

But…

On their way here, Filvis had protected Lefiya without a second thought. Their fast pace hadn't allowed the time for the magic user to cast her spells, so she had been forced to fight monsters physically with her staff, something she had yet to master. She had been on the brink of being overwhelmed many times, but Filvis had stepped in more than once to take the brunt of the attack and kept her safe. Almost like she was taking care of her.

This elf was not a bad person. Of that she was sure.

"M-Miss Filvis, thank you so much for your assistance earlier!"
Lefiya made up her mind to try one more time.

Their journey was far from over, and they couldn't simply over-power monsters with brute force on the deeper floors. There might come a time when teamwork would be required to survive.

Above all, Filvis was her kin. Elves always looked out for their own. It was Lefiya's urge to establish this bond that led her to con-tinue her attempts to engage her in conversation.

"You stopped that Minotaur's advance...To be honest, I have quite a great deal of trouble dealing with them..."

".........."

"Do you fight on the front lines, Miss Filvis? You use both sword and staff, right?"

".........."

"Are you, perhaps, a magic swordsman? I-i-if so, I hold you in even higher esteem!"

".........."

"Ah-ha-ha-ha-ha...Wh-what do you do in your free time?"

Lefiya's voice grew more and more strained with each passing moment as she tried harder than ever. Unfortunately, she received only the same silence in response. Filvis kept walking, her eyes glued to the path ahead.

Lefiya's spirit was on the verge of crumbling, but she had seen the fortitude of the other girls firsthand for so long that she urged herself to keep going. *Don't give up! This is nothing, don't be dis-couraged!* Finding strength, she tried topic after topic.

"Give it a rest already, would you? I've had enough of your yakkin'." Bete snorted before continuing. "We can cut her loose the moment she's useless. What's the point in trying to break the ice?"

Filvis's eyes flashed at the werewolf's unnecessarily loud remark.

"Uuuuuoh..." Lefiya moaned again, on the verge of tears as the mood took a turn for the worse.

Most likely, it was Bete's propensity to stir up fights that kept ruining the atmosphere.

"I, too, have no interest in becoming anything more than a reluctant acquaintance of yours, lowly werewolf."

"So you *can* talk, devious elf. Now you can sing monsters to their grave with your Magic."

Verbal jabs cut through the air of the crystal-filled forest. Even the distant howls of monsters didn't slow them down.

All this negative energy was taking its toll on Lefiya as Filvis quickened her pace. Not wanting to waste any time, she found the quickest path to the Central Tree's roots, which led to the nineteenth floor below.

"Oi, moron! We ain't got a clue where Aiz is headed. Rivira should be our first stop."

Bete called out to Filvis, insisting that gathering information took priority, but she didn't turn around. Getting fed up, he reached out and grabbed the back of Filvis's collar.

She whipped around in a flash, drawing her sword and swinging it forcefully.

"—Don't you dare touch me!!"

A high-pitched, metallic clang echoed through the forest.

Time stood still as the tip of Filvis's blade came to a stop— directly in front of Lefiya, who was frozen in place.

Bete had easily deflected the blow with the gauntlet strapped to his arm.

"Ahn?"

The metal armor still rang from the impact, just as Bete's eyes reflected his growing bloodthirst. The tattoo on his cheek warped as he seethed at the sudden attack.

One wrong move and blood would be shed—but Lefiya quickly intervened.

"M-Mr. Bete, please stay your hand!"

Arms opened wide, Lefiya stood with her back to Filvis and desperately tried to make Bete understand why she had reacted that way.

"It is elven custom to not allow members of other races to touch our skin! This was…how should I explain…a reflex!"

It was part of elven culture and their way of life. To be more precise, they didn't allow others to touch their skin without consent.

This custom was believed to have originated from their exceptionally high level of pride as a race. However, how strictly this was observed varied by region or sometimes by whether the individual doubted its necessity, meaning that not all elves had the same reaction to physical contact.

Lefiya's birthplace was located deep in a forest often frequented by travelers, so she grew up without this custom being part of her daily life. Compared to other elves, she'd had more contact with members of other races as a child. Consequently, she carried little to no prejudice against the outside world. On the contrary, she wanted to see it all with her own eyes.

It took a few long minutes, but Lefiya managed to convince Bete.

Of course, she thought drawing a sword was an overreaction, without question. But that didn't stop her from desperately defending Filvis.

"Keh," Bete spat, though his rage had subsided before the efforts of his familia member. "Even so, that's goin' too far. Ain't it just something wrong with *her*?"

Bete berated Filvis for her reaction that was out of hand, even for elves, then turned his back on the two and set off westward, toward Rivira.

"……"

The forest went quiet, as if it agreed with the young man's words hanging in the air around them. As Lefiya turned uneasily to look at the other girl, Filvis clamped her mouth shut and fixed her gaze firmly on the ground.

The three adventurers entered the town of Rivira.

Adventurers gathered at this small town, built on the front lines of Dungeon exploration, for all sorts of reasons. But this party had come for a singular purpose: to figure out Aiz's destination. The letter she had sent home stated only that she had accepted a quest on the twenty-fourth floor, and it contained no details.

Loki had inferred the quest was to investigate the source of the unusual number of monsters. That was their only lead, so the three split up to question as many people as possible and gather information quickly.

"Sword Princess? Yeah, I saw her."

"Y-you did?!"

"Pretty damn sure. She was walking with this group of weird-looking guys in hoods. A whole mess of them, really."

Lefiya had stopped to talk with a small exchange shop's Amazonian proprietress. She confirmed that not only had Aiz visited the town, but she was also working with an unidentified party.

Meanwhile, Filvis made her way through the rows of shops and talked with merchants.

"Did you recognize anyone with the Sword Princess?"

"Ehhh, didn't exactly get a good look. Shady-looking guys are nothing new here, and I didn't think it was worth checking into."

"How about their crest? They must've purchased something during their time here."

"The Sword Princess bought everything—using *Loki Familia*'s emblem, no less."

The only valuable piece of information she learned was how Aiz's group had been careful to leave no money trail, yet everything she heard brought them a step closer to learning the identity of the mysterious group. Aiz had flashed her identification to purchase several items while completing other transactions by bartering with magic stones and other items.

"Any idea where the monsters are spilling over from?"

"Y-yeah. They're definitely showing up on the main route that cuts through the twenty-fourth floor...But there're too many to tell from what direction..."

"Thanks for the useless tidbit, bub."

"S-sorry to disappoint…"

Bete kicked in the front doors of a bar. He set to work right away and began interrogating terrified patrons about the monsters that had appeared in the city aboveground.

One adventurer suggested that if they went to the source of the outbreak, they could meet Aiz and the unknown group there. Unfortunately, the monsters were so numerous and pass parades so frequent that it was impossible to discern their origin. It was so bad that even Level Three adventurers were desperately fleeing. Over half the patrons of the bar confirmed that they were waiting for the Guild to dispatch an extermination team before venturing back down.

"Of course *now* is when there's no high-level parties coming through here," said several frustrated voices of adventurers from around the bar. Overhearing them, Bete began to curse so hard it almost made him vomit. He roared that if they couldn't do anything but rely on someone else, they should hang up their armor and stop being adventurers already.

Leaving the now depressed atmosphere of the bar behind, Bete proceeded to the next one.

"So then, no one was able to find anything concrete…" muttered Lefiya after the three of them convened in the town square sometime later.

They shared everything they learned but were no closer to discovering where Aiz had gone than when they first started. Many had seen the Sword Princess pass through. She was a famous first-class adventurer, after all, and easily recognizable. Unfortunately, no one they spoke with could say any more than that.

On the other hand, they learned that the mysterious group had purchased several spare weapons and a large amount of potions. They were preparing for a long, drawn-out battle, most likely with an overwhelming number of monsters. There was no mistake. All of them were going to investigate the Irregular on the twenty-fourth floor.

They had left the town only hours before, so there was a good chance the small party could catch up with them—if only they could pin down the mysterious group's destination.

"If only we had just a little more information…"

Lefiya stood next to Bete and Filvis, scanning the area.

The three of them stood in the middle of town, a place known as Crystal Square. Its name came from the twin white and blue crystals in its center, and it was also famous for the large sand dial that showed the remaining amount of "daylight" left on the eighteenth floor. Quite a bit of sand had already built up in the bottom half. There were still a few broken signs and some jagged wood scattered about, leftovers from the flower-monster attack. Other than that, Crystal Square looked much as it always did.

The myriad crystals that covered this level's ceiling shone brightly overhead, illuminating adventurers as they came in and out of the square.

"You talk to the big buffoon yet?"

Eh? Lefiya turned around, caught off guard by Bete's question. Confused and unsure of who he meant by "the big buffoon," the elf listened to his somewhat reluctant explanation.

"You know, the guy who's always walking around like he owns the place? The big buffoon with the eye patch?"

"Ahh." Lefiya nodded, getting the hint.

"You bet I saw her. Sword Princess paid me a visit."

The three of them went to the proprietor of the largest Exchange shop in Rivira, Bors Elder.

With a body built like a mountain, the patch over his left eye gave him a sinister appearance. Adventurers are outlaws—that was his motto, and he looked the part. At Level Three, he also had the strength and skill to go with it.

As the man who topped Rivira's hierarchy, his information network spread far and wide. The three adventurers counted on it when they decided to speak with him.

Bors was sitting in a chair outside his Exchange shop when they arrived, busily sharpening and maintaining several axes and clubs.

"Asked me to hold some armor for her. 'Don't let it outta your sight,' she says. That's an odd warning, if ya ask me."

"Armor...?"

There was a facility in Rivira where adventurers could temporarily store weapons and other equipment. This service allowed them to reduce their cargo by leaving spares in town that they could pick up on the way back.

As the owner of the only such facility, Bors was raking in the cash. There was a cave just visible behind his shop, and even from a distance, the adventurers could see a great deal of ominous-looking sickles and large destructive bows piled up inside.

"Yeah, have a look."

Lefiya tilted her head as Bors pulled out the item Aiz had entrusted to him.

It was an emerald vambrace, its surface marred with deep gouges.

While it was pretty to look at, this vambrace was not a piece of equipment top-class adventurers would use. In Lefiya's eyes, its properties were far too weak, more befitting a lower-class adventurer.

Why would Aiz be carrying something like this...? Lefiya pondered the question as she looked up from the piece of equipment.

"If I may ask, did Miss Aiz say anything while she was here? We are trying to find her, and any detailed information you can provide would be greatly appreciated..."

"Ohhh? Ya want to know where the Sword Princess went, do ya?" The human stood up from his chair and looked down at Lefiya, placing a hand thoughtfully on his boulder-like chin. A small grin appeared as he laughed to himself, like he knew something they didn't. "Maybe my memory might work better if I heard the clink of a few valis?"

"......"

Lefiya took a small step back, surprised by the man's poorly veiled demand for compensation.

"—Out with it, meathead."

"Ah, sorry, sorry. I'll talk, just let me go!"

Bors immediately dropped the act as soon as Bete took a fistful of his collar and pulled his face in uncomfortably close.

As a bead of sweat rolled down Lefiya's neck at the abrupt shift in the power balance, the large man proceeded to reveal everything.

"Sword Princess and those hooded folks with her bought a lot of trap items for diversions and several sets of camouflage."

"Trap items? The ones that attract monsters...? In that case, there could be only one place Miss Aiz and her companions would go..."

"The pantry, eh?"

Bete finished Lefiya's train of thought.

Trap items triggered a monster's instincts to feed and drew them to one spot. Camouflage was designed to help adventurers blend in with the environs of a specific floor and hide users from nearby enemies. Both items were often used during ventures to a pantry—naturally occurring fertile spaces inside the Dungeon that provided monsters with sustenance. These two items helped the party avoid fighting large swarms of monsters all at once.

The group already knew the floor where Aiz was headed. Now Lefiya and her allies knew their exact destination.

"We're done here," Filvis said and walked away from the shop without another word. Bete also turned to leave.

Finally free of the werewolf's grip, Bors rubbed the back of his neck with one of his large hands and muttered, "Damn that cur," under his breath. "All puffed up, thinkin' he's all that. Outta all of *Loki Familia*, that werewolf pisses me off the most. Say, Thousand Elf, I'll make it worth your time if ya slug 'im for me."

"That is impossible..."

Bors leaned in close to whisper in her ear, but Lefiya flat-out rejected his offer.

She could only imagine the repercussions of doing so. Her life itself would be in danger.

"Oh, and by the way…"

Bors stood back up, looking past Lefiya.

In fact, his eyes were focused on the person beyond Bete—the elf, Filvis.

"Are you working with the Banshee?"

"Eh?"

Lefiya turned to him. Bors cocked an eyebrow as if to say, *You don't know?*

"Banshee…Is that Miss Filvis's title?"

"Nah…That's just what we call her. That elf's title is something else."

A completely different nickname that adventurers had decided among themselves. Even the word *Banshee* had an ominous ring to it.

Lefiya took a moment to steady her beating heart and worked up the courage to ask a question. "Did something happen to Miss Filvis…?"

Bors glanced in the other elf's direction one more time before returning his attention to Lefiya and started talking about the girl's past.

"Every party that's worked with that elf…they're all dead as dead can be."

"?!"

"She's always the only survivor. It doesn't matter if they were part of her familia or not, they all died."

The shock was so great Lefiya felt as though a bird of prey had snatched her heart out with its talons. While she stood speechless, Bete's wolf ears twitched to the side, and he came to a stop.

"Ever heard of the 'Twenty-Seventh-Floor Nightmare'? Happened about six years ago now."

"I-I'm aware of the stories…A great deal of adventurers lost their lives that day."

"That they did. It was back when the Evils were still around. The last of 'em lured a bunch of strong parties into a deathtrap."

The Evils. Although they had been wiped out by the time Lefiya joined *Loki Familia*, she'd heard them come up in conversation many times.

Apparently they despised peace and order. They were led by a group of malevolent deities, radicals, and extremists. Their only mission was to destroy the Guild. They wiped out many familias in the pursuit of this goal, earning the title "Evils."

Some said that of all the atrocities the Evils committed, the Nightmare was by far the most devastating. It had started when they leaked information about strange occurrences in the Dungeon, prompting a large crowd of adventurers to gather in a specific point on the twenty-seventh floor.

Then the ambushers sacrificed themselves to draw an overwhelming number of monsters into the area using pass parades. Monsters from across the floor, including the floor boss, joined the chaotic massacre, where it was impossible to tell friend from foe.

The sight was hellish—rivers of blood, an ocean of dark flames, and a mountain of mangled humanoid bodies, as well as bestial corpses, greeted adventurers who arrived too late. Many said that the remaining monsters feasted on the dead. However, the fact that stories existed at all meant there were enough survivors for rumors.

Influential familias on both sides, whether allied with the Guild or the Evils, suffered such horrific losses that the incident was still well-known as "the Nightmare."

"Filvis Challia was one of the few to make it out alive."

Bors said it while casting his gaze at the elf, who stood off by herself in the distant town square.

"She came back here to Rivira looking like she ran for dear life the whole way...Her face was like a corpse's."

He narrowed his eyes as if remembering what he saw that day.

"I've seen people who've lost their friends, who've lost one body part or another...I've seen all kinds, but never a face that awful."

Torn clothing, bloodstained black hair.

Lightless eyes.

No one dared approach her as she dragged her body along.

As if searching for her dead comrades. As if searching for a way to join them in death.

Like she could only keep drifting around Rivira.

"But yeah, ever since that day, every party she's joined has bit the dust sooner or later. It's like she's been *cursed* or something."

".......!"

"As adventurers, we know our time could come at any moment. When you gotta go, you go...Luck ain't got nothin' to do with it. But word travels fast. Fight alongside that elf and you'll die. Everybody knows."

Once Filvis returned to the Dungeon as an adventurer, she became connected to a string of misfortunes and earned a reputation. One party made a poor decision; an Irregular caught another party off guard; another had crumbled from within.

All these parties had only two things in common: Filvis was a member each time, and they had all been wiped out. She was the only survivor.

"And the rest is what I already told you. Some guys call 'er by that nickname, and many avoid her like the plague."

The party-killing elf—Banshee.

The mournful wails of this fairy had continued since the day of the Nightmare, guiding more victims to an early death.

Adventurers had come to hate and despise the seemingly possessed girl. Even the members of her own *Dionysus Familia* kept a good distance from their leader.

Filvis Challia stood out among her community for all the wrong reasons. Therefore, she had become known as a strictly solo adventurer in Rivira and aboveground.

"I doubt it's a reputation she likes havin'...Just...keep your guard up."

Bors rolled his shoulders before going back into his shop.

Lefiya was left speechless. She and Bete, who had heard most of the story, stared at Filvis even though she didn't return the gesture. Standing close to the railing at the edge of the square overlooking a cliff, her gemlike red eyes focused on something off in the distance.

Lefiya was deep in contemplation. *Just how much has she suffered since she lost her friends during the Nightmare?*

Bors said she had looked like a dead-eyed corpse.

Her pride as an elf would have compounded the pain—by not dying alongside her friends and surviving alone, every breath Filvis took would be more shameful than the last. Could there be any escape from such despair?

As another elf, Lefiya envisioned what it would be like to be in Filvis's shoes. Her body trembled as her sympathy rose.

—Don't you dare touch me!!

Is her violent overreaction a result of fearing the misfortune that follows her?

Did this series of events force her to isolate herself, physically and mentally?

Unable to save so many, being the one who led so many to die, she might very well have done this to herself.

Lefiya knew that these were only guesses, but even so, the idea weighed heavily on her heart.

She couldn't help but picture Filvis's face when she had resembled a soulless husk, when even her own familia put distance between themselves and her. Lefiya's chest tightened as she hurried to catch up with Bete, who was already walking toward the town square.

The two of them approached the waiting elf. Filvis slowly turned in their direction.

Now aware of her past, Lefiya had no idea what to say.

With Lefiya unsure how to proceed, Bete took a step forward with a smirk on his lips.

"I ain't got details, but I know you've left allies to die and live on in shame. Such a disgrace." He drily chuckled in her face as Lefiya continued to watch, stunned. "Why the hell are you still an adventurer? You would've been so much better off if you'd just died along with them."

"Mr. Bete!!"

His words were intended to open old wounds. It enraged Lefiya that Bete showed no mercy to those weaker than himself even at times like this…But Filvis said nothing.

Slowly but surely, the apprehensive front that she had kept during their constant quarreling thus far disappeared, replaced by a small smile.

"It's just as you say."

It was a smile of self-deprecation that twisted the beautiful face that wore it, to the point it bordered on self-mutilation.

"By not perishing along with my familia on that day, I feel shame with every breath I take. I am a disgrace."

Filvis didn't deny that she had abandoned her allies to their fate.

Bete and Lefiya stood completely still as Filvis turned the rest of the way to face them before continuing.

"The rumors have reached you, I suppose? What say you? Shall we part ways? I could very well be the reason you die."

In response to the voice laced with self-hatred…

Bete frowned and clicked his tongue.

"People thinkin' like that pisses me the hell off."

And with those words of disdain, he turned and strode out of the square. He left the elves behind, seemingly abandoning them.

Lefiya and Filvis were alone.

The noise of other adventurers going about their business enveloped them. Someone was playing a stringed instrument, its melodies blending with the various lively conversations drifting around the town. Lights from the crystals above glistened on their golden-yellow and silky black hair.

The two shared a heavy silence, cut off from their bustling surroundings.

Lefiya still couldn't find the words…Filvis avoided making eye contact but opened her mouth to speak.

"Lefiya Viridis...trying to empathize with me would be a mistake. Stay away."

The shock of hearing Filvis say her name for the first time made Lefiya's shoulders tremble.

The one who had gone out of her way to protect her since they began this journey issued her a warning. With her next words, Filvis attempted to shut out her kindness completely.

"I am unclean." A weak smile appeared on her lips as if she was all too aware of the truth. "I do not want to sully my own kin."

Lefiya's eyes widened as Filvis explained.

It was a declaration unbecoming of an elf. Her words hanging in the air, Filvis immediately turned to leave.

The cold shoulder should have been the last nail in the coffin, solidifying her rejection of Lefiya's kindness. The younger elf stood in stunned silence for a moment—then her eyes flooded with determination.

She reached out, fully aware of what might happen, and grabbed Filvis by the wrist.

"You are not unclean!!"

Now it was Filvis's turn to be shocked.

Looking over her shoulder, she stared directly into Lefiya's deep blue eyes. Her words had stunned Filvis but...after a moment, she knocked away the young girl's hand. ·

Lefiya stepped back, clutching her wrist and seeming flustered.

As though surprised at herself for taking so long to break away, Filvis looked down and stared for a while at her hand that Lefiya had grabbed.

"You are far more beautiful and kind than I will ever be!" Lefiya pressed.

It wasn't empathy or an attempt to cheer her up, nor was Lefiya trying to make herself feel better. She spoke sincerely.

The word *unclean* had triggered the reaction. Everything Filvis had said to Lefiya up until this point was for the younger elf's own good, and she couldn't stand to see her insulted, even if those insults came from Filvis's own lips. Elven pride was rooted deeply in the two girls' hearts, as was the kinship they felt with members of their race. A connection that could not be put into words was forming.

Most of all, she couldn't stand back and let the girl before her lock herself away.

As Lefiya made her feelings plain in no uncertain terms, Filvis eyed her in dismay.

She responded with a hint of anger.

"How could you possibly know? Do not speak of things you don't understand! We only just met."

"Gah…" Lefiya couldn't string words together in the face of Filvis's sound argument.

*To lose now would be…*Lefiya blurted out the first rebuttal that came to mind.

"I-I'll find many examples during our time together!!"

"……"

"……"

Her words blindsided Filvis.

Lefiya was still frozen in the same pose as when she spoke.

The reckless response of her kin left Filvis feeling like her efforts were pointless…"Heh." The sound slipped out of her after a few moments.

She quickly covered her mouth with her fingers in an attempt to hide her laughter, but it was useless.

"Heh-heh." Giving up, she let her lips grow into a smile as she pointed out the flaws in Lefiya's logic.

"Think about what you just said. That wasn't an answer."

"Ahh…"

Lefiya blushed as she acknowledged Filvis's point.

Seeing her reaction, the older elf fought harder to contain her laughter, shoulders shaking. A soft giggle like the chirping of small birds escaped from her dainty lips.

© Kiyotaka Haimura

This could very well be…

…the first time that she, a loathed adventurer, had laughed in a very long time.

Lefiya's face burned with embarrassment, but she couldn't help but smile upon seeing Filvis's expression.

I cannot explain it, but…

There were things that could be understood only between kin. The person standing in front of her was a proud elf with a beautiful spirit. Through their brief interaction, Lefiya was certain of it.

"…You are a bizarre elf," Filvis quietly remarked, her expression no longer tense.

Her demeanor was ever so slightly less thorny, and Lefiya couldn't have been happier.

The two young women made eye contact underneath the blue underground "sky."

"Hey, you elven slackers! Move your asses!"

—And got scolded for it.

The two turned in the direction of the yell and, sure enough, Bete was waiting for them at the edge of the town square.

Lefiya and Filvis exchanged another glance and nodded to each other before rushing to join him.

The three adventurers left Rivira together, just as they had come.

The silver saber Desperate whistled through the air.

"ROOoo—!"

It connected at an angle with the bladelike antlers of a deer monster—a swordstag—and cut straight into the creature's head.

The monster bucked its hind legs before collapsing to the Dungeon floor with a loud *thud*.

"Whoaaa. I knew you were strong, but…wow!"

Lulune observed Aiz's instant victory and was impressed.

Her target had fallen, but Aiz didn't let her guard down. Scanning the area for more threats, she glanced over her shoulder at her allies. Her new temporary party had already finished cleaning up the last of the wave of monsters they encountered.

The walls surrounding them were covered in tree bark, and patches of glowing blue moss lit their way. As monsters that had gotten stronger with each passing floor fell in their wake, Aiz and the members of *Hermes Familia* arrived on the twenty-fourth floor.

This floor was very close to being considered one of the lower levels of the Dungeon. While it lacked the intersections and twisting paths of the upper levels and the rest of the middle levels, it was much larger than any previous floors. In fact, the hallways and rooms were so wide, the sixteen-adventurer party could fight freely without feeling confined.

At the same time, the monster numbers and encounter frequency also increased. However, Lulune and the rest of *Hermes Familia* hardly broke a sweat as they systematically eliminated their targets.

"Lulune…your familia is quite strong as well…"

"You don't have to be so reserved. We're practically the same age, you know?"

Explaining that she was eighteen, Lulune said she wanted to keep things casual.

Aiz nodded in understanding while party leader Asfi issued orders from the front of the formation. "Advance," she commanded.

It took a few moments for the group to form, and then they pushed forward as a unit.

"Well, we're not hiding our Levels just so we can show off, you know. Of course I'm pretty good, but Asfi and the crew can fight as well as some of the best."

At their position in the middle of the formation, Aiz and Lulune were close enough to continue their conversation while they advanced.

Aiz had already known going in, but Lulune's acrobatic fighting style and knife skills were impressive. As a thief, she did not exactly enjoy engaging in intense, pitched battles. But when push came to shove, she assisted her allies with disruptive guerrilla tactics, aiming for monster limbs and landing one attack at a time.

All individually strong, exponentially stronger with well-organized teamwork...

When it came to *Hermes Familia*, it was difficult to point out any flaws. Even the supporters with backpacks strapped to their shoulders could hold their own.

A war tiger wielding both large shield and greatsword, prums with perfectly timed spells, elves with a wide array of short bows and hand axes at their disposal...They executed different formations and tactics in battle after battle on their way to this floor. The first time Aiz saw any action at all was downing that swordstag earlier, proof of *Hermes Familia*'s skill in combat.

Their teamwork reflected their leader's personality. Each part of their battle line—vanguard, center, and rear guard—had a specific role to play. Asfi took charge of the middle ranks herself, making it particularly fearsome. With jack-of-all-trades fighters like Lulune, they were extremely capable in coordinating attacks as well as quickly responding to the ever-changing tides of combat. With a solid and dependable center anchoring their party, the adventurers on the front and rear lines could focus on giving their all.

Eliminating meaningless movements and placing an emphasis on efficiency might be their doctrine, but above all else, they were strong.

In terms of their strength as a party, they were on par with top-class adventurers, including Aiz, and as strong as *Loki Familia*'s core troops, if not stronger.

Aiz had never paid much attention to *Hermes Familia*, but now she admired them.

Especially...

She looked ahead at the woman with aqua-blue hair and the white cloak over her shoulders.

Asfi usually issued commands during battle, hardly ever joining the fray. But when she did, the way she wielded her shortsword was a sight to behold.

Even as the leader of accomplished fighters, her abilities were head and shoulders above the rest.

"Oh? Asfi caught your eye?"

"…Lulune, what's her Level?" Aiz asked quietly, leaning in close.

"Level Four," answered Lulune without a second thought.

It was just as Aiz expected. However, she couldn't help but feel there was more to it. Asfi's skill in battle all but confirmed this, and doubtless she was cautious to reveal as little as possible.

Hermes Familia *is much stronger than everyone thinks*, she concluded silently.

Aiz decided to ask Lulune a question or two to figure out the extent.

"How far below have you gone?"

"The thirty-seventh. But those monsters are pretty damn strong, so we didn't make it far."

If she recalled correctly, according to Guild announcements, *Hermes Familia* had reached only the nineteenth floor. Their actual progress was almost double that. Hearing that *Hermes Familia* had set foot in the Deep Levels was surprising.

That brought Aiz to her second question, something she was very curious about.

"It's amazing you've managed to go so deep without other adventurers noticing…"

A party this large going that far into the Dungeon was sure to attract attention—and expose their secret about hidden Levels. At least, Aiz thought so.

Lulune grinned proudly and boasted, "Don't forget, our boss is *the* Perseus. She can make awesome magic items, and there's one that *prevents anyone else from seeing*—"

"Quit the chatter, Lulune."

Asfi cut Lulune off with a sharp warning. Her piercing glare from behind her silver glasses delivered the message loud and clear: *Don't say what can be left unsaid.*

"S-sorry, Asfi."

"Good grief…"

Lulune, who had been giddy with excitement a moment ago, tried to make herself as small as possible.

Asfi sighed, amazed that a thief could be so careless with sensitive information. She came to Aiz's side.

"Sword Princess, I would like your honest opinion about this quest."

"…What do you mean?"

"Lulune has informed me about the attack on Rivira, specifically how it began. A darkly dressed stranger issued a quest involving a mysterious orb…Do you believe this undertaking is dangerous?"

Asfi hinted that the involvement of Black Robe meant that the unusual monster outbreak could be linked with the orb as well. She wanted to know if this quest could lead to another event like the one that nearly destroyed Rivira.

Aiz waited briefly before giving an affirmative nod. At the very least, her opinion as an adventurer was that this was not to be taken lightly.

Asfi did her best to hold back another sigh upon hearing that.

"Well then, we got pulled into a real mess, didn't we…?"

Lulune heard the entire exchange, and her shoulders fell further still. However, Asfi didn't press the point. As the leader of the group, it was her job to keep everyone unified.

Hermes Familia used their superb teamwork to quickly dispatch the monsters that sporadically tried to block their path as Aiz and the party progressed through the twenty-fourth floor's main route.

The entrance to the nineteenth floor of the Dungeon sat under the massive tree in the middle of the eighteenth floor, the safe point. The area extending from there to the twenty-fourth floor was known as the Colossal Tree Labyrinth.

The walls and ceiling of the floors were covered in a thick layer of tree bark, and the pattern on the floor made it appear as though they were traveling through a hollowed-out tree trunk. Instead of the phosphorescent light sources that occupied the floors above, the Colossal Tree Labyrinth was lit by soft blue illumination from random patches of wall moss.

Strange types of leaves, large mushrooms, and flowers with silver sap lined the hallways and rooms that adventurers needed to pass through. Most plants here didn't exist on the surface. Every location adventurers visited had its own unique combination of colors, some rooms even containing lush flower beds.

At the same time, the monsters appearing on this floor were much more aggressive than those above, some equivalent to or stronger than Level Two adventurers. More than ever, precise teamwork and cooperation were required to safely pass to the twenty-fourth floor.

"Oh! Look at that! White Leaves! Asfi, mind if I grab a few?"

"Leave them. Monsters will ambush you the moment you try to collect any. We can't waste energy or resources before our quest is completed."

"Shops all over the city are running low on them, too. We could've made a killing...Such a waste."

Lulune had spotted a White Tree as they passed through a hallway and into the back of the room. She immediately moved to collect the leaves, but Asfi stopped her. The chienthrope was reluctant to pass on easy profits, her tail drooping.

This floor's plant diversity often provided ingredients desirable to chemists, resulting in many quests being issued for this area. Many of the leaves and roots had healing properties so potent that eating them raw could restore health or cure ailments on the spot. Useful as the main component for healing items, these collectibles were incredibly valuable. Even the luminescent moss growing on the walls could be sold for a decent price aboveground.

The group spotted an incredibly rare jewel tree—a tree that produced dazzling red and blue gems that could be sold for a great deal of money—sending a wave of excitement through the party. Even Asfi's eyes lit up. It pained them all to know they had to press forward without collecting a single one. These trees were protected by green dragons, the strongest monsters on the floor and a good match for even Level Four adventurers. As with the Cadmus dragons on the fifty-first floor, it was common for powerful creatures known as treasure keepers to guard rare items.

Aiz spotted a green dragon sprawled out at the base of the jewel tree. A shot of adrenaline rushed through her when its green eyes met hers. However, she didn't want to cause problems for her companions and didn't stop to challenge the beast.

The green dragon clamped its eyes shut the moment the blond, golden-eyed swordswoman left, its large body stirring repeatedly as if recoiling from fright.

"...!"

"Halt the advance."

Aiz was the first to pick up on the presence farther down the hallway, but the others weren't far behind. Asfi immediately threw up her hand, signaling their band to stop.

Two hallways intersected directly in their path. It was difficult to tell in the soft blue light of the moss, but countless shadows shifted within the darkness. The adventurers needed only a moment to recognize what they were seeing.

It was a procession of monsters so numerous that it was impossible to tell where one body ended and the next began. The wide passage was completely packed.

"Ughh..."

Lulune's voice trailed off next to Aiz.

The spectacle of the monsters crowding through the hallway was so overwhelming that the other adventurers reflexively took a step back. The hideous beasts continued endlessly as though from a hidden burrow, and the sight alone was enough to send a chill down anyone's spine.

Aiz observed them, thinking that so many monsters concentrated in one place could not be natural. She'd never seen this many together in one area, let alone proceeding down a hallway in a column.

The group briefly stood in awe before some of the monsters took notice. A few broke away from the stream, others following behind.

"Asfi, what do we do?"

"They must be dealt with eventually. We end it here."

Lulune's line of sight was fixed on the oncoming enemies as she addressed Asfi. The leader called out to her company: "Prepare for battle!"

Each member readied a weapon, and designated adventurers arrived in the front to take their places in the shield wall.

"Magic users, begin casting. We need to reduce their numbers before first contact—"

"Wait."

Aiz interrupted Asfi in the middle of her orders.

The blue-haired woman shot an angry glare in her direction, but Aiz calmly said:

"Leave this to me."

"What?"

Jerking Desperate from its sheath, Aiz charged into the oncoming wave at full speed.

"H-hey! What are you doing?!"

Hermes Familia's preparations suddenly halted as the Sword Princess advanced alone.

Aiz engaged her first opponents at about the same time Lulune's screams of disbelief reached her ears.

One wide swing of her silver saber, and the dying howls of several monsters signaled the beginning of the fray.

"OOOOOooooo——————————!"

The extermination was under way.

Monsters were eviscerated with every mighty cleave of her blade, many collapsing in lifeless heaps. One slash slew three at once as she dodged another beast's claws and counterattacked in mid-roll. She sprang up, golden mane splayed out behind her as she cut her attacker down in a flash of light.

She faced the swarm head-on, meeting claws and fangs with steel.

With every step forward, the beasts around Aiz vanished—more accurately, they littered the floor with their corpses and small mountains of ash.

Her saber was like a barrier. Any that entered its range met a merciless fate. Heads, limbs, and chunks of torsos flew in every direction.

The title "Sword Princess" no longer seemed appropriate. Aiz used pure force to overpower monster attacks and defenses, taking on multiple enemies at once and leaving a path of devastation in her wake.

The bloodthirsty roars echoing through the hallway only moments before had become howls of terror.

"......"

"......"

"...It would seem we can leave everything to her, no?"

"...Wanna head home?"

"You know we can't do that..."

As the rest of the party observed her mutely, Asfi mumbled to herself and answered Lulune's question quietly. She had fought back the urge to nod before rejecting the idea.

Watching the massacre unfolding before them, the members of *Hermes Familia* couldn't help but wonder if their presence was even necessary.

"!"

Aiz was vaguely aware of the many stares watching her from far behind, but she wasn't about to let up.

While she never allowed a single beast to deliver a clean hit, she did periodically need to go out of her way to block, pushing her body to move even faster.

If only there were more...

Despite the monstrous visages reflecting in her golden eyes, she was more focused on the sensations of her own body.

Aiz was testing herself, seeing what she could do. The ideal way was real combat with monsters.

She had just leveled up.

With her new Level Six Status, she needed to experience the dramatic boost in strength and speed firsthand.

Whenever an adventurer leveled up, their mind and body needed time to adjust. The sudden leap in their abilities could be disorienting. Aiz repeated the same actions over and over to fine-tune her senses and movements, speeding up the process of acclimating to her new body.

Aiz had rushed to the eighteenth floor after pursuing Bell Cranell. Add in the potency of *Hermes Familia*'s efficient teamwork, and she had hardly fought all day. This was her chance to cut loose, and she wouldn't waste it.

She didn't use her Magic.

Aiz piled on kill after kill with pure swordsmanship and physical strength alone.

"!"

"GHIII—!"

Slicing down monster after monster at dizzying speed, Aiz arrived at the end of the hallway, kicked off the wall, and flipped into the air.

She neatly cleaved the deadly hornet directly above in two.

Deadly hornets were known for their agility, but this one couldn't evade her saber. As the bisected corpse hit the ground, Aiz spun and dispatched two swordstags while in the air. The rest of the pack couldn't even press their chance to attack when she landed because Aiz was already racing out to meet them, ready to strike.

"GAAAAAaaa!!"

"SHAA!"

© Kiyotaka Haimura

The remaining monsters began to express their fear as the horde dwindled around them. Amid their fright, three lizardmen equipped with nature weapons—a hardened flower for a shield, its thorny stem acting as a shortsword—came to the fore and challenged Aiz to a duel. The three scaly warriors' display of courage was cut incredibly short, however, as their flawed swordplay was exposed with three quick flicks of Aiz's wrist.

Next in line to stop Aiz's merciless rampage were several mushroom monsters known as dark fungi. They flooded the air with a highly toxic pollen that was harmful to friend and foe alike—but to no avail. These middle-level monsters didn't have pollen nearly potent enough to overpower Aiz's advanced Immunity skill. The poison had no effect.

Aiz charged straight into the cloud of toxic spores.

Ignoring the pained cries of lizardmen and swordstags as they fell, she dashed through the poisonous cloud and skewered the dark fungi before finishing off the rest.

"OOOooooo..."

In a fierce battle where second-tier adventurers would have lost their lives, Aiz had overpowered her adversaries without taking a scratch. The monsters had never stood a chance.

The fight drew to a close with the dying rasp of a hobgoblin, a stronger species of goblin often found higher up in the Dungeon.

The large-category creature slammed down with a dull *thud*. Only then did Aiz place Desperate back in its sheath.

The stream of monsters had been completely wiped out in about ten minutes.

"...So that's...the Sword Princess?"

Asfi stood in the middle of the hallway, looking past the mounds of carrion toward the female knight standing at the other end.

Lulune gulped as her allies watched with awe. The chienthrope narrowed her eyes in a smile at her fellow adventurer's back.

"...W-well, that's the top class for you, strong as hell. Taking down a mob like that with no backup, no wonder everybody's always scared to death! Ah, need a potion?"

"No, I'm fine...Thanks."

It took Lulune and the rest of *Hermes Familia* a moment to return to normal, but they greeted the returning Aiz with warm smiles.

Realizing they had one of the best, most dependable allies in the world, they showered her with compliments and admiration.

Embarrassed by the sudden praise, Aiz wasn't sure how to react. However, she had a better sense of the new height she had achieved. Maintaining a similar pace for the same duration at Level Five would have been extremely taxing. But now, she didn't even need a recovery potion afterward.

Aiz was fully aware of her improved strength and speed, but it was her newfound endurance that made the largest impression on her.

"Well, the monsters are all cleaned up, but...what do we do now, Asfi?"

The hallway had become a morgue, with carcasses strewn as far as the eye could see. They couldn't just leave all the loot, so the supporters rushed out to collect magic stones and drop items. In the meantime, Lulune wanted to get Asfi's opinion.

Aiz stopped flexing her fists and gave her full attention.

"If we can trust Black Robe, the pantry's where we need to go. There are three of them on the twenty-fourth floor—to the southwest, to the southeast, and to the north. Where should we start?"

With a quiet rustling noise, she fumbled with the pouch at her waist and pulled out a sheet. It was a folded map of the twenty-fourth floor.

Sure enough, three massive areas were marked off—larger than any room on the map—in red ink circles. Aiz approached Lulune and peeked over her shoulder as the chienthrope scanned the map.

Seeing it drawn out like this, it hit her just how big the floor was.

Each floor of the Dungeon was larger than the previous one, and the twenty-fourth was at least half the size of Orario. Should they need to visit all three pantries, the sheer number of monsters they would encounter, plus the ground they had to cover, would take its toll.

The party waited for their leader's decision. Asfi proposed, "We'll let the monsters tell us."

"Huh?"

"We should find the source of the outbreak by retracing their steps. If what we're looking for is in a pantry, all we need to do is reverse the path the monsters took to get here."

"I see." Aiz agreed with Asfi's logic.

All their sources of information about the outbreak pointed to a pantry. Rather than investigate all three for irregularities, following the flow would allow them to find their goal by process of elimination.

Lulune and other members of the party caught on to the idea, exchanging glances and nods. They turned their attention to the remains of the monsters Aiz had wiped out only a few moments ago.

They'd been pushing one another, momentum carrying the procession forward. The slain monsters at the intersection had come from...

"...The north, huh?"

In the soft blue light of the moss on the walls, Lulune whispered as she analyzed the tracks and the heading the corpses faced. She peered farther down the hall in that direction.

The party set off for the northern pantry as soon as the supporters finished amassing loot.

"So we're going to the pantry after all...Just has to be a hotbed for newborn monsters. Any thoughts, Sword Princess?"

"I'm not sure...but..."

"But?"

"It's...probably not so simple."

Lulune and Aiz continued their conversation, occasionally interrupted by Asfi, as the party proceeded down the hallway.

They knew their choice to head north was correct after encountering more monster ranks traveling through the hallways. Asfi, wanting to conserve Mind, energy, and supplies, asked Aiz to take care of them each time. It went without saying that the Sword Princess did have a limit and accepted potions from a human supporter, periodically resting to recover her strength.

As they pressed on, the Dungeon's appearance began to shift.

The bark walls and ceiling became patchy, revealing rough areas of solid reddish rock. It wasn't long before their route transitioned into what seemed like a cave.

This change was proof their destination was close. A pillar of quartz stood deep inside every pantry. Hungry monsters came from far and wide to drink the nutritious fluid that pooled at the base of the pillars. The Dungeon focused on optimizing energy use around the pantries to provide this food, so the surrounding environment reverted to the most basic form.

What had caused the outbreak?

What was waiting for them at their destination?

Anxiety was starting to affect Lulune and the rest of *Hermes Familia*. Sensing the tension, Aiz stayed on high alert. The monster presence had all but disappeared, making the Dungeon too quiet. Still, the party pressed forward.

"Wha...?"

That's when the adventurers saw *it*.

"A-a wall...?"

"...Is that a plant?"

Something was blocking their path, a looming barricade large enough to plug the hallway.

It was an eerie sight, its strange appearance heightened by the squirming, pulsing movements on its surface. They came to a stop in front of the off-putting green-flesh barrier, unable to advance. The rocky walls of the Dungeon abruptly ended where the green monstrosity began. They were two completely different entities.

It seemed to be alive—plantlike, as someone had whispered earlier. Or maybe a cancerous growth afflicting the Dungeon.

Asfi had led her allies into the Deep Levels, and Aiz had traveled far deeper than this numerous times, but never had any of them laid eyes on something resembling this.

The jittery party talked among themselves, unsure of what to make of the thing.

"...Lulune, are we on the right path?"

"Th-this is it. I picked a direct path to the pantry straight from the map. This shouldn't be here...but it is."

Lulune quickly pulled out the chart again to check their position after Asfi asked for confirmation.

As the map carrier, Lulune was the party's guide. Aiz had been beside her the whole time and could confirm that Lulune had made the correct decision every time they reached a fork in the path. They were exactly where they should be.

The pantry should be just a little farther down this hallway.

Aiz stared up at the sinewy bulwark that barred their path.

"...We'll check the other routes. Falgar, Thane, make two squads and take the others to investigate. Do not go too far in. Report back the instant you find something."

On Asfi's command, the hulking war tiger and an elven man nodded. Extra maps in hand, they each took five adventurers to form small parties and doubled back on the path.

After watching them return to the previous fork in the road, Aiz and the remaining members of *Hermes Familia* again considered the wall.

The only four adventurers left in this location were Aiz, Lulune, Asfi, and a supporter. No one spoke as they individually investigated their surroundings.

There was nothing out of the ordinary with the exposed rock wall. It seemed less likely the problem originated with the Dungeon itself and more that the fleshy mass blocking the hallway was separate. Aiz decided to go near Lulune, who was visibly shaken as she paced back and forth.

The twenty-fourth floor's hallways were massive. Closing one off completely meant that the wall had a span of at least ten square meders. It also gave off a putrid stench, reminiscent of rotting flesh.

"Nasty…"

As a chienthrope, Lulune had to plug her nose to calm her stomach.

Aiz ventured closer to the repugnant barrier and slowly reached toward it.

Lulune immediately rushed over to stop her, but Aiz heeded no warnings as her fingers brushed against the wall's fleshy surface.

It's alive…

She could feel heat and a slight twitch through the palm of her hand. Eyes and ears hyperalert, muscles ready to react to the slightest inkling of danger, Aiz continued to peer at the meaty surface.

"Asfi, we're back."

"What did you find?"

Once the other groups of adventurers had returned from scouting, Aiz rejoined Asfi's group as they put some distance between themselves and the wall.

From what they'd seen, the other routes into the pantry were also blocked by the same kind of fleshy screen. Most likely, all paths that led into this pantry were now impassible.

It didn't take long for Asfi to develop her own theory.

"It appears that this outbreak is an Irregular…but it didn't originate from a sudden influx of monsters born from the Dungeon."

"Wh-what does that mean?"

Asfi pushed her glasses up against the bridge of her nose when Lulune asked for clarification.

"Hungry monsters gather at pantries on their floor. If, for instance, their path was blocked for some reason…what do you think these starving fellows would do then?"

"Ah…"

"…Travel to a different pantry."

Aiz answered the question in Lulune's place, and Asfi nodded.

"The monsters who came to the northern pantry had no choice but to change course and travel south to one of the other pantries. The large flows of monsters that adventurers have encountered over the past few days were not outbreaks but *migrations*."

Asfi concluded that creatures from this floor's northern half, unable to feed at this pantry, were stampeding southward—directly into the path of unlucky adventurers.

With these walls blocking the entrances, an extraordinarily large number of hungry creatures had joined the mass migration across every major pathway on the floor, including the ones adventurers normally used.

The sudden food scarcity was now clearly linked to the outbreak. The party members agreed as Lulune turned around. "Now we know why all the monsters were wandering around…So, what's on the other side of that wall?"

The unidentified greenish, plantlike boundary was the cause of everything.

The Irregular was right in front of them—whatever was on the other side was *not normal*, that much was certain.

"…Asfi, what's your call?"

"…Do we have any other choice but to go in?"

Lulune tucked her tail between her legs after asking her question. Asfi answered with a long sigh.

The chienthrope wasn't thrilled, either, shoulders drooping as she mumbled under her breath, "Yeah, yeah, I know."

"But doesn't that look kinda like a gate…?"

She pointed out a spot on the imposing wall that resembled a flower bud with all the petals turned inward. On closer inspection, it looked more like a mouth.

It was large enough to allow the most fearsome large-category monsters to easily pass through. If an entrance it was, then there was a possibility it would open automatically if they waited long enough, but…their chances were not great.

"It looks like destroying it is our only option."

Asfi took a long look at the opening as well as the rest of the fleshy wall before making her decision.

"Since it's probably a plant of some kind, fire magic might do the trick…"

"Shall I cut it down?"

"Please don't say things like that with a straight face, Sword Princess…"

Aiz had already pulled Desperate halfway out of its sheath. Lulune sent her an astonished glance over her shoulder.

Asfi took another few moments to consider before saying, "No," rejecting Aiz's suggestion.

"This is an opportunity to collect information. I want to see what we can do if we use our Magic. Merrill."

A prum spellcaster came to the front of the party at Asfi's call.

Everyone watched as the girl, barely taller than Aiz's waist, held up a short rod and began her spell. Her pointed hat rocked and swayed.

The skilled caster chanted as a magic circle appeared and expanded. The prum's voice was soft as a huge fireball blasted from her rod.

The mass of flames collided with the sinewy facade in a thunderous roar, igniting the structure.

An ominous wailing sound similar to a scream filled the air as flaming pieces of the wall scattered. The "gate" was now nothing but a gaping hole, and the mouth of the charred barrier was open.

Asfi made eye contact with each of her allies, who all nodded back. They lined up and faced the entrance.

Aiz and *Hermes Familia* entered.

"The wall…"

A strange gushing sound alerted the party that the situation was rapidly developing. Lulune looked over her shoulder and gawked as the structure started healing itself.

"In no way are we trapped. We simply need to open another hole on the way out."

Asfi was quick to put the uneasy minds of her allies at ease and shore up morale. Sure enough, Lulune and the others quickly calmed down. Aiz joined them, everyone scanning their new environment.

The sides, ceiling, and floor of the interior were the same shade of pale green. They couldn't help but feel they were walking *inside* something alive.

The odor of rotting flesh had grown thicker after they had burned down the door. Aiz walked near the internal walls.

Desperate in hand, she sliced the green surface open with a quick slash.

It gave way with almost no resistance. On the other side—reddish rock. The same rock face that should be here on the twenty-fourth floor.

Something's covering the Dungeon...?

Aiz thought it looked as though fleshy wallpaper had been affixed to the labyrinth.

"What the hell *is* this?" Lulune mumbled with a hint of disgust as the wall, too, started healing itself.

*Regeneration...*Aiz silently watched the fleshy mass exhibit a self-regenerating ability just like the Dungeon's, and she thought about what it meant.

"We're pressing on."

The party pushed through the greenish territory at Asfi's command.

The putrid, lingering scent took its toll on the animal people in the party. No one could hide their fear at this point.

A mysterious green space had suddenly appeared in the Dungeon. The fact that this was unexplored territory weighed on them with each heavy step deeper into the ominous atmosphere of this Irregular.

"Hey, mind if I say something scary? If all these twitching, wiggling bits are the gross guts of some monster…we're literally walking right into the belly of the beast, right?"

"Oi!" "Cut it out!" "Keep your thoughts to yourself."

Lulune's terrifying offhand comment stirred up a storm. Everyone agreed on one thing: there was no evidence to support her theory. At the same time, the tension that had been hanging over *Hermes Familia* suddenly lost its edge. Aiz listened to them bicker and kept her eyes open. She noticed something strange in her peripheral vision.

Flickering light illuminated the space.

It was dim, not much stronger than a candle. And climbing the walls and ceiling were wilting flowers.

Flowers. Vivid red flowers.

Aiz frowned.

"A fork in the path…It appears that the maps we have won't be of much use any longer."

They had traveled through the exceptionally dim passageway for several minutes.

Asfi came to a stop at the intersection. The hallway diverged into four directions: left, right, straight ahead, and up.

Apparently the green walls created a whole new layout within the Dungeon. Although the outer walls must have butted up against the Dungeon, the inner passages intertwined like plant roots in the ground. Their path was about to become much more complicated.

Aiz was caught off guard, unsure how to proceed. Asfi, however, addressed their chienthrope.

"Lulune, make a map."

"Gotcha covered."

The leader's voice was calm, cool, and collected. At her behest, Lulune opened her pouch and took out another sheet of paper and a red-feathered pen—the same kind that Aiz carried—and set to work.

First, she established their entrance point and traced the route taken thus far by using the size of her steps as a reference. She traced the twists and turns of the pathway with astounding accuracy.

In a word, she was a cartographer.

Aiz peered over Lulune's shoulder with visible shock.

"Amazing…You can draw maps."

"Oh? It's not a big deal. Sure, I'll take praise from the Sword Princess any day, but…I *am* a thief, after all."

A quiet giggle escaped her lips, and she blushed, but her hands never stopped moving. Aiz acknowledged the girl possessed a skill she did not have while watching her hand-drawn map take shape until it finally reached their current location.

Map data were available for adventurers to use at the Guild nowadays, so they enjoyed the ability to prowl wherever they wanted in the Dungeon without the fear of getting lost. That was all thanks to the brave people who had been exploring the Dungeon since the Ancient Times. They went into the unknown and put their lives on the line with no prior knowledge, pioneering the main routes through each floor and eventually mapping out every detail.

Aiz and other adventurers were able to enjoy a wealth of map data only thanks to the hard work of their forebears. As proof, the Sword Princess herself had no clue how to make a map or where to start. She was certain the other adventurers—with the exception of cartographers who went into unexplored areas to collect geography data to sell—didn't know what went into making maps, either.

For the first time in her life, the idea of exploring unknown regions made a chill run down her spine.

She had been so focused on fighting that she had forgotten the true purpose of adventuring. It was her occupation, and yet missing such a key piece of the puzzle gave her pause.

At the same time, she held a tremendous new respect for Lulune.

"You're…very good…"

"Ah-ha-ha, if you knew how many times Lord Hermes has taken me outside the city into some old ruins or through dark caves, you'd know why. I'm used to this kind of thing."

Asfi gave the order, and the party proceeded down the right path. Meanwhile, Lulune busily updated her map as Aiz watched with interest. The chienthrope recounted some of her experiences with her god, grinding her molars at the same time.

Checking passageways one by one, Aiz and *Hermes Familia* made their way through the skein of this complicated new labyrinth.

Despite being fully engrossed in her cartography, Lulune didn't forget to drop crystal shards she'd collected on the eighteenth floor every so often to mark their path. That way, they would always be able to retrace their steps.

"I hate to say it…but it looks like the trap items and camouflage we bought in Rivira won't be much use."

"You got a point there…Eh?"

It went without saying that there were no monsters inside this place, so an unnatural silence hung in the passageways. Just as members of the party were beginning to think they were overdue for a discovery of some kind, they stumbled upon one.

Unnaturally scattered piles of ash littered the floor right in the middle of an open passage.

"Dead monsters?"

"Yes. It appears so."

There were no magic stones to be seen in any of the piles of ash, but Asfi was quick to find a drop item.

"How would that get in here…?" Lulune wondered out loud.

Asfi answered that question as she drew a shortsword from its sheath.

"If my theory is correct, a group of monsters capable of penetrating the 'gate' made it this far…and were slain by *something else*."

Hearing that, the atmosphere around *Hermes Familia* drew taut once again. Aiz and others quick to connect the dots were already preparing their weapons as they searched for the slightest sign of trouble.

Monsters strong enough to tear a hole in the fleshy wall that barred their way to the pantry—were now no more than piles of ash. They had been stopped in their tracks.

Asfi directed her team to cover the more vulnerable party members in the rear. Everyone's senses were on high alert, muscles tensed.

The adventurers focused on every detail around them in the dark openings, the path ahead, and the path behind. As for Aiz...

...She was the only one to look up.

"—Above."

The sounds of shifting armor and fluttering fabric swept through the party like a wave as Asfi and the others looked toward the ceiling.

Guided by Aiz's voice, they spotted in the maddeningly dim light many *large slithering bodies.*

The monsters crawling across the ceiling far above their heads had richly colored flower petals, and several were leaking mucus.

A maw opened to reveal rows of jagged fangs—and the meat-eating plants dropped down a moment later.

"OOOOOOOOOOOOOOOOOOOOOOOOOOOOOOOOOOOO OOOOOO!!"

Roars like broken bells assaulted them from every direction as Asfi shouted:

"All units, attack!"

Dodging the falling creatures, Aiz and *Hermes Familia* charged into battle.

"Levis, we have intruders."

A man's voice sounded in an open chamber bathed in ominous red light.

"Monsters?"

"No, adventurers. I knew they'd come," growled a man dressed in white after the red-haired woman, Levis, asked for confirmation.

The two of them stood still even though many people dressed in robes hurried about in the vicinity. The people appeared to be concerned about the presence of adventurers, calling out to one another on the verge of panic.

Levis glanced at them for a moment, unamused.

"A midsize party…They appear formidable."

A bluish white liquid membrane in the shape of the moon covered a nearby flesh wall. The battle between plants and adventurers was reflected in its shiny surface.

Levis showed no interest in the display—that is, until a beautiful swordswoman with blond hair and golden eyes appeared. Her eyes flared.

She stood up with a start from her seat on the floor. "That's Aria."

"What?"

The woman's whisper got the man's attention.

His lips twitched in confusion as he realized that Levis's green gaze was glued to Aiz.

"The Sword Princess is Aria…? Impossible."

"Oh, she is."

The short, red-haired woman stood, acting like a completely different person. Her demeanor itself had become ferocious.

Like a hunter on the cusp of a kill or a messenger from hell set to unleash a calamity, her overwhelming presence was cold as ice.

She glared at the girl reflected in the liquid membrane.

"I'm going. Separate Aria from the rest."

"…Fine."

But the woman hadn't waited for a response. She already had her back to him, heading deeper into the chamber.

Illuminated by the bloodred light, the woman's ferocious visage melted into the darkness.

A fierce battle raged beneath a bluish white flower blooming on the ceiling.

The monsters charged into large shields, launching their bodies like battering rams. They hurled their whiplike roots at magic users mid-spell, only to have them swatted away by adventurers in the formation's center. As the enemies aggressively targeted the casters in the rear of the formation, it took everything *Hermes Familia* had to hold the monsters at bay. The two sides were evenly matched in a one-step-forward, one-step-back clash of steel and fangs.

"Lulune, where are their magic stones?"

Among the party facing an unknown opponent, the first to get a good grasp on the situation was Asfi.

Fending off multiple enemies with her shortsword, she cut deep into their large bodies whenever possible.

A series of broken howls drew the attention of the other creatures directly to her. However, none of the monsters could land a hit as Asfi jumped and spun between their attacks as if she were light as a feather, causing them to roar in frustration.

"Um, should be in their mouths!"

Lulune fended off her own attackers with a knife not much smaller than her leader's sword. She hollered the intelligence she had acquired during the attack on Rivira as loud as she could.

"Their mouths, you say," said Asfi with her eyes focused on the chin of a nearby monster. She deflected one of the whips with her cloak and produced a vial of dark-red liquid from her belt holster.

She flung it straight into the monster's open mouth in one swift motion—*BOOM!*

"―――――――――ah!"

The explosion going off in its throat prevented the beast's scream from ever being heard. Its magic stone caught in the blast, the predator fell to the ground in a heap of ash.

A special hand grenade that could only be created by an item maker: Burst Oil. Producing it required materials not found inside the city—Asfi had created this potent item using the flower called an obia flare that grew only around the volcanoes on the mainland's northern regions. One vial, filled with the red liquid that only Asfi could manufacture, was powerful enough to instantly reduce middle-level monsters to smoldering cinders.

Using the powerful items that she designed specifically for herself, Asfi took down one beast after another.

Her allies had adjusted to their enemies' movements and charged as one, slaughtering the plant monsters within their reach.

"Are you okay?"

"I-I'm fine!"

Aiz had fallen back to the rear of the formation to protect the vulnerable magic users. Any enemies drawn in by the presence of magic energy were laid low immediately.

The prum girl blushed as she looked up at Aiz, but the blond swordswoman was more focused on watching Asfi in combat.

She's very strong, Aiz thought as her eyes followed the item maker's white cloak dance while its owner attacked. She fell back to the rear guard as well after learning the monsters targeted people with high Magic, since there was no reason for her to fight alone in the front. Not only was she responsive to her comrades' plight, but her ability to calmly assess the battlefield and make quick decisions was also head and shoulders above the rest. Aiz couldn't help but be reminded of her own commander, Finn, as she watched her work.

Thanks to the war tiger's timely cover, Asfi caught the longsword a supporter tossed toward her and jumped into point-blank range of a carnivorous plant. Striking its head, she sent the beast flying backward.

"Only a few more to clean up..."

Throwing the longsword back to the supporter, Asfi surveyed the battlefield.

She saw Lulune deliver the final blow to the last monster. Her knife pierced its magic stone, turning the creature into a small pile of ash. "Whew," the thief muttered as she retrieved her knife and rejoined the party.

"If we keep cool during the fight, everything turns out okay, eh?"

"I was concerned when our attacks weren't getting through...but yes, I can work with these results."

Lulune did not have good memories of the battle of Rivira, but she was able to regain her confidence thanks to having strong allies at her side. Asfi was concerned about expending too much Burst Oil but was satisfied by how the battle turned out.

The supporters were surprised to see the rich colors of the magic stones but quickly did their jobs and collected the items. The party was on the move once more.

"You mentioned them before, but I'd like to confirm. That was the 'new species'...?"

"Hard as a rock, damn fast...and a whole mess of 'em. They're seriously a pain."

"Sword Princess, if you have any other information pertaining to these unidentified monsters, would you mind telling me what you know?"

"Understood."

Asfi and Lulune had a short conversation before including Aiz and asking her to share information. She started by saying that blunt force had little effect on them. These carnivorous plant monsters had a lower resistance to sharp weapons and pinpoint attacks.

Next, she confirmed that they responded to Magic and would immediately attack the source.

The party made sure to stay at full attention, constantly scanning their surroundings even as they listened to Aiz's soft voice.

"...One more thing. They might prioritize attacking other monsters."

To be more accurate, Aiz had witnessed this behavior only in the caterpillars she had encountered in the Deep Levels. While *Loki*

Familia's adventurers had been trying to escape from a horde of them on the fifty-first floor, the monsters had ignored them and instead devoured a group of black rhinos that appeared in the hallway. Even now, she could clearly recall every detail.

Although the same behavior had yet to be confirmed in the flower monsters, the two shared the same type of magic stone. Therefore, Aiz thought it was a good idea to inform her allies.

"Cannibalistic monsters? That's pretty rare."

Lulune lifted her head from the map she was still sketching. Asfi remained silent but adjusted the silver frame of the glasses on her face.

She then offered an explanation as to why.

"There are two main possibilities as to why one monster would attack another."

Asfi held up one finger.

"The first is a sudden fight. Either by accident or coincidence, one beast takes an attack from another and strikes back out of revenge. Some have seen this happen in swarms as well."

Aiz nodded in understanding as Asfi held up a second finger.

"As for the second, some monsters *develop a taste for magic stones.*"

The tone of her voice changed as if she was getting into the main point.

"By devouring the magic stone of another, the abilities of the feeding monster will increase in much the same way we receive a Status update."

"Enhanced species…"

"Indeed. Monsters that consume a large amount of magic stones acquire abilities that are a cut above their original power."

Aiz's quiet voice filled a small pause in Asfi's explanation.

Monsters were born with strong instincts similar across every species. One such instinct was a natural aversion to infighting. However, every so often individuals able to transcend those instincts appeared.

While adventurers gathered excelia to improve their Status, these exceptional monsters adopted a dog-eat-dog policy, consuming others of their kind to strengthen themselves.

In time, they became enthralled by the powerful sensation that eating a magic stone provided. They ended up wandering the Dungeon, craving the stones that lay inside their bestial kin. The ones that became too strong drew the attention of the Guild, who would issue a bounty. Then extermination squads moved in.

"The most well-known of these would be the Bloodstained Troll—a truly ferocious beast that slew many adventurers and hotheads who could only think about money. Even the elite parties called in were wiped out."

"Oh yeah, I remember that…Took five top-class adventurers to kill that thing, right?"

"Yes. The fact that *Freya Familia* was successful in the extermination is still fresh in my memory."

It was for Aiz as well. She remembered when stories about the Troll took root in Orario.

The Bloodstained Troll, a beast that became so powerful that the Guild couldn't classify its Level, was only an example. Studies found that monsters needed to consume only five magic stones before their increase in power became apparent.

"So what you're saying is that this new species goes after other monsters to eat their magic stones?"

"That's my theory, yes. It's appropriate to believe something has driven them to cannibalism. Correct me if I'm wrong, but there was a great difference in strength between individuals during that battle."

"Now that you mention it, they were definitely all over the place. Some went down with a flick, but others needed a lot more convincing. But an entire swarm aiming for magic stones? Is that even possible? Monsters born hungry for magic stones? That's no joke."

Aiz listened to Asfi and Lulune's conversation and thought about everything they had said.

Asfi's guess seemed to be the most logical explanation. Thinking back to the flower monsters she fought during the Monsterphilia and in Rivira, there had been quite a few individuals that were stronger than much of those in the ambush they had just defeated. There was so much variation among them that it was impossible to draw any conclusions.

And there was still one big question remaining: Why didn't they attack one another? Just as Lulune suggested, it could be that the monsters with the deeply colored magic stones hadn't developed a taste for them after the fact but hunted them out of innate instinct.

Aiz's train of thought reached that point before taking a hard detour.

Those plant monsters are here... That means somewhere up ahead—

There was a good chance *she* was here, too.

A head of short bloodred hair along with the snakelike bodies of the flower monsters came to mind.

Her left hand tightly clenched into a fist.

Aiz quietly prepared herself for that encounter.

"Forking again, haaah..."

The party came to a stop in front of another intersection.

Their path split into tunnels going left and right. Lulune turned to Asfi for a decision.

"Asfi, which way this ti—"

That's when they came.

The sound of massive bodies sliding across the fleshy walls interrupted Lulune in midsentence. The vivid flowery heads of the carnivorous plants appeared on the left and right.

"Two fronts? You gotta be kidding me..."

"Worse...they're behind us, too."

"Damn it...!" Lulune yelped shrilly after Aiz pointed out the severity of the situation, her head on a swivel.

Left, right, and behind. They were trapped in a three-way pincer. The creatures advanced along the floor, walls, and ceiling, and the other members of *Hermes Familia* watched their approach, frowning at their adversaries.

The escape routes were cut off.

"...Sword Princess, can you handle one side by yourself?"

"Understood."

Asfi phrased her order like a request, and Aiz agreed.

With a top-class adventurer like Aiz holding one flank, Asfi was free to supervise *Hermes Familia*'s counterattack in the other two directions.

The party leader's sharp voice cut through the air as she issued orders. Sixteen adventurers rushed to their positions.

Eight moved to the back, seven to the right, and Aiz to the left to meet the monsters head-on.

Then the Sword Princess charged. Desperate drew first blood.

As if something had expected this turn of events, a large pillar descended straight down from the ceiling directly above her.

"?!"

Aiz dove forward out of its path.

She kicked off the ground and into the air. *WHAM! WHAM! WHAM!* More gigantic pillars dropped from the ceiling in quick succession. Aiz continued to dodge them one after another until she realized what had happened.

The left path had been completely cut off. Asfi and her other allies were on the other side.

"We're cut off!!"

She could hear Lulune's muffled cry from the other side of the thick wall of pillars.

Aiz's golden eyes widened. The Dungeon never sprang this kind of trap. This possibility hadn't crossed her mind. And now she was completely secluded as her allies looked on with similar shock on the other side.

—*I've been isolated!*

Aiz was forced to fend off the monsters while still in disbelief.

"OOOOOOOOOOOOOOOOOOOOOOOOOOOOOOOOOO
OOOOO!!"

"!"

Severing their vine whips, Aiz dispatched the five monsters with
ease.

The last of them dissolved into ash behind her as she turned back
to the wall, intent on destroying it to reunite with Lulune and the
others.

That is, until the appearance of a murderous presence stayed her
hand.

"......!"

The overwhelming bloodlust made Aiz's shoulders tremble. She
spun around to face the dark end of the long tunnel.

She remembered the feeling coming from whatever was in the
black shadows at the end of the tunnel, a pressure far too powerful
to ignore.

Aiz steadied herself, knowing full well this wasn't an opponent
she could allow to see her back...She narrowed her eyes after a few
moments and started advancing, as if the darkness were drawing
her in.

The light from the flowers growing on the walls flickered, casting
shadows across Aiz's face.

The sound of her boots echoed, light reflecting off her silver breast-
plate and spaulders as she advanced down the straight tunnel.

She didn't have to go far.

Slowly, something approached like a mirror image.

Her opponent emerged from the darkness, matching her step for
step.

"—Never thought you'd come straight to me. Can't complain,
though."

The one who greeted her was the redheaded tamer.

Without any disguise, the woman's ivory skin and bloodred hair
were plainly visible. Her green irises locked onto Aiz.

—I knew she was here.

The woman's icy glare met Aiz's golden gaze.

The two women faced each other in the long, fleshy green tunnel.

"…What are you doing here?"

"Guess."

"This…What is this Dungeon? Did you make it?"

"You don't need to know."

Neither side blinked, both ready to lash out at any time as Aiz studied her adversary.

The tamer looked like an experienced bandit or battle-hardened marauder, the gear she wore frayed and damaged. Not only was she not wearing armor, the red-haired woman had no weapons on her person.

Judging by the way she'd responded, the tamer was not interested in discussion.

Similar to the last time they met, she spat her answers, keeping them as short as possible.

"Keep your mouth shut and follow me. There's someone who wants to meet you. You're coming along, Aria."

Aiz's gaze sharpened into a glare.

"I am not Aria."

Aiz's rebuttal only deepened the woman's frown.

"Aria is my mother."

"Cut the bullshit. Aria has no children. Even so…whether you are Aria or not, it makes no difference."

Aiz leaned forward during their brief exchange.

"How do you know Aria? What do you know about her?"

"Only her name. 'Bring me Aria, bring me Aria.' All I did was obey that annoying voice…and ran into you. That's it."

Even the display of emotion and unusual talkativeness did nothing to sway her.

Judging by her tone, it pained the red-haired tamer to use more words than necessary. She brought their conversation to a swift end.

"Enough useless chatter. You're coming with me."

With that, the woman *plunged her hand into the floor.*

She bent at her thin waist, large breasts swaying, and a sound like a whirlpool gushed out from beneath.

She yanked out her hand in a spray of red liquid as a long silver cylinder emerged from the ground in her clutches.

With a hilt at the end, there was no mistake. It was a longsword.

—*A nature weapon?*

Aiz watched in amazement as the woman drew the sword. The tamer assumed her stance and flicked off the last of the red fluid.

The weapon looked as though it had been molded from a living creature's flesh and bones. Its uncanny form lacked a hand guard or any embellishment whatsoever. The crimson blade didn't even have a cutting edge. An aura pulsed around the weapon, as if a curse would befall anyone struck by it.

Aiz kept her mouth clamped shut but quietly released needless tension from her body.

An impending battle was upon the two combatants. Aiz entrusted her fate to Desperate and faced the challenger.

"Here I come."

The woman charged.

Her short hair lashed around her head like splattering blood as she brought the strange longsword down with all her might.

Aiz blocked the strike head-on, using Desperate to knock it aside.

A complex echo bounced through the hallway, an odd mixture of the metallic *clang* and a dull *thud* not much different from a punch. The woman continued her assault, using the ferocious strength that had overpowered Aiz during the battle of Rivira. Her weapon whistled through the air in a gaudy display of power that Aiz dodged without difficulty. The blond swordswoman followed it with her own upward cut.

In a repeat of their previous battle, pure swordsmanship battled against sheer strength in a furious exchange of blows.

"......?"

A serious expression appeared on the woman's face amid the slashes and counterattacks.

One eyebrow rose as she realized Aiz's speed continued to increase, her attacks coming faster and faster—when suddenly, both eyes widened.

She could see only Aiz's afterimages stepping into close range. A flash of surprise passed over her face an instant before—!

The sword connected with such force that she lost her balance.

"Wha?!"

Aiz didn't allow her time to recover. Her follow-up attack was already on its way.

Barely able to keep pace with the incessant slashes, the woman struggled to block or dodge the first strike while the second was on its way. *SHING!* The last impact sent her reeling.

Unable to disperse the momentum of a full diagonal slash, her feet tore long gashes in the greenish floor.

The tamer was stunned when she finally came to a stop.

Slowly, very slowly, she brought her hand to her breast and trembled as she looked down at the glinting blood on her fingertips.

There was a shallow cut across her chest. She looked up at Aiz. "You—No way..." Returning a glare as intense as the other girl's, the tamer's face melted into a scowl. "You raised your Status...?!"

The girl standing before her was far more capable than she had been ten days ago. Of that the short-haired woman was now painfully aware.

A level-up meant a new level of strength attainable only through great accomplishment.

Aiz had broken free of her former limits after rising to Level Six as a result of her battle with the floor boss Udaeus.

The girl the tamer had overpowered in the crystal-packed town no longer existed.

"Gah, such a pain...!!"

The woman's voice dripped irritation as she spat the syllables one by one.

The sheer physical strength that had overwhelmed the girl ten days ago wasn't good enough anymore. She could hold her own now.

Aiz softly responded to the woman's hateful scowl.

"I just didn't want to lose to you."

The pain of defeat she'd felt under that dark night sky had given Aiz the boost she needed to reach higher.

Deep down, Aiz hated to lose as much as her friends in *Loki Familia* did. Harnessing her unbreakable spirit had motivated her to prepare for this moment. Now was her chance for revenge.

Aiz pointed a blade as sharp as her will toward her opponent.

"Tsk…"

The woman clicked her tongue as she brought her longsword back into position. The two glared into each other's eyes.

The woman's usual indifferent expression had been replaced by clear loathing, her gaze bearing down on Aiz like pikes tipped with hatred. The murderous aura that bore down on the blond swordswoman was thicker than ever.

The two combatants faced each other without a word until the red-haired woman broke the silence.

"Aren't you going to use it?"

The woman wanted to know if Aiz would use her wind.

Aiz's Magic—the spell Airiel—was her greatest weapon. It seemed unnatural to not use it.

"I don't…need it."

Aiz did not mince words.

Reflecting on her constant use of Airiel in their previous battle, Aiz was determined to return to the fundamentals. A swordswoman needed to win by her skill with a blade. She wanted to win this battle on that alone.

"—Don't get cocky!"

Rage burned in the woman's eyes.

The rest of her face was devoid of any expression, her murderous intent overflowing. She raised her weapon into position, cracks forming in the handle.

Showing more emotion than ever before, she leaped up in a flash.

Her opponent charged like a missile as Aiz raised her saber, racing out to meet her.

Silver and crimson blades crossed at breakneck speed.

Impact.

CHAPTER 4

WHITE-HAIRED DEVIL

Гэта казка іншага сям'і.

сівавалосы дэман

"Loose your arrows, fairy archers. Pierce, arrow of accuracy!"

A beautiful voice spread through the air like waves over water.

Lefiya cast a short spell and lifted high into the air a staff designed specifically for magic users: Forest's Teardrop. Made from a white ore called seiros that mages were rather fond of, the staff was capable of increasing the base strength of Magic. Compounded with a magic crystal and a rare item known as Tear of the Elder Tree, it was extremely suitable for elven magic.

The crystals at the end of her staff flashed at the same time a magic circle expanded.

"Arcs Ray!"

An arrow of light appeared at her forceful call.

The powerful spell barreled forward, supported by her Skill, Fairy Cannon, and filled the narrow hallway with a bright light. The twenty monsters in the target zone howled before disintegrating as the spell overwhelmed them.

Only scattered ash remained when the radiance faded.

Confirming there were no survivors, Lefiya lowered her staff.

"That's right, you're from the Wishe Forest—a homeland known for possessing high magic power even among our kin...With magic such as that, it's no wonder."

"I-I'm nothing special. This is the only job I can do..."

After neutralizing the monster band barring their path, the small three-member party continued ahead. Filvis looked at Lefiya with satisfaction.

They had arrived on the twenty-fourth floor. Their mission to catch up with Aiz had led them through a complicated tangle of twists and turns as they descended deeper into the Dungeon. At last, they had reached the appointed floor. Walking between Bete and Filvis, Lefiya could hear only the sound of their tapping foot-falls on the wooden ground.

The party had set their sights on the northern pantry. According to their information, the outbreaks were occurring along the main route that wound through this floor. They discovered piles upon piles of ash and some uncollected loot. Perhaps there wasn't enough time for the previous party to collect it all. It stood to reason that only top-class adventurers could take on so many monsters on this floor at once. They were almost certain that Aiz and her companions were behind it.

More monsters appeared on the main route, forcing the small group into battle—and costing them valuable time. So they chose a slight detour, which brought them to a narrow hallway sheathed in tree bark. However, the passage was narrow only compared to the main route. Over five meders in diameter, anything short of a big party would have no problem passing through.

The bluish green moss growing on the walls illuminated the happy smile Lefiya wore during her conversations with Filvis. The black-haired elf's praise and the sense that the barrier between them was eroding away were the reason for her expression.

"Enough blabber. We got company."

Bete rolled his eyes as he jumped in front of the elves.

He was on top of the monsters at the other end of the hallway in the blink of an eye. Flipping through the air like an acrobat, he nailed several deadly hornets in midair before driving his heel into the grotesque, plump body of a two-meder-tall hobgoblin, cleaving it down the middle.

Bete eliminated the monsters in their path as quickly as possible to not waste any time.

Crack! The walls around Lefiya and Filvis suddenly opened.

"!"

"Fall back, Viridis!"

Seeing Lefiya surrounded by newborn monsters, Filvis called out her name before rushing to defend her.

Drawing a shortsword, she slew the monsters bearing down on Lefiya. A lizardman led its brethren into combat with a deafening roar, but Filvis's combination of swift stabs and sweeps felled them quickly. Dodging their thick tails, she removed lizard heads from torsos.

Lefiya stood still, unable to join the fray as the enemy numbers decreased by the second. Filvis removed a wand from inside her belt.

"*Purge, cleansing lightning!*"

Still engaged in combat with the remaining two lizardmen, she formed an incantation on her lips.

As Filvis began Concurrent Casting, the two monsters fell to the floor in pieces.

Then she pointed her wand at three dark fungi expanding their mushroom umbrellas in a threatening manner.

"*Dio Thyrsos!*"

Her short-trigger-spell magic flared to life the same moment the dark fungi released poisonous spores into the air.

Sharp flashes of lightning roared through the hallway, roasting the dark fungi and burning the spores out of the air at the same time.

A-amazing...

Lefiya marveled at Filvis's prowess in battle, dispatching the entire swarm on her own.

Unlike the casters suited for the rear ranks, Filvis was a magic swordsman.

Sought after for mid-formation positions by many parties of adventurers—in demand and extremely popular—they could balance any combination of combat strategies. While able to fight on the front lines themselves, they could provide more powerful ranged support with their Magic than any arrows or thrown weapons ever could. They were magic users capable of holding their own with speed; Lefiya idolized that battle style. Even among magic swordsmen who fought with short-trigger spells, Filvis was exceptionally fast.

With sword and wand in hand, she excelled at short- and long-range combat. The ability to use Concurrent Casting made her a force to be reckoned with even in the fiercest of battles. Driving enemies back with her sword, feet moving like a rhythmic dance, burning them down with Magic, her elegant beauty—she shone like a jewel on the battlefield.

Lefiya stayed mesmerized for several moments after the battle was over, a feeling of inferiority overtaking her.

"Now if only you could pull that off."

"Uwhaa…"

Bete came up to her and delivered a verbal knockout punch.

Lefiya was a pure-magic user, meaning she couldn't contribute to a battle without the help of a Wall, practically helpless without allies for support.

Compared to the all-powerful Filvis who was fine in solo combat, the difference was like night and day.

Her head drooping with depression setting in, this time it was Filvis who came to her defense.

"It is cruel to expect that from a magic user who wields such firepower. It is highly likely Viridis's strength will be essential to completing our mission."

Filvis firmly pointed out that it was the party's role to protect magic users like Lefiya long enough to unleash that power.

Indeed, the technique Bete was referring to—Concurrent Casting—was an extremely rare ability among those who specialized in pure-magic power. So rare, in fact, that the only other person Lefiya knew of who could do it was Riveria.

Filvis pushed her point even further by saying that powerful magic users were a party's ace in the hole. Bete, on the other hand, took one look at the two girls and snorted.

"Gotten really buddy-buddy, haven't you, elves."

When Bete pointed out how much their relationship had changed in a short amount of time, Filvis clenched her mouth shut. Lefiya's cheeks turned bright red as she looked between the two.

The werewolf chuckled drily before focusing his gaze on Lefiya.

"You satisfied like this? Having to count on others 'cause you can't protect yourself?"

Amber eyes unblinking, he didn't pull any punches.

His voice might have been full of the usual contempt, but it was the serious look in Bete's eyes that made Lefiya's shoulders tremble.

"Those airheaded Amazons are spoiling you, but I ain't doing that. As long as your Magic is the only useful thing you got, you'll never be anything more than baggage."

"......"

"You are soft."

There wasn't a shred of kindness in the man's verbal onslaught. His amber irises bore down on Lefiya as if cornering her on the edge of a cliff.

Bete always chose the words that would hit someone in their weakest spot. He didn't pour salt on their wounds, he tore them open.

That was one of the reasons he wasn't well liked. His aggression and lack of restraint turned words into cutting instruments, opening old scars and drawing the ire of adventurers far and wide.

At the root of this was his own inability to face the scars of his past.

Lefiya had no response as she spiraled deeper into despair. Even still, a part of her knew that she had no choice but to change. It was the same part that had pained her during the incident at the Monsterphilia.

In order to not hold back her idol, Aiz, and the others—in order to be allowed to stand side by side with them, Lefiya had to find a way to reach a new height. She must never forget the tears she'd shed at her own powerlessness, nor the burning desire to catch up. It would be a lie to say that Bete's words, with his amber eyes glaring down at her, didn't sting.

Lefiya felt Filvis's concerned gaze on the side of her face as she held her staff in both hands, squeezing as hard as she could.

"......?"

At that moment, Lefiya looked up from the floor.

After saying all those things, Bete was walking away. Filvis, too, was a few steps down the hall, although she was looking back over her shoulder at her.

A strange feeling crept over Lefiya as she watched their backs.

Magic...?

Rooted to the spot, she had a look around.

"Um, Mr. Bete...?"

"Yeah?" He responded verbally first. "What?" He then turned to face her but apparently didn't sense anything wrong.

"Is something the matter?"

"Ehh, um, well..."

Lefiya failed to string words together after Filvis asked as well.

Just my imagination? she thought, tilting her head and observing the other two. They weren't sensing it.

"If it's nothing, then we're going. The pantry ain't that far away."

Bete started walking again, his mood worsening because they'd lost even more time. Filvis followed close behind.

Lefiya examined the path behind them, paused for a moment, and then hurried to catch up to the other two.

The girl's golden-yellow hair swished as she disappeared down the hallway.

"......"

A figure in the darkness watched her leave.

It emerged from the corner of the path Lefiya had been look-ing at.

This figure, clad in a violet hooded robe and hiding its face behind an ominous mask, followed the adventurers' footsteps far-ther into the Dungeon.

"Sword Princess! Hey, can't you hear me?!"

Lulune yelled loudly enough to be heard over the roaring monsters.

Separated from Aiz, *Hermes Familia* was doing its best to fend off the pincer attack from two swarms of man-eating flowers.

But with wave upon wave charging in from farther down the hallways, the swords and spears constantly plunging into monster flesh weren't enough.

"What the hell just happened?! Asfi, what do we do?!"

"…If you have the energy to be concerned about her, use it to protect yourself. We must evacuate this location the moment a path is clear!"

"Have you no heart?"

"She's the Sword Princess!!"

No matter how loud Lulune yelled, there was no response from Aiz on the other side of the wall of pillars. Fearing for the girl's life, Lulune pleaded with Asfi for help. But their leader would not budge, saying that it was a waste of time to worry about a top-class adventurer, and quickly issued orders. Aiz Wallenstein was an experienced veteran, with enough skill to warrant the label War Princess. Asfi's first priority was the safety of her party.

New monster reinforcements were still arriving from both the front and the back.

"New enemies on the rear flank! Five of them!"

"More from the front, too!"

Hearing the frantic calls of her allies, Asfi made a swift decision. "Scatter the magic stones!"

At their leader's command, the entire party took a deep breath.

Each of them had a small pouch tied to their belts. Thrusting their hands inside, they pulled out handfuls of the purple crystals and threw them against the walls.

Suddenly, the carnivorous plants weren't interested in the adventurers anymore. Ignoring them completely, the monsters went straight for the magic stones.

"All units, forward!"

Thanks to Aiz's information, Asfi knew how to manipulate these monsters' predilections and guided the party ahead. Motioning for Lulune and the others to keep going, she wanted to use this window of opportunity.

Falling back to the rear of the party, Asfi drew three vials of Burst Oil from her holster to make sure this encounter ended here.

"Nelly, a magic sword!"

She hurled the liquid grenades directly into the swarm of monsters still devouring the magic stones.

The human supporter did as she was told, drawing a magic sword and swinging at the beasts.

A stream of fire erupted from the dagger-shaped, magic-infused blade and collided with the three vials of Burst Oil, setting off a gigantic explosion.

The defeaning blast drowned out the roasting monsters' cries of pain as a mushroom cloud formed in the passageway, eliminating the possibility of counterattack.

"Asfi, there's a ton coming from the front!"

Lulune called out to alert her of another wave coming in.

She did not, however, slow down as she shouted. Her blades flashed as she jumped between the massive creatures. Monster blood sprayed in her wake. Thanks to Lulune's distraction, other party members carrying larger weapons had a clear shot at the monsters' heads. Most of the bud-like appendages split on impact.

"Apparently, they don't want us going any farther down this hall...!"

Asfi's eyes narrowed, and the corners of her lips turned upward as she looked past their enemies.

Judging by the increased intensity of the monsters' attacks, she was certain there had to be *something* worth protecting on the other side. She moved from the rear of the party up to the front lines and forced the wall of monsters back with her own blades. Her allies followed, steadily advancing at the same pace.

Asfi and the war tiger Falgar, who was wielding a greatsword, drove the swarm of enormous creatures out of the way.

"…What is this place?"

It was after they'd plowed through more waves of monsters than they could count.

The party saw bloodred light at the end of the long passageway, unlike the dim light from the flowers.

"Could that be light from the quartz? So the pantry is up there?"

Just like her allies, Lulune examined the view ahead.

Pantries were located in the deepest corners of many floors in the Dungeon. These vast caverns all had one thing in common: a towering pillar of quartz crystals. The pillars produced a nutritious fluid that monsters traveled from far and wide to consume. They also constantly generated a mysterious light.

The quartz pillars on the twenty-fourth floor gave off red light. That telltale sign at the end of the tunnel let everyone know their destination was just up ahead.

"Asfi."

"…We advance at full speed."

The party followed their leader's order without question.

Slaying the final flower monsters in their path, they dashed through the passageway of green flesh.

The smell of rotting tissue thickened with every breath. At long last, the party made it to the exit near the source of the red light.

Their boots hit the ground of the cavernous pantry floor.

"—"

What awaited Asfi and the others once they made it inside took their breath away.

The same disgusting green walls they had seen up to this point also encased this large, open space. The only major difference they could see was the thousands of flower buds sticking out of the walls.

However, what quickly captured all their attention were the enormous *monsters* on the pillar of quartz inside the pantry.

"Parasites...?"

Three in all, they looked like overgrown plant monsters. What's more, they were firmly attached to the pillar, which stood over thirty meders tall.

Three gigantic, richly colored flowers bloomed in different spots on the pillar. In terms of length and girth, these creatures were at least ten times the size of the carnivorous flower monsters. A vast network of vines sprouting from their bodies connected them to the pillar.

It could have been due to the bloodred light, but the vines themselves looked like veins traveling up and down a giant limb.

"Don't tell me...It's sucking the goo straight out of the pillar?"

SLURP! A low sucking noise echoed through the cavern every so often. Asfi's eyes trembled as she watched every drop of the liquid from the quartz disappear.

However, the gigantic flower monsters' roots and vines didn't stop there. They extended to the walls, ceiling, and floor to create the soft green surface that the party knew all too well. There was no doubt in their minds that these gigantic flower monsters were behind the dramatic changes around the northern pantry.

They fit the definition of a parasite exactly.

The Dungeon constantly produced a nutritious liquid. The monsters were able to exponentially grow their bodies by using it as an energy source. The resulting abomination changed the Dungeon's very structure.

"Th-that's..."

Asfi and her party were not the only people inside this vast green cavern covered with countless flower buds. An unknown group was already there.

Each member wore large robes that hid their upper bodies from view as well as masks that left only their mouths exposed. The sudden appearance of *Hermes Familia* startled the unknown faction hiding their faces and origin. At first, they looked to one another in panic, until one of them pointed to the newcomers and started yelling orders.

The atmosphere in the chamber quickly turned much more serious, even deadly. However, Lulune was still looking past the unidentified masked group to something attached to the quartz pillar.

Specifically, the base of the structure, covered in the vines and roots of the three gigantic flower monsters.

There was a green sphere containing a feminine fetus attached to it.

"The orb from before...?!"

"So they made it this far."

While Asfi and her party were trying to recover from shock...

The ones already there were figuring out how to deal with them.

A man dressed in all white stood at the base of the quartz pillar, staring at all fifteen of the intruders. His white hair peeked out from beneath the skull drop item he'd fashioned into a helmetlike mask.

It was the tall man who had spoken with Levis, the red-haired tamer, not too long ago.

"How? What have you been doing?!"

"The violas weren't enough to stop them."

A human approached the man dressed in white and offered an explanation as he kept his gaze concentrated on the intruders.

This newcomer was clad in a different color from the rest of the masked faction. The man in white did his best to contain his anger as he responded to the excuse.

"Fill your role, Evils' Remnant. Become her shield."

After sending a glare in the human's direction, the man dressed in white cast his gaze up at the pillar.

Specifically, at the green orb containing a feminine fetus attached to its base.

Protected by several thick vines from the gigantic flower monsters, it, too, was absorbing the nutritious liquid produced by the quartz.

The Dungeon was known as the "mother" of all monsters. Now, it was nursing a child.

However, this selfish infant cared nothing for the struggle of its mother.

Paying little attention to the constant groans coming from the weakly glowing quartz, it kept growing as it consumed all the nutrients the pillar could provide.

The man watched, a look of ecstasy in his eyes every time the fetus kicked.

"...That's a given!"

The man dressed in white didn't take his gaze off the shifting orb as the other masked human frowned before turning on his heel.

The man in white and the female fetus watched as the human issued orders to the other Evils' Remnants. The group of masked warriors was quick to draw blades.

"Let no intruder survive!"

An angry roar cut through the din.

It came from a man wearing a robe different from the rest—those around the human followed his command. The masked faction inside the cavern sprang into action.

Weapons held high, they charged forward to engage Asfi and her party.

"Hey, these guys aren't playing around!"

Lulune could see the intent to kill on their faces and warned her friends.

Hermes Familia was still at the cavern entrance, watching their new, unknown enemies charge at them at full speed.

"We shall meet them in battle. It doesn't look like we will get any information out of them without a little persuasion, now does it?"

The enemy's strange energy made Asfi's skin crawl. She quickly looked to all her allies in turn.

The green walls hosted many exits besides the path they had used to arrive in the cavern. A large, black, cage-like apparatus was located next to each of them, housing carnivorous plants.

At the same time, more monsters were being born from the fleshy green walls. The flower buds started to bloom, mature ones sliding forward with their bodies dangling from the wall surface before flopping to the ground and slithering across the floor. Apparently, the green coating from the gigantic flower monsters had the ability to bear live young just like the walls of the Dungeon itself.

The question now was whether the enormous floral creatures had been artificially created or if they were purely a new species of monster. Were all plant monsters born this way?

Every hypothesis passing through Asfi's mind sent shivers down her spine. No matter the answer, she didn't have a good feeling about it.

The leader took another look around the unrecognizable pantry, her mind working overtime.

There were still many questions that needed answers, such as how this space was created and where they would take the cages lined up at the exits.

"Kill them!"

"Engage!"

Leaders of both companies issuing their final orders, *Hermes Familia* clashed with the group of masked warriors.

Large robes and masks concealed the identities of the faction that held a considerable numerical advantage over *Hermes Familia*. Their front lines descended on the adventurers like a storm, blades and war cries bearing down on their targets. In response, Lulune led the other demi-humans in the middle of their formation up to the front lines, matching the attackers' intensity with their own.

The war tiger's shield knocked swords and spears to the side, opening a lane for several elves to engage the robed warriors at point-blank range.

Every time enemy archers unleashed a wave of arrows into the air, magic users were quick to respond with short-trigger spells. The air was clear in moments.

Hermes Familia combined their capacity to cover one another's weaknesses with the exceptional strength of their individuals to overwhelm an opponent trying to win on numbers alone. Robed warriors late to enter the fray saw the strength of upper-class adventurers among the intruders and lost the will to fight.

With their teamwork, the familia steadily advanced against the bloodthirsty ranks of the masked faction.

"One! Two!"

"Argh!"

Lulune inflicted precise cuts on all four limbs of her opponent before driving her knee square into his chest.

The masked figure, likely human, cried out in pain as he was removed from the fight.

"Now then, why don't you tell me your familia?"

Hauling the man up by his collar, Lulune's interrogation began.

The man's bleeding arms hung limp at his sides, his eyes glaring at her from beneath his mask. Though the battle still raged, he kept his cloth-covered mouth shut tight.

"......!"

"Shoulda figured. But silence will get you nowhere."

A vicious smile appeared on Lulune's face at the man who refused to say a word. She grabbed a vial from beneath her combat gear.

It was filled with a clear red liquid and had a small crystal floating inside—Status Thief. It had the ability to pick the "lock" that deities could use to hide the Blessings on their followers' backs, their Statuses. With this, it was possible for her to figure out not only what familia the man belonged to but his name as well.

The man's eyes trembled when he caught a glimpse of the vial between Lulune's fingers.

"……"

Determination appeared in the man's eyes almost immediately, as if he'd come to an important realization.

"My Lord, I shall follow through on our pact…"

Muffled words sounded beneath the kerchief over his mouth.

It happened in an instant.

The man's eyes flashed as he reached up with his bleeding arms and grabbed the robe at his waist, tearing it away from his body—to reveal what lay beneath.

A dark-red rock that looked as though a flame had been petrified mid-burn and sealed in stone was strapped to his chest.

"—"

The sight of it made Lulune forget to breathe.

—An Inferno Stone.

This drop item could be obtained by defeating monsters called flame rocks in the Deep Levels of the Dungeon. Unaltered, these pieces of the monster's body were highly flammable and could easily explode.

The man's Inferno Stone was especially large compared to the others she had seen. What's more, there was more than one, all of them tied along one long rope against his skin.

Her blood ran cold as she saw his hands move.

The stones were attached to a small box at his waist—a detonator with a string attached. The man grabbed hold and gave it a sharp yank.

Lulune immediately let go of the man's collar and jumped away with all the strength her legs could muster.

"My life for Iris—!!"

Flinging his body backward, the man crossed his arms over his chest.

Sparks emerged from the detonator a moment later, igniting the stones.

"_____!!"

The resulting explosion launched Lulune even farther. The heat blast overwhelmed her, followed by a shower of ash. She landed flat on her back, burns peppering her exposed skin.

Willing her body to sit up, the first thing she saw was a mass of smoldering flesh not too far away. The words fell from her lips.

"...H-he *blew himself up?*"

The charred remnants of the human body on the ground were still burning.

She stuck out both arms as she collapsed back to the ground. With that much damage to his skin, there was no point in using Status Thief. Of course, the man could no longer be counted among the living.

The man had sacrificed his life in order to prevent an information leak.

His level of devotion stunned Lulune.

"—May this unworthy vassal find salvation!!"

Suddenly, more of the robed warriors started exploding all around her.

The first ones to pull their cords were too injured to continue to fight. Then the ones who had lost hope of their chances of survival self-ignited. Still others decided that if they were going down, they'd take someone with them, and lunged forward with their arms extended. With each burst of flame came a blinding flash and thunderous roar filling the cavern.

And the cries of *Hermes Familia* were right in the middle of it.

"Asfi, these guys are zealots!!"

Having lost her composure, Lulune screamed as loudly as she could.

These warriors had committed everything to completing their mission.

A group of fighters prepared to face the ultimate fate—death.

Screams echoed through the chamber as a small army of warriors willing to turn themselves into bombs advanced on their position.

—"Syle's down!"

—"Someone, heal!"

—"Oi! Stop theeeem!"

The sight of explosions swallowing her allies one by one reflected in Asfi's stunned eyes. While her cloak protected her from the intense heat waves, the stench of gunpowder and burning flesh stung her nose. The entire battlefield was drowning in it.

"My brothers, fear not death!"

A new voice swept over the battlefield from behind the masked warriors.

A man in a robe different from the others urged his comrades forward, dark light pulsing in his bloodshot eyes.

"All we have dreamed of lies on the other side of death! Our Lord makes it so—show him loyalty!!"

The eyes behind the masks of the robed warriors changed at the voice. Their fear was gone.

They advanced as one, their half-covered faces already dead. Together they moved like a somber white inferno.

"Forgive me, Sophia!"

"Reina, I will now atone—!!"

"Alas, Julius!!"

Lives provided the sparks to ignite a chain of explosions.

The thunderous booms rendered hearing useless. A flabbergasted Asfi watched as the detonations showed no sign of stopping.

Names of deities…No, people?!

The last shouts of men and women on the other side of the explosions began to die down. Asfi's blood ran cold as soon as her ears recovered enough to catch what sounded like people's names echoing in the air between explosions.

Was this a sign of complete and total loyalty to a deity? Or was this the will of a deity they were being forced to obey?

Just what kind of familia were they fighting against? That thought sent another chill up Asfi's spine.

At the same time..."Should this kind of thing be allowed to exist?" she wondered aloud in a shaking voice.

"Such broken souls. Fools bound to a deity...Disgraceful."

—Elsewhere in the chamber, at the farthest corner away from Asfi's party...

The man clad in white scoffed at the battle unfolding in the distance and raised one hand.

Aiming his palm at the battlefield, the eyes behind his white skull mask narrowed.

"Violas."

Every monster in the chamber looked up the moment that word left his lips.

As if they were connected by one mind, one overarching will, their heavy slithering movements broke the silence in the cavern.

Monsters contained within the black cages broke free and joined the rivers of green flowing directly for *Hermes Familia.*

"Wha—?!"

"Monsters, too?!"

A joint attack of masked warriors and plant monsters was now under way.

As the monsters jostled to advance on their position, the adventurers cried out in terror. Vine whips and gigantic fangs mercilessly bore down on them.

"UWA-AAHHHHHHHHHHHHHHHHHHH!"

The floral rampage was not only aimed at Asfi and her allies. The tendrils wrapped around anything they touched, and the remaining robed warriors directly in their path were first. The last human was soon halfway down a monster's throat, screaming and thrashing about as his blood splattered everywhere.

The monsters were on track to wipe out everything, friend and foe alike.

"This is a massacre...!!"

The battle had turned into pandemonium.

However, the army of zealots paid no attention to the carnivores feasting on their allies and continued their attack on Asfi and her party. They ignited their Inferno Stones the moment they were in a creature's grasp, catching as many combatants in the blast as possible. *Hermes Familia*'s teamwork and defenses were not enough to hold the devastation at bay. Chaos was spreading, the battle deteriorating into a nightmare.

Barely able to defend herself, let alone the casters in the back of the formation, Lulune cried out as the overwhelming number of monster whips caught up to her.

"Not good…!"

With her carefully constructed battle formation in ruins, Asfi's eyes flared to life.

Allies and enemies were dropping one after another; there wasn't enough time to tell which was which.

At this rate, annihilation was just a matter of time. The relentless attacks of the monsters and the fear of the remaining robed warriors detonating their stones kept the still mobile members of *Hermes Familia* from advancing.

Retreat was close to impossible in this situation. The party would be mowed down the moment they lowered their weapons to run.

That white-robed bastard…!

Shortsword in hand, Asfi rushed to the aid of her allies. Breaking through the front lines of the enemy, she slew masked warriors and monsters alike on her way forward.

The mysterious man in the white robe and drop-item mask stood far in the distance, well behind the man in the unique robe. Asfi managed to catch a glimpse of the man moving his arm an instant before the plant monsters launched their attack.

—A tamer, no doubt!

Asfi developed her own theory about their enemy's true identity from her limited information.

It was illogical for one tamer to have so many large-category monsters under his command at one time. However, if this tamer was also behind the mutation of the pantry, a theory could start taking shape. That would also explain their current situation.

The destruction of friend and foe was the enemy's—no, the man in white's plan all along.

Even if the zealots failed in their mission, the easiest way to clean up the mess was to set the monsters loose.

If only she could destroy the "head," including the man in the unique robe guiding the zealots.

Asfi kicked off the ground, determined to put an end to the chaos.

"Falgar, take command! Gather everyone together and hold your ground!"

Even before she finished issuing the order, Asfi tossed a vial of Burst Oil directly into the fray.

Her target was one particular robed man. His eyes opened wide as the vial hit him square in the chest, flared, and ignited his own Inferno Stones.

Monsters, masked warriors—everything in the immediate vicinity was caught up in the blast and launched into the air. That provided a window for the war tiger to reestablish formation and for Lulune and the others to catch a breather. Asfi, however, charged directly through the cloud of smoke in front of her.

Wrapped in the cloak that she designed herself for protection, the swirling heat of the explosion had no effect on her. She cut through the blazing battlefield like a streaking arrow.

Surprise and horror spread over the face of the man in the unique robe as she broke through the wall of zealots and monsters under the cover of smoke.

By the time he had drawn his own weapon and braced for combat, it was already too late.

"GAH!"

Asfi was already past him, the man collapsing into a pile behind her.

Aqua-blue hair streaming behind her, she left his bleeding body in her wake.

She maintained that momentum with her eyes focused directly on the man dressed in white.

Asfi's course was set for the ominous figure standing at the base of the quartz pillar, shortsword tightly locked in her grip.

"You would have been spared so much pain if you'd only let the violas consume you...You are delaying the inevitable," her target mumbled from the corner of his mouth as he ran to meet her head-on.

Leaving the feminine fetus at the base of the pillar, the man didn't back down.

The distance between Asfi and him disappeared in a heartbeat. Asfi thrust her blade toward the still unarmed man and increased her speed before jumping at her target.

"Now."

"?!"

In that moment...

When she was only five steps away, green spears erupted from the ground.

Sensing danger from beneath, Asfi roughly threw her body to the side. Her desperate change in direction allowed her to dodge the surprise attack by the slimmest of margins.

When she regained her footing and faced her enemy, the man was already protected by a thick mass of vine whips growing directly out of the floor. What's more, the surface below was cracking open to reveal more floral beasts.

Had they been lurking under their feet the whole time? Either way, this new swarm of monsters stood in front of Asfi like an elite guard protecting the master.

"You move well, adventurer...or should I say Perseus."

"Geh—?!"

"But you shall die."

The man spoke in a calm, cold voice as he manipulated the monsters.

Just as Asfi returned to her feet after her emergency evasion, the swarm charged forward at the man's command.

Their fanged blossom heads rained down on her in quick succession like the legendary hydra. Never able to truly regain her balance, Asfi desperately flipped and contorted her body to evade. However, the countless whips swiping at her cut off every escape route.

She retreated while using her white cloak as a shield, but blows assailed her from every direction at once.

Asfi grimaced and clicked her tongue before reaching down and stroking her sandals with the tips of her fingers.

"Talaria."

With that word, Asfi disappeared from the path of the whips and fangs.

The green flesh of the floor shattered on impact, its groans of pain echoing throughout the chamber.

"What?"

The eyes behind the skull mask widened in surprise.

There should have been a corpse lying where the whips and fangs connected, but it wasn't there. Asfi had disappeared without a trace, leaving the monsters confused as they searched for her. Meanwhile, the man's gaze had turned to the ceiling.

There he spotted a figure seemingly floating in midair, standing on white flapping wings attached to her sandals. Asfi.

"In the air..."

The man in white couldn't hide his surprise. Even the remaining masked zealots raised their eyes as Asfi stared down at them.

Talaria—a magic item created by Perseus herself.

Each sandal was equipped with two white wings, allowing the wearer free movement through the air. It was the crowning achievement of prodigy Perseus's inventions thanks to her Advanced Ability Enigma.

Asfi adjusted her silver glasses while observing the swarm of monsters and the man dressed in white, who were all staring back at her.

"You have forced my hand. This ends here and now."

With those words, she thrust her hand beneath her cloak.

Her hand emerged with an entire holster-load of Burst Oil between her fingers. Flinging her arm open in a wide arc, she spread out the hail of vials, including her spares, over the targets below.

The eyes beneath the skull mask opened as far as they would go.

The crimson liquid grenades triggered a new wave of explosions over the area.

"_____!"

The destruction had begun.

Each burst of brilliant red flame hurled monsters haphazardly across the room. Even their dying cries were drowned out by the explosions. Shreds of deeply colored flower petals, fangs, pale-green flesh, whip-like roots, and snakelike bodies were strewn about the floor.

The rain of Burst Oil was composed of everything Asfi had left.

She watched the carnage unfolding below with a stoic expression on her face.

"Tsk!"

Even from beneath his hastily formed shield of plant-monster bodies, Asfi's flaming claws drew ever closer. Crimson light dominated his entire field of vision, and the monsters that had absorbed the blow in his place were peeling away.

The carpet-bombing rattled the very walls of the cavern.

"—!!"

Only now did Asfi descend into the plumes of smoke rising toward the ceiling.

Making it through the outer layer of the hazy dome, she picked up speed. Her knowledge as the creator of Talaria allowed her to move through the air at any speed or direction she wished. She descended into the devastation like a bird of prey searching for its next kill.

The white smoke filling the air provided her with cover. It was time to strike.

Too slow!

She swooped in to ground level directly behind the man dressed in white.

He had been scanning the space overhead, but she used the smoke to her advantage to attack from a blind spot. He moved to defend himself, but Asfi was faster.

Now that it was impossible for him to dodge, Asfi thrust her blade toward the chest of her unarmed enemy.

—You're mine!

The sharp blade of her shortsword flashed through the smoke.

"—"

But...

"?!"

He stopped her blade by grabbing it with his *bare hand*.

"Huh...?!"

Asfi's eyes went wide, stunned by what she was seeing.

The man was only halfway turned in her direction, his left hand around the blade of her shortsword. Her momentum died.

Grabbing a weapon with an unprotected hand was a reckless, desperate defensive tactic. But even so, the man had, with one arm, completely shut down an aerial strike at Talaria's full speed.

It defied comprehension. Even though the man's fingers bled, the sharp edge did little more than penetrate his skin. All the power that Asfi's Level Four strength could muster was unable to propel the weapon any farther.

Staunch muscles and a terrifyingly strong grip.

Two frigid, inhuman eyes fixed on her from beneath the white skull mask.

A chill colder than anything she'd felt before swept through Asfi's veins.

Alarm bells blared inside her mind. She released her sword in a last-ditch attempt to escape, but her enemy didn't allow it.

"Nha!"

"Gah!"

Grabbing hold of her collar with his free hand, the man in white slammed her to the floor.

Strength that surpassed comprehension sent Asfi rolling after the impact. Colliding with the charred remains of flower monsters that littered the floor, her body flung chunks of black flesh into the air.

Searing pain shot through her shoulder. She managed to slow down by digging her feet into the floor, grimacing as she clenched her molars together.

She leaped to her feet, straight into a cloud of smoke that still hung in the air.

The man was gone from her line of sight. Head on a swivel, she desperately tried to find his figure in the smoke and scanned every detail in the ever-shifting cloud.

Just then.

SHING!

"—!"

A sickening sound came from her torso.

Time stood still for a moment as a burning sensation spread from where the sound came from.

A red blotch spread out from beneath her combat gear. Only then did she notice the glimmer of the blood-spattered blade protruding from her stomach. Trembling, she looked over her shoulder.

The man in white was right behind her.

He held the familiar blade piercing her body, white hair shifting with his momentum.

Asfi had been run through. Knowing that her opponent got behind her faster than her eyes could see sent a bead of cold sweat down her cheek. Blood spilled from her mouth a heartbeat later.

SHUCK! She collapsed to the floor, a bloody mess, the moment he pulled the blade out of her.

She cursed her weakness, and the fact she hadn't been able to tell the difference in their power, as she fell.

"Asfi?!"

Clatter. A metallic echo filled her ears as the man discarded her shortsword.

Lulune screamed from far away. The sight of their leader collapsing threatened to break the spirit of *Hermes Familia.* The ranks they had so desperately held in their attempt to fend off the enemy attacks started to fall apart.

Amid the distant sound of clashing blades, the man in white approached Asfi.

First, his gaze went to the still extended wings of Talaria, and he smashed them underfoot. Next, he grabbed hold of her neck.

"Ga-ha, gahh…?!"

"So, you still cling to life?"

He proceeded to lift her body high into the air as if she weighed nothing. Asfi's feet dangled limply above the floor.

Her combat gear and white cloak had been stained red with her blood, making her look like a crucified martyr. Yet even now, she possessed an undeniable beauty.

The blood dripping off her boots started to form a red puddle beneath her feet.

A grin appeared on the man's lips as his fingers wrapped all the way around Asfi's thin neck.

"Be at ease. Adventurer's tenacity runs deep within you…I'll suffocate it."

Fingers plunged into her skin as he tightened his grip.

Her weak struggling came to a sudden end, her face contorting. A sadistic gleam in his eyes behind the skull mask, the man squeezed again in an attempt to break her warm neck in half.

However—that was the moment that the rumble of lightning echoed through the cavern.

"?!"

The man in white searched for the source of the noise. What he saw was a werewolf kicking everything in sight—and two elves carrying magical staffs.

"Proud warriors, marksmen of the forest. Take up your bows to face the marauders. Answer the call of your kin, nock your arrows."

Lefiya entered the cavern just behind Bete and started using her Magic the moment Filvis's spell was complete.

The three adventurers had entered the pantry by the same route Aiz and *Hermes Familia* had, by breaking through the fleshy "gate" and wandering through the passages. The appearance of this mutated Dungeon—the foul plantlike walls and ceiling—was enough to make them feel physically sick, providing even more incentive to quicken their pace.

The larger party had left a trail of crystals. That, combined with what they could discern from the slain monsters left in the passageways, guided them directly to the main cavern.

"The hell's goin' on in here?!"

The first thing Bete saw upon passing through the entrance was a party of adventurers engaged in a desperate fight with a strange group of masked warriors and a swarm of flower monsters. With a surly shout, he raced headlong into the fray.

He made a split-second decision to eliminate the monsters bearing down on the party. Lending his strength to their cause, his boots connected with the first of the vicious plants at the same time that Filvis unleashed her Magic to cover him. Surprised adventurers watched in shock as he single-handedly pushed the front line back with a flurry of attacks.

"Bring forth the flames, torches of the forest. Release them, flaming arrows of the fairies."

Every enemy on the attack was now Bete's target.

The remaining masked warriors started to scream in the face of his onslaught and reached for their cords. But it was already too late. Before they could detonate their payloads, Bete punched and kicked them high into the air, knocking each one unconscious with a single blow.

At the same time, Filvis dealt with the beasts drawn to Lefiya's magic by generating her own as a distraction and finishing them off with precise swordwork.

"Fall like rain, burn the savages to ash!!"

The moment her chant ended, a golden magic circle illuminated her in a bright light.

A prum caster in the adventurers' rear guard looked over her shoulder when she saw the flash. Then her expression changed as she yelled, "E-everyone, take cover!"

As a specialist herself, she knew the Magic packed into that spell was greater than normal.

Heeding her warning, the party immediately fell back. Lefiya unleashed a spell powerful enough to frighten another magic user the moment they were clear.

"Fusillade Fallarica!!"

Innumerable flames appeared high above her head before descending as a downpour over the battlefield.

The wide-range offensive spell wiped out the monsters trapped beneath in a matter of moments as a tremor passed through the battlefield.

Lefiya had pushed both the power and range of the spell to its absolute limit. The surviving robed warriors fled the fiery rain in a panic, leaving the plant monsters behind. Some managed to get away from the inferno by the skin of their teeth. The blazing salvo spread out to cover almost half the cavern, incinerating every large monster that happened to be in the area.

The vision of all present burned red.

"Wha—?"

The man in white took his eyes off Asfi for a moment to gaze at the destructive spell's aftermath.

Just barely out of range, a few of the flaming missiles had landed right in front of him. The floor split open at the point of impact, sending tremors under his feet as the man used his free arm to shield his face.

As the tide of battle turned, Asfi's blue eyes cleared and locked onto the arm holding her aloft by her neck. Whipping her body in one swift motion, she drew a knife from her holster and slammed it into the man's wrist.

"Nah!"

"‼"

She drove her heel straight into the man's chest the moment she felt his grip weaken.

With missiles still falling behind her, blood continued to flow from the hole in Asfi's stomach as she broke away from the man's grasp.

"Damn you..." The man yanked out the knife impaling his wrist while cursing Asfi's feeble escape attempt.

She gained a bit of distance before collapsing in a fit of coughing and falling to her knees in pain. The man held his bleeding wrist and took a step in her direction...when a large explosion and another flash of light caught his attention. He stayed still.

Ignoring the dying girl at his feet for a moment, the man focused on the new intruders instead.

"*Haah, haah...*What...what is this place...?"

Lefiya muttered as she lowered her staff and took a look around the cavern after eliminating the swarm of monsters.

The area was composed of relatively soft green walls, and three gigantic flowers bloomed on the quartz pillar. Her Magic had done immense damage to the floor, but it was beginning to heal with stomach-turning gushing noises. More flower buds than she could count dotted the walls and ceiling while the open, vividly colored flowers wiggled their way free. New plant monsters were being born.

Every one of those buds was a new enemy—that realization made Lefiya's face turn pale. The mysteries of the living labyrinth were only increasing.

The sight of human bodies among the corpses of monsters left her lost for words.

"There were several factions in the battle…?"

She saw the smoldering corpses of what looked to be adventurers and an incredible number of flower monsters. Filvis stepped up next to Lefiya, frowning as she spoke.

"Don't I know you…? No way. Lefiya?!"

"Eh? Miss Lulune?!"

A chienthrope—Lulune called out to her, and Lefiya rushed to her side.

The two had met just prior to the attack on Rivira. The elf was concerned, seeing her acquaintance and her allies covered in injuries.

"Why are you here—?"

"Oi, is Aiz here or not? Answer me!"

Lefiya was interrupted by Bete, who stepped in front of her and approached Lulune.

Down on one knee, the chienthrope did her best to string words together under his furious gaze as her tail trembled.

"Sh-she was with us, up until a while back…We got…separated."

"Huhh? Whaddaya mean, 'separated'?"

"B-b-but right now, please save Asfi!"

Lulune fell forward, desperately pleading for Bete and Lefiya to leave the questions for later.

She looked toward the opposite end of the cavern to where the man in white stood. The other adventurers could see a blood-splattered female body on the floor near him.

The sinister figure looked their way, white hair peeking out from under his mask.

"This screwed-up pantry, all those freaky monsters—he's behind everything! It's all his fault!"

"...!"

"We'll tell you anything you want to know! Just please, save Asfi first...!"

Confirming Lulune's assessment, the man raised an arm, causing two flesh-eating plant monsters to emerge from the wall and start slithering toward them.

Bete narrowed his eyes at the man capable of manipulating monsters. A stunned Lefiya stood next to him.

The stare from underneath the skull mask was enough to let them know he was their enemy. Bete braced himself for battle beside the elves.

"Oi, my blades."

"R-right away!!"

Bete didn't take his eyes off the white-dressed man as he issued Lefiya a command.

The jittery elf quickly took the tubular backpack off her shoulder and drew twin blades, each fifty celch long. Bete had prepared them before they left home.

"It's a pain in the ass, but why the hell not. Can't stand that look in his eyes."

The man had thrashed Asfi within an inch of her life, and Lulune knew the rest of them didn't stand a chance. Her only choice was to plead with the elite adventurer. Bete's amber eyes flashed with intensity and locked with the masked man's gaze. He knew in an instant that their enemy had no intention of letting them walk away whole.

The carnivorous flowers thundered their broken-bell howls, as if Bete's equipment change was the signal to attack. They lunged forward from their positions beside the man.

"Leave the guys in the robes to us! We'll manage somehow! Both of you, please, go!"

"O-okay!" Lulune shouted as she watched Bete race into battle.

The last survivors of the robed faction that managed to regroup were renewing their attack. While Lulune and the rest of the party consumed their healing items and took hold of their weapons, Lefiya nodded.

Filvis also dipped her head affirmatively before joining her in a race to catch up with Bete.

The curtain had risen on the second battle within the transformed pantry.

"_____!!"

"Outta my way!"

Bete held the twin blades in a reverse grip as he charged straight toward the oncoming flowers.

Jumping between them, he inflicted fatal gashes along their bodies with two silver swipes. He left Filvis and Lefiya to put the writhing monsters down and continued his advance toward the man in white.

Filvis begrudgingly fulfilled the job pushed onto her before following suit.

"Got any more tricks up your sleeve?"

"More than you could ever imagine, filthy adventurer!"

Bete had come within striking distance of the man dressed in white.

Jumping into the air and bringing his blade down like a scythe, Bete missed his furious target. Dodging the attack with ease, the man made a move toward the werewolf's exposed back, but the ash-gray adventurer was faster.

A quick pivot on his plant leg and Bete unleashed a fully extended sweeping kick. A tinge of surprise flashed over the man's face as he was forced to use his right arm to block it.

"Gah!"

A shocked grunt escaped his lips. The blow was powerful enough to make his arm go numb.

"Tsk!"

Bete clicked his tongue, frustrated that his opponent not only blocked the kick but did so with his arm in one piece.

"Vanargand…A member of *Loki Familia*! You came in pursuit of the Sword Princess!"

"Bastard, what have you done with her?!"

A grin appeared beneath the skull mask. Bete bared his fangs and intensified his assault.

Dodging the twin-blade strikes by a hair, the man commenced his own counterattack as he answered.

"My associate is seeing to her. She should be all but subdued by this point, and I'm sure the Sword Princess is in great hands."

"—You die, now."

An aura more threatening and murderous than any monster's emanated from the werewolf as his attacks reached a fever pitch.

His body became a blur, his frenzied attacks struggling to reach his enemy. The man dressed in white smirked, moving his powerful arms at the same rate and knocking Bete's blades away.

"Mr. Bete!"

"Viridis, stay back! Ready support—!!"

The two elves had arrived in time to witness the hand-to-hand brawl between Bete and the man. The two began casting to assist their ally.

However, their desire to help was pointless because their target was moving too fast. Every time they caught a glimpse of him and pointed their staffs, the enemy was already gone.

H-he's so fast—

Aiming is impossible!

The high-speed battle overwhelmed Lefiya and Filvis. Neither could get a clean shot.

Their eyes could hardly follow the exchange of powerful blows and counterattacks. The instant an attack was blocked, the defender had already wheeled around to strike from the exposed side. By the time one of the elves had lined up for a ranged attack, the battle had already moved to a different location. The two elves spent so much time lining up their sights that neither could pull the trigger.

Afterimages of gray werewolf fur and white streaks of hair behind the skull mask streaked across the battlefield.

"On par with a strong upper-class adventurer..."

Filvis's red-gem eyes shook with fear. Lefiya's dark-blue irises were also trembling, but out of disbelief.

—*A match for Mr. Bete?!*

The man in white clearly matched the fastest member of *Loki Familia* blow for blow. Trying to comprehend how this man was competing with a captain of the strongest familia in Orario was too much for her to handle.

He might have been slightly slower, but there was no mistake the man was physically stronger than Bete. Even more disturbing was his ability to endure damage and continue attacking.

The werewolf's metallic silver boots landed hit after hit all over the man's body, but it did not faze his enemy in the slightest. Bete snarled with rage as his opponent countered from every angle with enough force to tear the werewolf limb from limb should he connect. Each near miss ripped long gashes in Bete's combat gear, sending bits of fabric to the floor below.

It was the same feeling—Lefiya had seen that strength before.

The battle between Aiz and the red-haired woman in Rivira replayed in the back of her mind.

The Sword Princess had failed to defeat the woman who was also able to block Lefiya's magic with her bare hands.

The raw power of Bete's opponent was extremely similar to what she saw on that day.

"Violas!"

The battlefield changed once again while Lefiya was lost in thought.

On the plantlike ceiling, several red flower buds far above the combatants' heads bloomed. The creatures opened their mouths wide, baring their fangs at the battle below, and dropped down at the man's call.

Bete was quick to dodge the massive incoming shadows. A chorus of dull, thudding impacts filled the chamber as the monsters rose from their landings and began their pursuit.

"You bastard!"

Four of the monsters charged him in unison. Bete was forced to divide his attention, defending himself with his twin swords and sending their gigantic frames flying with a flurry of kicks as the man in white charged in.

The man smirked and punched with all his might. Bete blocked the straightforward attack with his metal boots.

The force of the blow knocked him off balance, providing the reinforcements with an opening to flood the battle with vine whips.

"Mr. Bete!"

Even though all the whips were sliced down before they could connect, the man had already renewed his assault.

Lefiya watched in horror as Bete was forced to contend with the man's flurry of attacks without finishing off the monsters surrounding them.

"—My apologies, Miss Filvis. Protect me!"

Lefiya raised her staff and started casting without waiting for Filvis's response.

"Unleashed pillar of light, limbs of the holy tree!"

Her magic circle expanding, Lefiya's chant rose high into the air.

The only way to help Bete now was to take advantage of the plant monsters' instinct to pursue magic energy. By offering herself as bait, she could take some of the pressure off her ally.

"Pay her no mind, violas! Kill the werewolf first!"

"!"

However, the man's voice cut through the chamber the moment the monsters paused to look in Lefiya's direction.

They followed the man's command and prioritized Bete, continuing their attack. The tamer's quick reaction thwarted Lefiya's plan.

"Enough of this!"

Wand and sword at the ready, Filvis charged headlong into the fray.

Lefiya watched and realized the only thing left for her now was to provide ranged support. She continued her trigger spell.

"You are the master archer!"

Feeling Lefiya's concerned gaze behind her, Filvis cut her way through a never-ending stream of monster vines.

Broken-bell howls rent the air one after another as a streak of pure-white combat gear made it to the other side. Harnessing the powerful mobility that magic swordsmen were known for, Filvis swiftly beheaded the closest beast without losing her forward momentum.

She dispatched another monster with the sword in her right hand before bringing the wand in her left forward.

"Loose your arrows, fairy archers—!"

"Purge, cleansing lightning!"

There was no hesitation in her voice as Filvis ended her short-trigger spell.

Concurrent Casting executed to perfection, she aimed her wand—at the man dressed in white.

"Dio Thyrsos!"

A thick bolt of lightning blasted forth.

It tore into the flesh of monsters that happened to be in the line of fire, a jagged stream of golden plasma on a collision course with the eyes behind the skull mask.

"You idiot!!"

Bete roared as soon as he caught a glimpse of what was happening.

While he was occupied beating the remaining three creatures to a pulp, the man in white grinned and ran toward the lightning. ·

Filvis's red-jewel eyes went wide, quivering at the sight.

The palm of the man's left hand stopped her golden lightning cold. Unable to continue forward, the bolt split left and right. Although it was a short-trigger spell, it was powered by Level Three magic energy. Time slowed to a crawl for the elf girl as she watched the man demonstrate his immense power, literally cutting her magic in half with his bare hand as he charged right for her.

Lefiya was unable to scream during her incantation, but she turned pale as a ghost, lips frozen in place.

"So weak!"

Filvis saw the fist sweeping up at her and reflexively moved to avoid it.

Raising her sword at an angle to guide the blow away from her body did nothing. Her weapon provided as much resistance as a toothpick, shattering at the moment of impact. The man's fist broke through her defense, connected, and sent her flying.

The man charged after her, catching up to the tumbling elf and reaching for her neck.

"Dammit, elf!"

"GaHA!"

It happened the instant before the man's hand reached its target.

Bete's foot collided with Filvis, sending her into the air once again.

The elf's limp body arced through the air as the man in white watched with a sneer. Bete's tattoo rippled across his cheek.

As if ridiculing the werewolf who rescued the woman, the man in white raised an arm to finish it.

Lefiya's magic would arrive too late. The tide of battle had turned too far in the man's favor.

All he had to do to end it was deliver the blow. Bete was defenseless, desperately trying to protect himself.

"—"

From out of nowhere…

The eyes beneath the mask widened mid-leer.

The attacker took evasive action.

His forward movement came to a halt, body tilting backward ever so slightly as a red line appeared across his chest. *Eh?* Lefiya thought in surprise, unable to voice it.

The sound of a blade slicing through flesh had come from the space where there shouldn't be anything.

The red line cut deepest just below the man's neck, and a stream of blood sprayed into the air.

Lefiya, Filvis, and Bete watched in shock as the man in white wildly swung at the air with one arm in a rage.

"Wench!"

His extended fist hit something with a sharp *WHAM!*

A string of loud cracks rang out after the impact, and a young woman's body materialized *out of thin air.*

—Perseus!!

Glistening aqua-blue hair reflected in Lefiya's eyes, allowing her to discern the woman's identity.

A renowned item maker famous throughout Orario, and also the person Lulune had begged them to save. The leader of *Hermes Familia*, Asfi Al Andromeda.

Despite her serious injuries and being on the brink of death, she had likely made herself invisible—*with a magic item that hid her from sight*—and ambushed the man.

"—Look at you, now!"

A dark-black helmet had been destroyed, disabling her invisibility, and its fragments were scattered about the floor. Her voice was weak despite the faint smile on her face as she collapsed. The short-sword clenched in her fist glinted next to her, the man's rage-filled eyes reflected in its blade.

That was the weapon that had inflicted the wound in the man's neck, which was still gushing fountains into the air.

The werewolf, already out for blood, licked his lips as he saw the enemy lose his balance.

Eyes flashing, Bete renewed his attack with a vengeance.

"GRAHHHHHHHHHHHHHHH!!"

"GOAH!"

A front kick, straight and sharp as an arrow, accompanied by whirling twin swords.

The kicks kept coming—a storm of sharp slashes and powerful blows pummeled the man dressed in white.

The force of each impact sent him staggering backward. The blades cut through the cloth covering his body, splitting the skin beneath before the metal boots hammered the man's body like rampaging wrecking balls.

For the first time, the man allowed one of Bete's kicks to connect with his face. A web of cracks instantly spread out over his mask.

"Don't—PUSH YOUR LUUUUUUCK!!"

Consumed by a new wave of rage, the man started to fight back against Bete's onslaught.

As if the grotesque number of cuts covering his body weren't there at all, he took hold of the extended twin swords and drove his fist into the flat part of the blades, breaking them in half. Bete howled as he threw away the now useless weapons and coaxed even more speed out of his feet.

Neither side was backing down.

"—*Pierce, arrow of accuracy!*"

The combatants matched each other blow for blow as Lefiya finally completed her trigger spell.

The bow had been drawn, the arrow nocked, and all that remained was to let it fly.

The man had yet to show any sign of pain despite the terrific strikes his body had absorbed. Unable to overcome a staunch defense that was reminiscent of a floor boss's, Bete couldn't deliver a decisive blow. If she was going to use magic, it was now or never.

—But how?

However, Lefiya was wavering.

She'd seen the man physically overpower magic with her own eyes. What if what just happened to Filvis happened to her, just as the red-haired woman had done in Rivira?

That woman's ferocious visage overlapped the man in white, sending fear down Lefiya's spine and freezing her hand in place.

"The hell are you waiting for?!"

"!"

Bete's yell made Lefiya's shoulders jump.

Despite being in the middle of an intense brawl, he made eye contact with her for a split second. His voice echoed through the cavern around the frozen Lefiya.

"Do it, shoot!!"

The look in his amber eyes provided the push she needed. The hesitation was gone.

She pulled back on the loaded bow and let the arrow fly.

"Arcs Ray!!"

A flash of light from the magic circle accompanied the pillar of glowing energy hurtling toward her target.

The man in white saw the straight beam approaching and moved to block it head-on.

"When will you learn your lesson?!"

The man thrust out his right arm to block the magic—when the beam of light *started to turn.*

"?!"

As for where the arrow of light was headed, it was now on course to collide with Bete's metallic boots.

Frosvirt: a second-tier Superior weapon. What set these mythril boots apart from the rest was their ability to absorb magic.

"Now *that's* what I'm talkin' about!"

Lefiya's offensive spell, Arcs Ray, had the ability to hone in on its target.

The elf was not targeting the man in white. This magic arrow would twist and turn until it connected with Bete.

The man swiped at open air as the beam of light curved around him. Lefiya had correctly interpreted what her comrade had been trying to say. The corners of the werewolf's lips curled upward.

His right boot pulsed with magic energy as the arrow disappeared into it.

"Rot in hell."

"!"

His target in sight, Bete closed in at breakneck speed.

The man in white spun to evade, but Bete didn't give him the chance.

Moving into point-blank range, he slammed his shining boot directly into his opponent.

"_____!"

The man in white disappeared into the explosive impact of the magically enhanced boot.

His smoking body blasted out of the plume a moment later, arms crossed defensively over his chest as he streaked through the chamber like a comet.

The man landed on his back, but his momentum carried him deeper into the chamber, ripping holes in the fleshy green floor as he went. His path through the piles of monster ash sent black clouds into the air in his wake, all the way until he came to a merciful stop at the base of the quartz pillar.

Just as the high-pitched echoes from the impact began to fade in the chamber, the sounds of battle on the other side also came to an end. Lulune and the rest of *Hermes Familia* had managed to dispatch the remaining robed warriors once and for all.

"Asfi!" Lulune was the first to dash across the chamber, shouting, her allies not far behind. Everyone had uncorked high potions in hand the moment they reached where Asfi fell, and Lulune dumped a virtual waterfall of Tiger Cub Elixir on her leader's body. Light from magical healing spells enveloped the woman's body.

Asfi, completely drenched in liquid, slowly but surely opened her eyes. Lulune was almost in tears as she dove in for a hug filled with pure joy and relief.

"Did you get him...?"

"I aimed to kill when I hit the bastard."

Filvis returned to the group, staggering as she clutched her injured shoulder while Asfi climbed weakly to her feet. Bete looked past the elf toward the clouds of ash.

Having unloaded every bit of magical energy into that one kick, Frosvirt had returned to its normal appearance.

No matter how good the man's Defense attribute was, it was unlikely anyone could walk away from a hit like that.

The awe-inspiring power was possible only because of Bete's physical strength and Lefiya's magic. The elf nervously waited as moments passed.

A plume of smoke formed from the disturbed monster ash. The cloud expanded to overtake the chamber, blinding them. Only the sloshing sounds of the gigantic flower monsters absorbing the liquid from the quartz pillar could be heard in the darkness.

"—?"

The ash began to settle, a red light penetrating through the smoke.

The ones who'd been watching the fading plume with bated breath suddenly trembled.

A human figure stood in the middle of it. It took a few steps forward a moment later.

"What kind of monster *is* this guy...?" mumbled Lulune as she lent her shoulder to Asfi, who was also frowning.

Most corpses looked healthier than the man in white did, but he stood on his own two feet nonetheless.

His arms were barely recognizable after taking the brunt of Bete's attack. His forearms were broken in several places, the skin was burned to a crisp, and blood leaked from open wounds. His combat gear was in tatters, its once-white surfaces stained with blood in several places, especially across the chest.

His white skull helmet hadn't survived. The man's dull-white hair flowed freely.

"...That was a nice try."

The man's pale lips opened.

Though his face was downturned, mostly hidden behind hair, his devious smile was just visible.

"However, bodies endowed with Her love don't crumble so easily."

He raised his head with his mouth slightly open in a sneer. That's when the adventurers saw it.

The man's body was changing.

It started with the arms that Bete had all but destroyed and the cut from Asfi's blade that had nearly taken off his head.

The wounds were *closing on their own.*

"Impossible—!"

Lefiya couldn't believe her eyes.

The same was true for Filvis, Asfi, Lulune, and Bete.

This was no healing magic but pure self-regeneration. Lefiya and the adventurers watched in horror as all traces of their battle started to disappear from the man's body. Sparkling fragments of light—residue from magic energy—rose from his body like steam.

No one present could say a thing. The last of the ash cloud dissipating, the man stepped into the light and revealed his identity.

"Wha...?"

Asfi was the first one to react.

His face, paler than a dying man's, was such a shock that she couldn't move.

"Mi...Miss Filvis?"

"...Why?"

Filvis had the same reaction as Asfi.

Lefiya knew something was wrong immediately when she saw the expressions on the two women's faces and sensed the tension in the air.

Feeling Lefiya's gaze at her side, Filvis's lips trembled as she spoke.

"Olivas Act..."

The atmosphere became grave the moment that name reached the other adventurers' ears. The man in white had their full attention.

The group began to stir as confusion descended upon them.

"Olivas Act…? The White Devil, Vendetta?! It can't be!"

Voice going up an octave, Lulune blinked many times as she studied the man's face.

It was as though her memory were arguing with her eyes. It took all she had to squeeze words out of her dry throat.

"B-but Vendetta is…!"

Lefiya looked around in confusion as the only one who had no recollection of that name. She desperately tried to meet someone's eyes to get an explanation.

Asfi was flabbergasted, absolutely stunned—until she couldn't take it anymore and howled at the top of her lungs:

"Impossible! A dead man cannot possibly be standing here!"

Her high-pitched voice echoed throughout the chamber.

Lefiya couldn't quite comprehend the true meaning of her words. However, the intensity of her expression, as well as those of Filvis and all of *Hermes Familia*, made her blood run cold.

"A…a dead man…?"

Lefiya felt her lips shaking, but she was barely aware of her own voice as it spilled out.

Asfi attempted to dispel her own doubts by voicing what she knew about the man under the red light of the quartz pillar.

"Olivas Act…Estimated to be Level Three, he was a wanted man who was given the title 'White Devil, Vendetta.' His god returned to Tenkai, and the rest of his familia was wiped out."

Stepping away from Lulune's shoulder, she took a defensive stance with her eyes locked onto him.

"A known Evils disciple…and the mastermind behind the Twenty-Seventh-Floor Nightmare."

"—?!"

Lefiya immediately turned to Filvis.

The Twenty-Seventh-Floor Nightmare. A calamity of immense proportions brought on by the Evils who had claimed countless lives. It was also the event that had robbed her friend of her allies and taken her pride as an elf.

Lefiya saw all the color drain from Filvis's face. The elf was frozen in place.

"Familias fighting in the name of the Guild cornered him during the battle, and he was consequently devoured by monsters...His death should have been confirmed when the shredded remains of his lower body were discovered."

Her gaze never left the man in front of them while she described his gruesome end.

In the midst of her waking nightmare, she spoke to Olivas directly.

"Did you survive...?"

"No, I died. However, I have been revived from the brink of death."

Olivas answered with great pride.

At the opportunity to show them his badly injured body—that is to say, the self-regeneration keeping him alive—a look of joy bordering on ecstasy appeared on his face. He then began to run his fingers up his legs, over his stomach, and up to his chest, caressing every curve.

The sudden change in Olivas's demeanor sent another chill up Lefiya's spine.

Her eyes followed his hands, leading her to notice something very unusual about him.

The skin on his lower body, beneath the torn combat gear...

Both his legs were the same shade of yellowish green as the plant monsters'.

What's more, shining through from under the skin healing just beneath his neck was a crystal.

No, *a richly colored magic stone* was buried deep in his chest.

"—!"

This time, Lefiya screamed.

Others around her had noticed, too. Each of them had turned pale.

Olivas's devious grin widened, his eyes flashing. Lefiya and the adventurers had lost all sense of calm, and the man wanted to press his advantage. Holding the wound open, he made certain that everyone could see the vivid magic stone in his chest.

"I have been granted a second life by none other than Her!!"

The red glow of the quartz pillar behind him made the man's visage only more menacing.

BA-DUM. The feminine fetus encased in the orb at the base of the pillar kicked its legs.

CHAPTER 5

Hell
and Hell

Гэта казка іншага сям'і.

Пекла і Пекла

Darkness overtook the man's vision.

The only sounds to reach his bloody inner ears were a muffled mix of human screams and the howls of monsters on a rampage.

The screams came from all angles, so many echoes that it was impossible to discern where one began and another ended.

The man dragged his upper body across the floor, senses overwhelmed by the pandemonium that surrounded him.

Both his eyes had been crushed.

Tears of blood flowed from behind closed eyelids as he fumbled through an endless abyss.

Everything below his waist had been severed from his body.

Using his arms to pull himself forward, he moved like a nearly deceased creature that had forgotten it had once been a man.

A body that was unrecognizable. Moans of pain. A consciousness in turmoil.

He felt intense heat.

His throat was so dry it stung.

Even his jaw wouldn't shut comfortably.

Each time he shuffled forward, some essential part of him spilled from his open abdomen.

The literally half-dead human man had no idea where he was as he proceeded deeper and deeper into the Dungeon.

Whirling pain and suffering unknown to this world finally consumed his mind.

Any normal person would have already died in this hell. But the Falna in the Status on his back wouldn't let him easily pass into the next realm.

A new sound filled his ears: the crude laughter of gods. Although not real, he could hear them laughing at him, as though he were a freak for their entertainment. Even if this was just some hallucination the exitless Dungeon was tormenting him with, it was nothing more than a curse.

Anger and rage filled the tears of blood still pouring from his eyes. The will to live had yet to break.

The man who hated everything outside himself was swallowed up by despair from which there was no escape.

The man could go no farther, lost in a vast ocean of darkness.

He lay completely still, leaking the last of his blood into the red puddle beneath him.

There were no sounds of people, no sounds of monsters. Only silence.

His body turned cold in a corner of the Dungeon completely cut off from the rest of the world—

Slither.

A sound wafted through the air as something reached out to the man on the brink of death.

A single root grew toward him from even deeper in the Dungeon.

A richly colored glow sparkled at the end of its tip.

It glided ever closer as if inviting him to come to the other side of the darkness. Wrapping itself around his lifeless body, it flipped the man over onto his back.

The vivid glow disappearing into the legless human's chest, his eyes closed.

The man awoke with a start a moment later, crushed irises taking on a greenish yellow hue.

A beastly roar echoed through the darkness.

Lefiya shook in fear as Olivas's yellow-green eyes warped into a diabolical smile.

A threateningly intense glow emanated from the object in his chest. That, combined with a lower body the same off-green color as his eyes, proved that this man was no human.

His overpowering presence was enough to make Lefiya forget where she was, her eyes spinning.

She also felt extremely nauseous.

Lefiya the elf was afraid of the thing in human form before her eyes—utterly revolted by it and overcome with an urge to put as much distance between them as possible.

"This has to be some cruel joke..."

Asfi swore under her breath. The rest of *Hermes Familia* was equally perturbed.

Was their enemy human?

Or a monster in human form?

Feeling vomit build up in her throat, unable to take it anymore, Lefiya pressed for answers.

"Just what are you...?"

Olivas's lips curved into a smile, his white hair swishing around his shoulders.

"I am both and neither, a combination of strengths that has ascended beyond human and monster!"

The man shrouded in white sneered at Lefiya and the other adventurers as he proudly declared his origin.

No sooner were those words out of his mouth than the last of the light coming from the magic stone disappeared behind a healing wound, accentuating his point.

"How can the likes of you, who only fight with a deity's Blessing... win against one such as I?"

Olivas chuckled with contempt.

As for Lefiya, her mind frantically tried to make sense of what she had just heard.

The strengths of man and monster.

Intelligence with Status, contained in a body equipped with monstrous strength and ridiculously high defense.

There were several instances in the previous battle where those abilities had been on display.

Lefiya had seen him take several direct hits from Bete, a top-class adventurer, and not even flinch. That unfathomably thick skin had repelled magic and possessed a terrifyingly fast self-regeneration ability that was still at work as they spoke. The idea that all these things came from a Status felt too strange to be true.

If Olivas's words were to be believed, then whoever "She" was had transformed a dying man into *something* completely different.

The feminine fetus at the base of the quartz pillar was visible just behind the man in white.

Human and monster—a hybrid.

The man in front of her—and most likely the red-haired woman as well—was the same type of absurd abomination.

Creature was the only way she could describe it.

"…Are you a remnant of the Evils?"

Asfi, who had recovered enough to speak, narrowed her eyes as she joined the conversation.

The entire party focused solely on Olivas. The man laughed off that idea, however.

"Do not confuse me with the scum who refuse to let go of the past. I am not some puppet who will dance for a god."

Yellowish green irises surveyed the landscape.

The cavern floor was dotted with scorched corpses, as well as a few robed warriors who had been denied that fate. Although he didn't say it directly, Olivas's expression was enough to let the adventurers know that the zealots whom *Hermes Familia* and Lefiya's party had dispatched were part of the still active Evils organization. Based on his choice of words, Lefiya guessed they were merely cooperating with him, nothing more than pawns in a larger plan.

An eerie silence filled the chamber.

The gigantic flower monsters still attached to the quartz pillar emanating red light and the fetus created the only sounds in the cave. This time, it was Asfi who broke the quiet.

"What is this place? What is it that you and your conspirators were planning to do here?"

"This is a Plant."

"Plant…?"

"That is correct. A pantry infested with parasites forcing it to bear violas…A vessel to bring monsters from the Deep Levels to higher floors."

Lefiya was unable to hide her shock.

The plant monsters originated in the Deep Levels, and—

"Monsters giving birth to other monsters…I have never heard of anything like it."

The Dungeon gave birth to all monsters as their "mother."

That was an absolute truth.

Even the gods clearly stated it was a law of this world.

The gigantic flower monsters' infestation of the pantry, the flesh walls that spawned flower buds. Even now, more buds opened, and the brood's broken-bell howls started filling the chamber once again. Lefiya fell silent, speechless.

"In other words, you used your skill as a tamer to instruct those monsters to create the space?"

"No, incorrect. I am no tamer."

Olivas's voice intensified.

"The violas, myself—all of us are one entity under Her. As Her representative, the monsters obey my will."

The man spoke as though he had been given a great honor, his voice brimming with delight.

Asfi donned the scowl of a disbeliever in front of the faithful and pressed right to the heart of the matter.

"What is it you're trying to achieve?"

Olivas's greenish yellow eyes smiled once again, glinting.

"Destroying Orario."

That declaration sent a wave of fear through the adventurers as they stood like statues.

Lefiya gulped. Those around her did the same.

Whether she was aware of it or not, Lulune's trembling hand took hold of her tail and squeezed as she spoke for the first time.

"D-do you know what you're saying…? What that means?"

Orario was a large city built directly on top of the Dungeon. It was also a fortress that kept the Dungeon in check. The Tower of Babel stood directly over a large hole in the ground, like a lid that prevented monsters from reaching the surface. Built in the Ancient Times, it was a barrier that separated the Dungeon from the rest of the world. Calling it humanity's last bastion wouldn't be an exaggeration.

If Orario fell, the world would be plunged into the darkest days since the Ancient Times.

The tragic days of war between monsters and the various races of humanity would begin again.

"Of course I do!!"

Olivas shouted his response to Lulune's question.

"I would destroy Orario voluntarily!! All to make Her dream a reality!"

He gestured to the pillar behind him in front of the adventurers' horrified faces.

"She speaks! Can you not hear Her?"

His outstretched hand pointed directly to the base of the column, to the fetus contained in the orb.

"She wants to see the sky! She longs for it! That is Her wish, and I will do everything in my power to grant it!"

His voice steadily reached a fever pitch.

Skin paler than a sick man's wrinkled as an exultant smile appeared on his lips.

If there was one thing that the adventurers understood from the nonsense that spilled from his mouth, it was that this man possessed loyalty to "Her" that bordered on obsession.

"The city blocks her view of the sky from deep underground! The metropolis that blocks the hole must be obliterated!

"Inept humans and powerless deities have no right to control the surface! She should reign supreme!

"She is not the same as deities who merely crave amusement, letting chips fall where they may so they can be entertained, whittling the time away, doing nothing themselves! No!! She granted me a second life and bestowed an even greater joy upon me!"

Lefiya's and the other adventurers' glares intensified as Olivas unleashed an avalanche of scorn.

"I have been chosen by none other than Her!! And I—we—will see Her dreams come true! I will stop at nothing to give Her anything She desires!!"

One look at the man's expression was enough for Lefiya to know.

—*A fanatic.*

Olivas had a blind faith in the "Her" who gave him a second life.

That was a feat that even the "philosopher" who created the Philosopher's Stone—an item that granted eternal life—had tried and failed to accomplish many times. Gekai was bound by a set of rules that even the deities who loved the children had to abide by, one of them being that reanimation of the dead was impossible. Olivas Act had committed himself to "Her" because she transcended these rules for his sake.

A soul that had forsaken the gods themselves willingly chained his existence to this new entity.

"She is my everything!!"

Olivas declared this with the female fetus as his witness.

No one could say a word in the face of this man's unwavering devotion to an unidentified being known as "Her." Asfi stood transfixed with a searching gaze. Lulune weakly shook her head, trying to convince herself this was just a very bad dream. Filvis was still shaken to the core, unable to speak or move.

Lefiya continued to stare at him, horrified.

"Shut up already."

Bete suddenly broke the silence.

The young werewolf was clearly unamused and stepped out in front of the group.

"Just find a resting spot an' die...'Cause you can't fight for shit right now, can you?"

Voice arrogant, the werewolf's eyes burned with a wild fire as he made his claim.

Lefiya and the other adventurers stared at him, jaws slack with surprise. Olivas said nothing in response, closing his mouth.

The top-class adventurer Bete realized that this lecture was nothing but a way to buy time to heal. Recovering from those injuries would have required a considerable amount of Mind and physical energy, meaning that the man wouldn't be able to fight with the same ferocity as before.

"Hmph," mumbled Olivas with a grin in the face of Bete's sharp glare. "My strategy deciphered by mere humans, how troubling."

Olivas admitted to Bete's claim.

However, his reaction was quite the opposite from someone whose ace in the hole had been discovered: a calm smile.

Bete sensed something was off in the relaxed demeanor of his enemy and snarled.

"This body is nothing but a thing that She saw fit to grant life...It is as you say. I cannot fight as I am now.

"—*I* cannot," he added with a smirk.

Asfi's and Bete's eyes shot open a heartbeat later as something entered their line of vision.

Not giving them time to react, the man with the title "Vendetta" raised his arm into the air with such force that his white hair swirled to the other side of his body.

"Now—viskum."

The quartz pillar behind him immediately began to shake, filling the chamber with wavering red light.

One of the three gigantic flower monsters attached to the crystal shook its threatening petals as it shifted toward the adventurers below. Rather than roaring, it screeched like nails on a chalkboard as it broke away.

A new stench coming from the vivid flower filled the air—putrid, rotting flesh.

Time slowed to a crawl as a gigantic shadow above the adventurers' heads grew larger by the second. The beast was descending.

"—Scatter!!" screamed Bete as everyone took off running.

They sprinted as fast as their legs could carry them. Filvis was the last to react, taking action only when Lefiya grabbed her wrist and half dragged her outside the beast's massive shadow. Their enemy Olivas ran off in the other direction, safely exiting the landing zone with a few light strides.

The gargantuan body of the monster slammed into the floor a moment later with the force of a meteorite. The entire cavern shook with the strongest tremors of the battle.

"~~~~~~?!"

"You gotta be kidding!"

Arms up to protect their faces, Lulune and Asfi braced themselves against the shaking.

Pieces of the green floor exploded, falling like rain. Another ash plume filled the air, concealing the massive creature inside.

Every upper-class adventurer looked upon the gigantic shadow in the middle of the cloud, easily larger than a floor boss.

"Obliterate them."

Following Olivas's command, the gargantuan flower monster lumbered forward.

The beast was far too heavy to raise its upper body like the violas, so instead it slithered toward the adventurers like an overgrown worm.

"!"

Separated from Filvis, Lefiya watched the massive green body approach and immediately moved to get out of the way.

An enemy this large left no room for error. Kicking off the ground, she dove headfirst to avoid its initial body slam, only to get caught up in the burst of wind that accompanied the impact and roll across the floor for several meders.

Other members of the party didn't fare much better. Since each twist and turn of its gigantic frame could result in a fatal blow, every adventurer was quick to put some distance between themselves and the monster.

· "Can we even hurt this thing?!"

Lulune screamed as she dodged round after round of ivy-like whips from the monstrous roots.

One of *Hermes Familia*'s human supporters also evaded a slew of ivy tendrils as she extracted a magic sword from her backpack. She unleashed the full power of the fire-infused blade onto the beast, but the monster didn't seem to notice. Flames bouncing off its incredibly thick skin, the gigantic flower continued its series of plunging body slams unfazed.

Brave adventurers drew their weapons and attacked, but the monster's incessant wiggling knocked them back over and over. Magic users busily cast their spells in an attempt to overwhelm the beast with their power, but they were silenced by waves of ivy whips in their vulnerable state. Even worse, the magic energy attracted a swarm of violas. There was no time to complete their trigger spells.

The chaos on the battlefield prevented *Hermes Familia* from using its formations and teamwork.

"Over here, piece of shit!!"

An airborne Bete landed a devastating kick.

The hastily attached knife on Frosvirt opened up a large gash in the monster's flank, but it was nowhere near enough to bring it down. Although it writhed in pain, a raging bull would never fall to a toothpick.

The beast's movements and attack speed weren't all that impressive, but its mass and scale were just too immense.

Bete clicked his tongue in frustration as he glared at the enemy that no one in their right mind would ever willingly engage in battle.

"FUA-HA-HA-HA-HA-HA! Go, my viskum! Eliminate the adventurers who have set foot on this holy ground!!"

Olivas watched the battle from a short distance away, his laughter echoing through the chamber.

Knowing he had two more of the beasts in reserve, the man couldn't have been more confident of victory. Satisfaction appeared on his face as he waited for the last of his injuries to heal.

"Olivas Act!"

"......?"

A cry of rage reached his ears.

Turning to face its source, he saw an elf with long, shiny black hair wearing pure-white combat gear.

"How have you lived with yourself after causing so much pain and suffering?" Her murderous visage obscured her elven beauty. "Because of you, my allies...I...!"

"...Oh, you survived that plan, too?"

"How dare you!"

The thirst for revenge in the elf's eyes let Olivas know the girl had been directly affected by the Twenty-Seventh-Floor Nightmare.

The man lifted his chin, head tilted as he calmly smiled at her.

"Although the plan was executed according to my design, I am also a victim—I perished, after all. And now I finally awaken from the nightmare of the gods...We can share this pain."

"Go to hell!!"

Filvis wouldn't have any of Olivas's mind game and shot it down.

Her arms and legs trembled with fervor. Rage rolled off her thin body, and her mind was far away. Any semblance of reason had long since disappeared.

Her shortsword gone, she made a fist out of her open right hand and raised her wand high with her left.

Filvis's loathing was not only directed at the man responsible for her pain but also at herself for not being strong enough to take revenge while he was in his weakened state.

"So long as you die, nothing else matters…!"

Dark flames of indignation burned within her red eyes as Olivas accepted her hate with open arms.

At the same time, he shifted his gaze to look directly behind her.

"While entertaining you does pique my interest…can you abandon your kin to her fate, elven maiden?"

"—!"

Her eyes quivered.

She looked over her shoulder at the viskum's onslaught.

Among the adventurers desperately fighting for their lives was another elf with golden yellow hair, trapped between the gigantic flower monster and several smaller plants.

Filvis's expression contorted once again.

The irony in the man's taunts brought her back to herself, awakened her ability to see reason.

"Your friends have already perished…and now, can you let the same happen to her?"

A series of vicious attacks had left cuts and gashes all over Lefiya's body. Filvis's red eyes landed on each one.

She was faced with a decision: forward or backward.

Would she take the forward path and slay the enemy with the burning rage within her?

Or would she extend a helping hand backward to rescue a fellow elf on a precarious edge between life and death?

—"Banshee."

A horrid nickname that she'd never once paid any attention to now tormented her in the back of her mind.

She didn't know how many elves had forsaken her after learning of her past, calling her an "embarrassment to their race" before today.

It was the truth.

Never once had her heart felt pain.

That is, until someone called her "beautiful" despite knowing everything.

The girl who was willing to speak kindly to someone as unclean as herself, even if it was only consolation and sympathy.

Just like Dionysus.

She had looked upon Filvis with sincere, honest eyes, gorgeous enough to make her envious.

Would she leave that beautiful young girl to die...?

The dilemma dug deeply into her soul, posing the same question over and over.

The voices of her deceased allies came to life in her ears.

—*Run for your life, Filvis!!*

—*Go...go now!*

—*AARRGHHHHHHHHHHHHH!!*

—*Yes, Filvis...you must...go.*

—*Run, Filvis.*

—*Fil-vis...*

—*Save me.*

The voices of allies lost to the Nightmare kept coming. Memories that had been eating away at her from the inside began to flash before her eyes, staining the chamber red.

Their sad voices, bloodcurdling screams, and mournful final whispers seized her heart.

I—...

The one responsible stood in front of her, watching her inner conflict and enjoying every twinge pass across her face. Directly behind her was a fellow elf desperately fighting to stay alive.

She stood at an impasse. Then—

"Damn! Damn it all...!!"

Turning her back on Olivas, she rushed back into the battlefield.

"!"

Lefiya guided the ivy whips away from her body with her staff.

Her special robes were getting torn to shreds, but she was managing to keep the rain of creepers from making a direct hit.

Her ability to protect herself in a situation where casting was impossible was thanks entirely to Riveria's tutelage. Magic energy was volatile, and its wielders possessed a great deal of it. They must be able to physically defend themselves should the time come. Riveria had taught her to have the resilient spirit of a towering tree, keeping her mind calm amid the chaos. As long as she focused on her enemies and harnessed the many bow-staff techniques that had been drilled into her, Lefiya could deflect monster attacks on her own.

And, of course, she had plenty of experience dealing with plant monsters.

Lefiya dodged oncoming attacks well before they reached her by calling upon her many battles with this species of late. When the impact of a nearby ivy whip knocked her off balance, the carnivorous plant monsters saw their opportunity and swarmed her. Although able to avoid a direct hit, Lefiya was tossed high into the air.

She landed on her back, fighting through the pain and struggling to breathe as she forced her body up off the floor.

Not good! She could feel the bloodthirsty eyes on her as she got to her feet—when a yellow lightning bolt passed just in front of her face.

"Viridis!"

"Miss Filvis!"

Filvis dashed to Lefiya's side as the smoldering monsters fell away, done in by her magic.

Lefiya had feared the worst after the two became separated, so she breathed a sigh of relief upon seeing the other elf's face.

"Are you hurt?"

"I am all right, thank you."

Filvis's relief was evident as well when she saw Lefiya stand on her own two feet.

"Do you have any blades?" asked Filvis. Lefiya immediately removed her backpack and flipped open the lid. Filvis stuck her hand into the tubular container and pulled out a one-handed longsword.

Ditching the sheath, she moved in front of Lefiya to protect her.

"What do we do, Asfi?!"

—Elsewhere, a group of adventurers were directly engaged in battle with the enormous parasite.

Lulune yelped from inside the swarm of monsters too numerous to kill. Asfi did her best to defend with a shortsword, but she'd lost too much blood to go on the offensive. Rivers of sweat poured down her face and neck as she desperately knocked away oncoming vines.

"...Now would be the perfect time to have Thousand Elf incinerate it with magic, but maintaining a Wall is impossible against an enemy of this size."

She could order many of her allies to raise their shields in a line, but the entire group would be crushed under the gigantic body. Whether or not they could block wasn't the issue.

Asfi glanced over her shoulder at Filvis fighting tirelessly to protect Lefiya before facing forward once again.

"It appears our only option is to aim for its magic stone."

Destroying it would turn the entire monster into a mountain of ash. Drawing out the battle would only work against them. Going for an instant kill at the monster's "core" was their only choice.

The problem was finding where the magic stone was located.

Was it in the central chest area as was normal for monsters in the Dungeon, or was it in the back of the throat like the violas?

Bete called on every muscle in his body to knock the monster off course. Asfi used these brief windows to examine its body for clues. But once they found it, could their blades penetrate deep enough into the gargantuan body to break the stone? Asfi did everything she could to drive that scenario out of her head as she issued orders to Lulune and her allies.

"Pointless."

Olivas chuckled to himself as he watched the party of adventurers fight back against the monsters.

Absorbing the nutritious liquid from the quartz tower had allowed the viskum to grow to a scale that outclassed other monsters. Each one would take more than a fortnight to conquer.

Deciding to end the battle before the adventurers devised a new strategy, Olivas narrowed his leaf-colored eyes and prepared to summon another of the gigantic beasts into battle.

Then, as he was about to raise his arm, it happened.

A new explosion from the other side rocked the cavern.

"?!"

Every inhabitant of the chamber turned around to find the source of the deafening boom and the cracking that followed.

They immediately spotted several columns of smoke rising—and the red-haired woman directly beneath them.

She had hit the wall of the cavern with the force of a cannonball, shattering its surface with her back on impact. *THUMP THUMP THUMP!* She tumbled down the wall and slammed into the floor.

Her body had flown like an arrow to the other side of the chamber, away from the rampaging viskum.

"Kagh...!"

Grunting in pain, she tossed what was left of her heavily damaged crimson blade to the side.

Despite the numerous injuries covering her from head to toe, offering a clue as to the intensity of her battle, she propped herself up onto one knee.

"Haaahh...haaah...!"

Everyone looked toward the wall she had come through and saw the unmistakable blond girl with golden eyes—Aiz.

The girl's armor and exposed skin were also covered in cuts, and her shoulders rose and fell with each breath.

"Levis!"

"Miss Aiz!"

Olivas and Lefiya yelled at the same time.

Aiz lifted her silver saber into a defensive position as she took her first step into the cavern. Cautiously scanning, her eyes popped open in surprise to see Lefiya before nodding to her right away to indicate she was okay.

It had been over half the day since they last saw each other. The sight of Aiz alive and well made Lefiya's eyes water with joy. Asfi, Lulune, and all of *Hermes Familia* couldn't help but smile as they fended off the latest round of attacks. Even Bete flashed a grin.

Lefiya quickly wiped her tears with her sleeve and refocused her attention on the new arrivals.

There was no doubt in her mind that this red-haired woman called Levis was the one who'd led the attack on Rivira. Judging by her sudden appearance in the cavern, Aiz had managed to deliver a direct hit at full strength during a fierce battle. Unable to withstand the blow, Levis had been launched through the wall and into this chamber.

Both combatants were covered in cuts and bruises, their armor and combat gear heavily damaged, and they were sweating up a storm.

Neither was anywhere close to peak condition, but Aiz held the advantage because of her weapon's special characteristic.

Aiz didn't let her guard down, keeping her focus squarely locked on to the now weaponless Levis kneeling on the floor.

"...All talk, Levis? Disgraceful."

Olivas observed the new arrivals just like Lefiya. The red-haired woman was supposedly his ally, but he only jeered at her.

Levis's green eyes flicked toward him.

Aiz followed suit as Olivas's sneer deepened the wrinkles on his brow.

"This child, 'Aria'?...Hardly, but it matters not. If that is Her will."

There was an air of hostility in the man's voice, almost as if he were jealous of Aiz.

Face contorting even further, he lifted his right hand high above his head.

"Viskum!"

He looked over his shoulder at the quartz pillar behind him and roared at the top of his lungs.

One of the monsters still leeching liquid from the quartz pillar started to move, detaching its body from the towering structure until it fell from it like a collapsing building. It hit the floor with a deafening crash, pieces of the broken surface scattering in all directions as it arched its lumbering body forward.

The last remaining viskum watched from above as its companion leveled the petals of its blooming head toward Aiz.

"Miss Aiz!"

Lefiya screamed as the second monster was summoned into battle.

The elf started to rush to her aid, but the first creature on the floor unleashed a wall of ivy whips, most likely at the behest of Olivas, to bar her path.

Reaching Aiz was now impossible.

"Corpse or not, I will bring the girl to Her."

With the monsters keeping the adventurers at bay, Olivas decided to approach Aiz himself.

The girl had sustained considerable injuries just as Levis had. A conniving grin grew across his lips as he thought about how easy it would be to kill her in this state.

"Hey, back off!"

"Do not attempt to get in my way, Levis. I will take care of the enemy you could not handle."

Levis shouted at him with one knee still firmly planted on the floor, but Olivas wouldn't listen. Subdued white hair swished back and forth with each step, his eyes unblinking and focused on the blond girl.

The man watched as Aiz quietly leveled her saber at the gigantic dark-green body slowly slithering toward her.

The difference in scale was so dramatic that it looked as though she were holding a toothpick toward the massive beast. The absurdity of it all made the man chuckle.

"Die, Sword Princess!"

Olivas roared as he thrust his arm in her direction.

The monster under his command picked up speed, carving up the floor as it closed in on its target.

"—Fool."

Levis snapped from her vantage point.

"—Here we go."

Aiz whispered to her weapon of choice, Desperate.

Then she *cast* her spell.

"*Awaken, Tempest.*"

Immediately, swirling winds burst through the chamber at her call.

Maintaining eye contact with the monster in front of her, Aiz bestowed Desperate with the strongest winds her magic could muster.

Slash!

The viskum's head was severed with one arcing slice.

"———"

Olivas, the adventurers in the cavern, and Levis all fell silent.

The power of the sword enhanced with magic. The flash of silver light. The howling wind.

The viskum's head fluttered through the air, riding the air currents created by the sword's single slash.

Time slowed to a crawl as the soaring mass of flesh was reflected in Lefiya's dark-blue eyes.

Blood splattered in all directions. The moment between the

beheading and the dull thud of the projectile hitting the floor felt like an eternity.

"_____—Aaa!!"

The feminine fetus at the base of the quartz pillar released an earsplitting scream.

The quartz itself seemed to writhe in pain in response to the magic wind howling through the cavern.

As soon as time returned to normal for the adventurers, Lefiya and everyone else focused on Aiz with shock. The girl was standing still, Desperate still extended after her follow-through.

One blow.

She'd ended the fight with one blow.

Although not as strong as a floor boss or either of the female-figured monsters they had faced before, she had just taken down a monster of that scale with one blade.

Unlike Aiz's Status or swordsmanship, there was no way to measure Airiel's true power.

The red-haired woman watched the events unfold with a cold stare. Bete's eyes were wide open while Asfi and Lulune stood transfixed, muscles in their faces twitching. Filvis stayed completely still, a speechless Lefiya at her side. No one moved. The only sound was the cry of the feminine fetus.

Its head gone, the gigantic flower monster was nothing more than a motionless mountain of green flesh.

Aiz slashed her saber down toward the creatures's limp body. Howling winds once again tore through the area.

Her beautiful, long blond hair swirled in the currents.

"Wha...what...?!"

One step, two steps. Olivas shrank away from the battlefield, his sickly white skin losing even more color.

His assured victory gone, the unyielding confidence he'd carried was a thing of the past. Losing the viskum in the blink of an eye shook him to his very core.

The residual magic wind whispered through his white hair.

"!"

Redirecting her first Level Six Airiel wind around her body like armor, Aiz shifted her attention to the man in white.

Olivas immediately thrust a shaking hand into the air and desperately called out.

"V-violas—!"

Following his command, the remaining flowers disengaged the other adventurers and swarmed toward Aiz.

Aiz looked around at her new opponents. With the wind as her ally, the swordsman charged into battle.

And so began a one-sided massacre.

She hit the line of approaching monsters with the speed and ferocity of a hurricane. Slashes similar to the one that slew the viskum cleaved several violas at once, pieces of their bodies soaring through the air. Instant death. The whirlwind surrounding Aiz deflected oncoming whips into other monsters. Victims of friendly fire, they were either blown backward or cut into pieces by the appendages of their allies.

"......!!"

Lefiya shuddered, struggling to comprehend the overwhelming force that was the magic wind whirling around Aiz.

—It was *not normal.*

Simultaneous offense and defense; power that granted her the ability to face the floor boss on her own; a strength that went far beyond any enchantment. No enchantment could produce an effect of this magnitude.

How was she, a human without the inborn magical talents of the elves, capable of producing that much power?

Miss Aiz as she is now is...!

The reason that Aiz had been considered to be among the upper echelons of adventurers while still at Level Five was due to her command of this magic, plain and simple.

This "wind" placed her on the same stage as Orario's elite, Level Six adventurers.

In terms of pure swordsmanship in a one-on-one duel, Lefiya was certain Aiz had surpassed Finn and the other leaders.

No one here could stop her.

"...Damn, she's leavin' me in the dust."

The Level Five werewolf watched Aiz fight, and a fire lit in his heart. He clicked his tongue. "Ahh, shit."

He turned his head back to his allies.

"Oi, we still got shit to do!"

The adventurers called out to one another, regrouping to face the gigantic flower monster in their way.

Seeing Aiz literally tear the monsters apart had done wonders for their morale. Bete led an invigorated counterattack as *Hermes Familia*'s superior teamwork began to come together.

The adventurers took the fight to their enemy.

"Everyone, I found it! The magic stone is in the head! Aim for its flower!"

Lulune had used the lull in the action to investigate the severed head of the first monster Aiz took down. She swiftly passed on the information.

When the thief's yell reached their ears, everyone quickly descended on the location of the surviving beast's magic stone.

"That's all well and good...but we are still unable to use magic as it is. We lack sufficient firepower."

Asfi muttered to herself as she watched the magic users prioritize the ivy raining down from above.

The slithering viskum wasn't about to allow them the time to cast a powerful spell, but without magic strong enough to pierce its thick skin, there was no hope of destroying its core.

Watching the casters be interrupted over and over and catching a glimpse of the desperation on Lefiya's face—determination appeared in Filvis's eyes.

"I shall go myself!"

"Miss Filvis!"

She left Lefiya behind her and raced forward.

Tightly gripping her wand in her left hand, she weaved in and out of the tendrils and into point-blank range of the enormous creature.

"Werewolf, open a hole!"

"…Tsk, don't go telling me what to do!"

The elf and the werewolf made eye contact before putting on a burst of speed.

The friction between them was still there, but they had a common goal, and the situation called for teamwork. Bete took the lead, slicing the vines out of their way. Filvis was close behind, following the path he cleared for her.

The two of them reached the top of the beast's body in no time flat and advanced toward the looming petals that formed the viskum's head.

Lulune's information led them directly to the vivid blossom, and Bete launched himself into the air.

"Eat this!"

Flipping, he brought the heel of his metal boot down directly into the beast's skin, tearing open a long slit in its head.

Filvis had her target. She jumped forward the moment Bete was clear of the gash.

"*Purge, cleansing lightning!*"

She was on top of the open wound just as she finished her trigger spell—and thrust her wand into the hole in the monster's flesh.

"*Dio Thyrsos!!*"

The lightning from the tip of the wand ripped through the gigantic monster's innards.

The creature flinched unnaturally several times as the skin on its belly flashed randomly from the inside. Electrical current found its way to the other gashes inflicted by the adventurers and escaped as streaks of golden plasma. Powered by an enormous amount of Mind, the spell continued to work its way through the monster's body, searching for the core.

After no more than a heartbeat, it went still.

The electrical current had pierced the magic stone. Unable to let out a dying cry, the viskum turned to ash.

Cheers erupted from the ranks of *Hermes Familia* as the monster became nothing but a pile of black soot in their wake.

Just before Bete and Filvis slew the gigantic flower monster...

Aiz cut down the last remaining viola.

Releasing herself from a self-imposed restriction on her own magic, she used Airiel to its fullest extent. Now, only mountains of ash remained on the battlefield.

"This...this isn't possible...!"

With Aiz's full power on display, Olivas couldn't stop his extremities from trembling.

A beautiful yet aloof knight stood before him. The sight of her slaying monsters with wind and overwhelming strength was worthy of the heroes who had become immortalized in legendary tales.

The strength the man possessed would not be enough.

Greenish eyes shaking uncontrollably, he heard an explosion from a different direction. The second viskum had been eliminated.

Two of his best cards gone, Olivas began to lose his composure.

"I refuse! Losing...I will not allow it!"

He kicked off the ground, charging directly at Aiz.

Since her back was to him, he had the element of surprise. The magic stone in his chest provided him with strength that surpassed the realm of human comprehension. Focusing all of it into his hands, he reached up with the intention of snapping her neck.

However, the fight against Bete and Asfi had taken its toll. His hampered movements were far too slow to contend with the new Aiz Wallenstein.

"—"

A golden eye caught a glimpse of Olivas's diving approach.

A flash of silver light, her saber a high-speed blur…

"~~~~~~!"

Cuts and gashes covered Olivas again.

It seemed unnatural that a body with that many wounds spewing blood could still be in one piece.

The yellowish green flesh of his lower body and his human torso shredded beyond recognition, Olivas fell onto his back. His eyes stared blankly toward the ceiling.

"Inconceivable…I, who have ascended beyond man and beast, who was chosen by Her…?!"

Olivas howled into the air as the agony of defeat started to set in.

Terrified, he looked up at the War Princess standing over him. He was so scared that his vision blurred.

"—Ridiculous."

"!"

It happened just as Aiz approached the now helpless man on the floor.

Levis burst onto the scene like a gust of wind to come to his aid.

Aiz jumped back out of reflex and watched the red-haired woman grab what was left of the man's clothes and carry him away. Levis came to a stop at the base of the quartz pillar and tossed Olivas's body unceremoniously to the floor.

Monsters had all but disappeared from the cavern, meaning there was nothing to distract Aiz, Lefiya, Bete, or the remaining adventurers who were starting to gather around them. Now the center of attention, they were the last two left alive.

"Th-thank you, Levis…"

"……"

Olivas pulled his body up to his knees even as he gasped for breath.

Caring little for the blood still leaking out of his body, he desperately focused on breathing. Levis didn't respond to the words he managed to squeeze out.

The adventurers spread out into a half circle, cornering the two.

The woman, illuminated by the ominous red light of the quartz, looked at each of the adventurers in turn with eyes hidden by dark shadows. Her green irises quickly returned to the kneeling man.

She reached out to him, her face blank.

She grabbed ahold of his collar and lifted him with one hand as if to make him stand.

Then—

She drove her knifelike hand directly into his chest.

"!"

"Wha—?"

Aiz and the adventurers forgot to breathe.

Her hand plunged into his broken rib cage. Bones and muscles cracked as she forced her hand deep.

Olivas himself was the most surprised by this turn of events, gaping at his "ally" in shock.

"L-Levis, what is the meaning of this...?!"

"Use your eyes, look around."

Aiz, Lefiya, Bete, Filvis, Asfi, Lulune.

The woman flipped her blood-colored hair out of her eyes as the line of upper-class adventurers watched.

"I need more strength. That's all."

Her voice was passionate, then cold.

"No matter how many I consume, no amount could ever *satisfy* me."

He must have realized what she intended to do with those words alone.

Olivas was petrified.

"You cannot be serious! I am the same as you, one chosen by Her...!"

"Chosen...? Do you think *that* is a goddess or something?"

"......!"

"There's no reason to put it on a pedestal."

Levis scoffed through her nose.

"You and I, we're nothing but pawns."

Levis's assertion made Olivas's eyes go wide, perfect circles of despair beneath his white bangs.

Desperation taking over, he used both hands to grab the woman's thin arm sticking out of his chest.

"D-do you mean to kill your only associate?!"

Levis flexed her fingers deep inside his chest, completely ignoring his words.

All the strength of the man's body instantaneously disappeared, like a puppet that suddenly lost its strings. Even the hands that gripped her arm fell to his sides.

It was as if every muscle, every tendon's strength had been rooted in his chest.

"With me gone, who will be able to protect Her—?"

Levis violently ripped her hand out of him, effectively silencing him mid-scream.

A brilliant magic stone drenched in blood was clasped tightly between her fingers.

Without his core, Olivas disintegrated into a pile of ash, just like any other monster that met the same fate.

"Don't get the wrong idea."

Practically spitting the words at the pile of ash by her feet, Levis looked away.

Aiz stood completely still with her gaze straightforward, unable to speak after witnessing the gruesome turn of events.

"I protected it all along. That's not about to change."

Levis brought the magic stone up to her mouth and crunched it between her teeth.

Slurp. She ran her tongue over her lips, cleaning the last fragments off her mouth.

Filvis stared, speechless, at this unimaginable betrayal. *Crick!* Lefiya squeezed her right hand into a fist, keeping her composure out of sheer will. The woman's red hair stood on end, fluttering in a nonexistent breeze.

One heartbeat later—the floor exploded at her feet as Levis charged directly for Aiz.

"!"

She left the other adventurers in her dust, her powerful fists aimed directly at the girl.

Aiz lifted the magically enhanced Desperate into the path of her oncoming opponent for defense. Even so, she was knocked off her feet and thrown backward a moment later.

Bete and the other adventurers only now noticed what had happened and turned toward the sound of impact, but Levis was already in pursuit of the blond swordswoman.

"You're...?"

"You can still talk? Let's fix that."

The woman's bloodred hair reflected in Aiz's trembling golden irises.

A richly colored magic stone. A man who'd turned to ash. An absorbed crystal. A monster.

Aiz had no knowledge of Olivas's or Levis's true identities, but the information that was in her head began swirling, connecting the dots in her mind. It led her to one conclusion.

A powerful kick came down from above—a kick strong enough to contend with a leveled-up Airiel. Levis's heel tore through the air, launching a blade of wind down at her. Spinning out of the way with ease, Aiz moved to counterattack. It was all the woman could do to defend before, but now she was going on the offensive.

—Enhanced species!!

Aiz had no choice but to accept that explanation for her opponent's sudden boost in strength and speed.

It was the natural order for monsters that consumed magic stones, a dog-eat-dog world diametrically opposed to that of humans with a Status. The being in front of her now was a monster in the shape of a human.

What was truly frightening was that Levis had become physically stronger and faster than Aiz at Level Six by devouring Olivas's magic stone. Only with the addition of Airiel's power had Aiz managed to keep the onslaught at bay.

A flash of silver. A gash appeared in Levis's shoulder.

Ignoring the blood spewing from the wound, Levis lifted her fist high into the air and used every muscle in her body to bring it down over Aiz's head. The girl dodged at the last possible second, but the fist kept going. It crashed into the floor and a small crater appeared where the blond girl had stood. Levis's fist stayed in the fleshy green depression for a moment before...*crick crick CRICK!* She pulled it free with all her might.

A crimson greatsword emerged from the ground, a nature weapon from the floor.

Holding the weapon with both hands, Levis charged once again. Aiz responded with a thrust of her saber.

"‼"

The wind-coated silver blade and the massive crimson greatsword collided in a thunderous impact.

"Just what is she...?...'Cause...holy shit!" said Lulune between gulps, transfixed by the battle between Aiz and Levis.

Just like the monsters that had acquired a taste for magic stones, the woman was matching Aiz blow for blow, on equal footing with the blond swordswoman who'd slain a viskum with one slash.

The battle was so fierce that it looked impossible for anyone else to join the fray. Bete was the first to make an attempt, dashing toward the battle with Lefiya and Filvis close behind.

"The situation may be dire, but...!"

As Bete led reinforcements toward Aiz, Asfi took off in the other direction by herself.

She made a beeline for the base of the quartz pillar in the deepest part of the pantry, where the orb containing the feminine fetus sat unprotected.

That orb was at the center of everything—this incident, the

attack on Rivira, and possibly many more events to come. Whether or not it was related to the "Her" Olivas kept going on about, there was no doubt in her mind that the fetus was the key to it all.

She was determined to acquire it no matter the cost, when— *WHAM!*

A sudden impact from out of nowhere.

"!"

"Wha—?!"

A hooded purple robe, a bizarre mask.

Asfi had no idea where this mysterious newcomer had been hiding, but his sneak attack knocked her off course.

Mind-blowing strength and a pair of metal gloves delivered a blow powerful enough to penetrate Perseus's custom white cloak.

"Asfi!"

"There was another one?!"

Lulune and the rest of *Hermes Familia* rushed toward their leader even before she hit the ground.

Even Lefiya's group came to a stop, looking back at what had just transpired. All three of them stared at the masked attacker.

"While not complete, it's grown enough! Take it to Enyo!"

Levis shouted to the newcomer between strikes as she continued to fight against Aiz.

The attacker wrapped his hands around the orb in its root cage while it shrieked in the presence of Aiz's magical energy. It fell silent in his grasp. From there, he ripped the entire thing off the pillar with one swift jerk.

"I understand."

The masked attacker spoke with a voice so deep and layered it sounded like several people speaking at once. With that, he made a quick exit.

The orb safely tucked into his arms, the man in the purple robe was well on his way to vanishing into one of the many exits in the cavern walls.

"Lulune, stop him!"

Asfi shouted at the top of her lungs in a desperate attempt to prevent his escape.

Lulune gritted her teeth and groaned as she took off in full-speed pursuit.

"Viskum!"

However, Levis's voice rang out.

Forcing Aiz away with a powerful swing of her blade, she issued an order to the last gigantic flower monster still attached to the quartz pillar.

"Keep bearing monsters!! Don't stop until your strength is spent!"

A howl echoed through the cavern a second later.

"…!"

Aiz paused mid-charge to look up at the ceiling.

The group around Bete and the group around Asfi and Lulune felt a tremor pass beneath their feet and came to a stop.

They all turned their attention toward the source of the howl, only to see the remaining viskum shifting from side to side. Only then did they hear the sucking sounds coming from beneath it, as though it was drinking every last drop of the liquid from the glowing red quartz all at once.

Crack! A series of fissures ran up and down the pillar of crystals.

At the same time, burgeoning lumps popped up all over the thick roots that worked their way around the cavern. The viskum convulsed as the lumps began to pulsate at an alarming rate.

Moments later…

All the flower buds located on the ceiling and walls of the cavern *bloomed* in unison.

"_____"

Every single one of the richly colored buds—every single one of the violas—came alive.

Each was in a different state of maturation, some buds larger or more colorful than others. The plant that had absorbed an immeasurable amount of nutrients from the Dungeon itself was now attempting to birth all the monsters it had created in one go.

The viskum withered at an alarming rate, turning a dull brown before its large body became weak and went limp. The monster's flower head folded in on itself.

The apocalypse had arrived in the form of an off-green tidal wave. The newborn monsters' broken-bell cries swelled within the dying pantry, echoes coming from everywhere. All color drained from Lefiya's face as she watched the approaching wall of green, her eardrums throbbing.

All the adventurers had the same thought, as much as they didn't want to believe it.

Aiz and her comrades watched in horror as the terrifying violas bared their fangs and fell from the ceiling and walls.

—Monster party!

Next came a series of tremors beneath their feet as the monsters touched down. Their heads rose high into the air, ready to attack moments later.

The adventurers watched in shock as monsters descended upon them from all directions in one furious wave.

"OOOOOOOOOOOOOOOOOOOOOOOOOOOOOOOOOOO OOOOOOOOOO!!"

"!"

Many of the adventurers couldn't get the screams out of their throats in the face of such overwhelming numbers.

They could see only flowers, flowers, flowers no matter where they looked—forward, left and right, backward. Even the space overhead was blocked out by yellowish green bodies. Cacophonous howls bearing down on them, the adventurers took off at full speed to avoid getting swallowed up by the wave. The viskum had sacrificed itself to completely inundate the cavern with monsters.

The swarm was so intimidating that even the strongest second-tier adventurers were on the brink of losing their will to fight.

There were hundreds, possibly thousands of them. Normal monster parties paled in comparison.

This was much, much worse.

"Keh…!"

The masked man made it into one of the cave entrances and left the hellscape behind.

Asfi saw him easily escape with her own eyes.

"No, no, no! This is frickin' impossible!"

"Stay close or you'll get crushed!"

Lulune wailed as she ran around in a panic, trying desperately to evade the massive walls of green bodies and seemingly infinite whips. The war tiger Falgar forced words out of his mouth in an attempt to reach her, but the monster howls swallowed his shout.

The violas attacked everything in their path. Upon seeing an adventurer, they either attempted a slithering body slam or unleashed a rain of whips. However, the monsters were also attacking one another. Amid the chaos, the last living members of the robed faction were devoured on the spot. "GAHHHHHHHHH-HHH!!" came one dying scream through the carnage as the remaining Evils' Remnants vanished from the cavern. Even the remains of the man in the off-color robe disappeared down a monster's throat.

Violas followed their scattering prey. Several isolated battles commenced. Bete spun through the air, slaying monster after monster with powerful kicks. Other frontline fighters wielded large weapons, slicing monsters in half with each swing. No matter how many of the monsters died to their blades, more kept coming. The adventurers could not make a dent in their numbers.

The battle became an all-out brawl.

"Violas!"

"!"

Meanwhile, Aiz was trapped in Levis's monster-pincer attack.

No sooner had she blocked her opponent's crimson sword than the violas at her command thrust their vine-whips at her like spears. Surrounded by a ring of endless enemies, she had nowhere to escape to. Levis used her limitless supply of disposable pawns as distractions to launch her own hit-and-run attacks. Even with the added strength of Airiel, Aiz was losing ground.

Neither Aiz's nor Lefiya's group of adventurers could come to each other's aid. They had their hands full just staying alive.

"—!!"

"Wha—?!"

Levis made her move after Aiz's wind had felled twenty, thirty, forty or more of the violas and blown them into the air.

She positioned herself behind one of their massive frames before cutting it out of her way. Caught off guard, Aiz wasn't able to react to the ambush in time as Levis appeared from among the pieces of the monster's body. She lost her grip on Desperate on impact, and it was knocked from her grasp.

—*Oh no!*

Aiz's weapon spun through the air in diminishing flashes of silver. Intense heat ran through her veins.

The knight was disarmed, a swordswoman without a sword. Aiz's capability in battle decreased dramatically without Desperate in her grasp.

Levis wasn't going to let this opportunity go to waste and charged in.

"You won't escape!"

"~~~~~~~~~~!"

Aiz did everything in her power to knock Levis away, but the monsters barred her path to Desperate.

That one-step delay was enough for the red-haired woman to close the distance and put Aiz on the defensive once again.

Forced into hand-to-hand combat, not her strong suit, the blond girl was in dire straits.

Just like the adventurers around her screaming at the top of their lungs, Aiz had her back against the ropes.

The monsters were becoming more aggressive.

Lefiya and the other adventurers managed to regroup in the cavern's center and desperately held the violas at bay.

Their only saving grace was that these monsters had been born prematurely, making them physically weaker than normal.

Even so, that didn't change the fact they were fighting for their lives. They were trapped in a nightmare, surrounded by fanged, vibrant blossoms. There were so many of the beasts that all exits were hidden from view.

It seemed like after every monster shriek, one of the adventurers fell to the ground.

"Ahh! Oh no…!"

Lefiya and the other magic users were trapped in the middle of the chaos, unable to harness any of their power.

Trying to cast magic in the middle of the swarm was the same as suicide. None of their allies was willing to form a protective Wall. They all had their hands full as it was, leaving Lefiya powerless to assist and cursing her uselessness.

The war tiger Falgar, caked in his own blood, howled. Elf fighters blocked oncoming attacks with their swords, barely able to repel them. A dwarf had lost his weapons in combat and instead slammed his broken fists into one monster after another. Asfi and Lulune engaged the violas with a flurry of slashes as Bete kept his feet moving, piles of monster corpses around him. Hearing their yells—no, screams tormented Lefiya as she watched their battles from a distance.

—Why can't I…

Why can't I fight side by side with these brave people?

Why can't I pick up a sword and slay monsters, pick up a shield and protect my allies?

I just run away, get saved, watch helplessly.

My chants only hold them back.

I'm useless.

The magic staff she clutched to her chest had never felt so heavy.

If only I could be like Lady Riveria or more like Miss Filvis...!

Visions of the overwhelmingly powerful high elf came to the forefront of her mind as she caught sight of the elegant young elf woman fighting valiantly.

Just like the blond swordswoman she idolized, the master elf was still far beyond her, and the beautiful magic swordswoman was still out of reach.

If only she were capable of fighting like the elf Filvis.

If only she were armed with sword and song, she could be slaying monsters that very moment.

Lefiya glimpsed Filvis taking down yet another beast. In that moment, Bete's words flared up in her mind.

—*"You'll never be anything more than baggage."*

She no longer felt any pain from those words, just a deep-seated sense of powerlessness.

"Aiz...!"

While Lefiya wallowed in despair, Bete caught a glimpse of the other battle.

He snarled at the sight of the blond swordswoman with golden irises fighting alone against Levis and a swarm of monsters.

Bete had lost track of how many of the premature, weaker monsters he had slain and quickly scanned the battlefield—and spied the young elf.

"Oi!"

"Eh...?"

He didn't bother announcing himself until he was right next to Lefiya.

"I'm going to help Aiz. You figure out a way to take care of this!"

Lefiya's shoulders jumped as the werewolf grabbed her collar.

"B-b-but I am just—"

"A bottom-feeder, I know! But I also know how ridiculously powerful your magic is!"

Bete interrupted her with a rage-filled lecture.

"All bottom-feeders say they want to be strong but run away

from it! Is that all you're ever gonna do? Prove me wrong! Make all of us regret doubting you!"

Bete's amber eyes glared deep into Lefiya's dark-blue irises.

"Don't admire the old hag, surpass her!"

—*Surpass Riveria Ljos Alf.*

Bete said it, loud and clear.

That absurd goal that no one else ever said. Even Aiz, Tiona, and Tione had never uttered those words.

They weren't the words of the abrasive, never-satisfied-with-his-current-strength werewolf, but they were Bete's true thoughts.

—*Are you satisfied with how you are?*

The question came right from his heart.

Bete, always irritated by the mere sight of weak adventurers, gazed at her with passion and roared with the power that lit a spark within Lefiya. That spark grew into flames that spread throughout her body.

Burning emotion filled her heart. It was a new pain, the pain of wanting to do exactly what the man in front of her was asking but not knowing if she could. It made her very soul shake.

As Lefiya unknowingly clenched her fists, the werewolf leaped into the fray.

He said nothing, provided no encouragement or smile as he turned and dashed away.

Lefiya watched his retreating form for a moment—the powerful back of a man worthy of fighting at her idol's side.

That image of his back burned into her memory. She frowned a moment later, her shapely eyebrows bristling.

The young elf came to a decision amid the howls and screams of man and beast.

"—Please protect me!!"

Lefiya's voice was powerful enough to cut through the chaos.

She held the one weapon allotted to her high above her head, signaling to her allies that she was preparing to cast magic.

The other adventurers' eyes went wide upon seeing her take that stance.

"P-protect you? And do what? A half-assed spell isn't going to do jack shit...!"

"Believe in me!!"

Visibly shaken by Lefiya's request, Lulune squealed between slashes.

Lefiya knew that she had to dispel thoughts of herself as a weak, cowardly magic user right here and now.

"I am a magic user! Protect me and I'll save us all!!"

She put the raw energy she had received from Bete, the flames burning in her chest, and the desire to reach a higher level into her voice. It was all an attempt to take a step closer to Riveria, a strong magic user anyone would want to have behind them.

That majestic tone and strong stance were enough to sway both Asfi and Filvis.

"All units, gather around Thousand Elf! I trust her!"

"......!"

Filvis led the group of adventurers entrusting their fate to the young elf into a group in front of her, to hold back the swarming monsters.

Lefiya began to gather Mind energy and issued one more plea.

"Surround me! Please hold for five—no, three minutes!"

She did her best impression of Riveria. The adventurers followed her command.

The violas' infighting came to an abrupt end as all of them zeroed in on the elf in the middle of the ring of adventurers. Lefiya lifted her gaze and started to cast.

A three-minute countdown that would determine their fate had begun.

"I beseech the name of Wishe!"

A golden circle grew under her feet, illuminating all the adventurers in magic light.

Blocking out the violas drawn to her like moths to a flame, Lefiya focused solely on her spell.

"*Ancestors of the forest, proud brethren. Answer my call and descend upon the plains.*"

Sing. Sing. Sing.

No unnecessary breaths, every syllable loud and clear, there was no doubt in her mind that Riveria could do this in less than a minute.

That wasn't something she could do as she was now—only sing.

A song of hope to save her friends—a song of victory.

"*Connecting bonds, the pledge of paradise. Turn the wheel and dance.*"

She selected her Summon Burst.

The magic she was calling forth would duplicate Riveria Ljos Alf's in a spell capable of destroying everything in sight.

Using the power of this incredible magic, she could wipe out every single monster at once.

"*Come, ring of fairies.*"

The adventurers in formation around her blocked one attack after another as the monsters broke into a frenzy.

The shield-wielding war tiger and dwarves refused to back down despite their injuries, ignoring the searing pain of their bleeding shoulders.

Elves equipped with twin blades and animal people sacrificed their bodies to hold back the surge of monsters. Lulune and Asfi were a blur behind them, knocking away the countless whips that came in over the heads of everyone manning the Wall.

Filvis and *Hermes Familia* faced the omnidirectional assault head-on.

"*Please—give me strength.*"

Lefiya's eyes shone with faith in her allies, allowing her to eliminate all distractions from her mind. She increased the tempo of her song—and triggered the spell by calling its name.

"*Elf Ring.*"

Her golden magic circle suddenly turned emerald green.

Lefiya then began to cast the summoned magic. New hope surged through Asfi and her allies, more determined than ever to buy Lefiya enough time. That is, until they saw something that made their faces go pale.

"Big ones! And a shit-ton of them!"

The newcomers must have been wandering about the green hallways of the transformed labyrinth. This new flood of enemies surged in from the many cavern entrances.

Lulune's scream sounded above the battle as more of the massive creatures encroached every time they slew their immature counterparts.

"Viridis—!"

Lefiya's spell was far from complete. Filvis peered over her shoulder at her kin and saw the young elf continuing to chant—determination once again burned in her eyes.

"Out of my way!"

"S-sure!"

Pushing her way past, Filvis charged directly into the path of the oncoming monsters.

Lefiya's gorgeous refrain sounded behind her as she opened her lips.

"*Shield me, cleansing chalice!*"

A short-trigger spell.

Asfi and Lulune watched in amazement as a second spell manifested.

Filvis thrust her left hand straight forward at the incoming tidal wave of violas.

"*Dio Grail!!*"

A pulsing white sphere appeared.

The first wave of monsters slammed into it. The field held against their whips and body slams.

Each impact sent sparks of magical energy flying into the air. Asfi's and the other adventurers' shadows danced, Filvis in the center of it all.

As the sphere of white light illuminated one part of the cavern, Aiz's wind was being overwhelmed.

Violas hindered the girl's path forward, and Levis relentlessly slashed with her crimson greatsword.

Dodging it by a hair, Aiz used her momentum to spin and land a devastating kick.

"That's nothing compared to that sword of yours."

"!"

Every ounce of wind Aiz could muster went into that kick, but the impact landed on the hilt of the crimson greatsword. Completely unscathed, the red-haired woman regarded her with cold confidence as she launched a counterattack of her own.

All the unarmed knight could do was evade. Airiel alone was not enough to contend with an opponent like Levis, especially when the heavy greatsword was fast enough to leave crimson afterimages.

If only I had a sword…!

Desperate had landed in a corner of the chamber not too far away, piercing the soft floor. Every time she caught a glimpse of the silver blade, Levis moved in to block her path. Aiz frowned in the face of this enemy who would not let her retrieve her weapon.

The two had been engaged in combat for quite a while at this point. Aiz's physical strength was waning, and the constant use of magic ate away at her mind and body. On the other hand, her opponent possessed seemingly limitless endurance, worthy of the title "monster."

"Let's finish this already!"

A bead of cold sweat rolled down Aiz's neck as Levis rode the front of a charging viola with the crimson greatsword held high.

A searing-hot pain shot through her chest as the blow connected. At that moment…

"—*A blaze shall soon descend.*"

The elf girl's song reached Aiz's ears through the monsters' howls.
"!"
—*Lefiya!*
The spell powerfully resonated as if Riveria herself were casting it in her beautiful voice. Aiz momentarily gawked at the elf's song.

At the same time—a flash of gray fur entered the fray.

"Get lost!"

Bete had arrived.

Forcing his way through the walls of monsters, he finally caught up to the furious battle with a series of vicious attacks. Aiz and Levis watched in surprise as the werewolf made a beeline to the girl's side.

"Hand it over, Aiz!"
"!"
That was all Aiz needed to hear to understand.

"Wind!"

A wind current glided from her outstretched hand and into Bete's metal boots as he passed by.

The yellow jewels built into the metallic greaves flashed as powerful vortices enveloped both his feet.

"*Approaching flames of war from which there is no escape. Battle horns blaring on high, all atrocities and strife shall be engulfed.*"

Aiz immediately made her escape from the battle after giving Bete the power of wind. Lefiya's song in her ears, she made a break for the silver saber protruding from the floor in a corner of the cavern.

Bete took her place in battle, blocking the red-haired woman's path.

"You!"

"Damn it, woman, stay down!"

Levis saw what Aiz was trying to do and gave chase. However, Bete wouldn't let her.

The clash of the woman's greatsword against Airiel-empowered boots reverberated through the open arena.

"*Come crimson pyre, merciless inferno. Become hellfire.*"

Bete rode the air currents to deliver a meteor shower of powerful kicks.

The werewolf devoted everything he had to allowing Aiz time to retrieve her sword. He had to keep their opponent in place for as long as possible.

Levis snarled in frustration. Sending the violas in the area to bar Aiz's path, she confronted him with every intention of killing the man in her way.

"Move!"

"…!"

The crimson slashes descending on Bete dyed his vision red. The wind allowed him to evade, kicking each strike out of the way at the last possible moment with the knowledge that he wouldn't survive if that blade hit home.

Even with the assistance of Aiz's Airiel, Bete was no match for Levis's enhanced physical strength. All his skills and techniques combined weren't enough to overcome her power. Ax kicks, sweeping kicks, reverse cyclone kicks—it didn't matter. The red-haired woman simply dodged and blocked his wind-infused feet, spinning like a top.

The werewolf's onslaught tore her combat gear to shreds. One of her gauntlets went flying as the wound in her shoulder reopened, spraying blood as she spun.

"I said move, werewolf!"

Voice shaking with fury, she swung her sword even faster.

Bete jerked his body into a defensive position. Attacking was no longer an option.

"*Purge the battlefield, end the war.*"

A girl's song reached Bete even as he lost ground.

Out of the corner of his eye, he caught sight of the group of adventurers surrounded by a white light. The men were covered in blood, and the women fended off monster attacks with magic staffs. Their screams and the monsters' howls sounded over the field of death.

An elf magic user stood in the middle of it all, shining like a beacon.

Bete gritted his teeth and sneered as he violently forced his body forward.

"Take this!!"

He knocked the blade back.

Bete knew he didn't stand a chance but refused to surrender any more ground. If his opponent wouldn't give him time to attack, he would take it.

Bete howled and bared his fangs in a crazed smile.

"The riffraff's standing tall! And they're not gonna see me get my ass whipped by the likes of you!"

It was the pride of the powerful and the iron will of a man.

The sight of the weak putting up a fight lit a fire within Bete, and he pushed his own limits to the point of shattering.

He poured all he had into his kicks as his feet rode torrents of wind. Back on the defensive, Levis widened her eyes before flashing an irritated scowl. Adjusting her grip, she reared back with her crimson greatsword held high.

Bete responded by jumping up with enough force to blast a hole in the floor beneath him as he spun and extended his left leg with incredible speed.

"HAAAAAAAAAAAAAAAAAAAAAAAAAAAAAAAAAAA!!"

Bete's ferocious roar filled the air as he drove his foot straight toward his enemy.

The crimson sword came down toward the wind-infused kick.

Impact.

"—"

The vortex of wind provided little resistance against the crimson blade, instantly giving way.

A web of cracks raced through the metal boot from where the two weapons collided.

The leg inside the boot snapped. Blood spewed into the air as skin and muscle tore asunder and bones splintered.

Intense pain quickly followed the shock of impact. Bete's eyes bulged in their sockets.

"Incinerate, sword of Surtr—My name is Alf!"

—That was the moment Lefiya completed her spell.

A sudden flash of emerald light reached Bete and changed the color of the battlefield.

Magic had been summoned.

"Rea Laevateinn!!"

A towering conflagration erupted from the magic circle.

The pillars of flames started where Lefiya and the adventurers were holding the line. Reaching all the way to the ceiling, the hell-fire narrowly missed the other combatants while consuming all the violas in one giant blaze. The roar of the flames was so loud it drowned out their final howls.

The incredibly destructive magic left no trace of the monsters behind, burning their magic stones and ashes into oblivion. The chamber had been turned into a realm of fire.

"—Heh!"

A grin formed on Bete's lips as red light illuminated his face in the immense heat. The monsters' fiery demise, the girl responsible, and her protectors' cheers—his amber eyes reflected it all. Focusing everything he had into his badly hurt left leg—spewing blood, about to give way to the crimson sword—Bete howled loud enough to rival the weaklings' cheers.

"AWWWOOOOOOOOOOOOOOOOOOOOOOOOOOOOOO!!"

The silver boot pushed back the crimson sword.

"Wha—?!"

An unforeseen reversal.

Although the collision launched Bete into the air, the weapon's momentum knocked back Levis's upper body as well. Her green eyes went wide in the fire-scape.

Bete's sacrificial, all-in attack had been strong enough to knock Levis off balance.

Then.

A swift shadow dashed toward the woman, surrounded by swirling sparks.

Squeezing her way between the towering pillars of flames, a blond, golden-eyed girl returned to battle with a silver saber clutched in her grasp.

The tip of the blade was pointed at Levis.

"Awaken, Tempest!"

The swirling air currents around her body blasted Aiz forward like a cannonball.

Her ally had given her a window and she wasn't about to let that go to waste. Desperate in position, she struck.

"GaHA!"

The blade arced diagonally through the air—

And sliced through the weapon that had been hastily brought up to defend.

"!!"

Her technique was flawless.

Just barely missing the center of Levis's chest and her magic stone, the blade created a new wound that sent droplets of blood into the air as the red-haired woman hurtled backward.

"—AAAHHHHHHHHHHH!!"

One final arcing slash to end the fight.

Both hands firmly grasping the hilt of Desperate, Aiz focused air currents down the blade to create a raging whirlwind as she jumped into the air.

And brought the weapon down—directly onto Levis beneath her.

"‼"

Levis crossed her arms in front of her chest and took the full force of the blow.

The air itself around the weapon screamed with the strike's incredible power as the blade bore down on its target.

A heartbeat later, Levis careened backward, as though trapped in the current of a raging river.

Even slamming her feet into the floor didn't stop her momentum. Two long gashes appeared in the floor as Levis's one-way trip to the back of the chamber continued unabated.

She finally came to a stop with her back against the base of the quartz pillar. Once bright enough to illuminate the cavern, its feeble red light flickered silently overhead.

Victory was in Aiz's grasp.

"Haaahh…haaah…"

She caught her breath, saber clutched in her right hand.

The protective air currents around her body going quiet as she released them, the blond swordswoman walked steadily toward the base of the pillar where Levis was waiting.

The magic Lefiya had summoned to the battlefield had turned the pantry into a charred, burning wasteland filled with sweltering heat. The birthing apparatuses that once dotted the ceiling and walls crackled as they burned away and fell to the floor. The rocky surface of the original Dungeon walls began to reappear. The adventurers, this time certain that the enemy forces had been eliminated, collapsed to the floor well behind Aiz's back.

Levis, propped up on one knee as the blond girl approached, slowly stood up.

A shining vapor drifted from the wounds that covered her blood-speckled body—magic energy residue—as she began to heal. Eyes a bit wider than normal in disbelief, she opened her mouth to speak.

"...Seems I can't beat you right now."

Her green eyes showed no emotion at all while she spoke.

Levis openly admitted that consuming Olivas's magic stone didn't give her enough power to overcome Aiz's wind. She was alone with no allies or monsters left, yet she still spoke with a calm confidence.

Aiz kept her distance, eyeing the red-haired woman with suspicion as her opponent looked up at the quartz pillar behind her.

"This is a weight-bearing pillar. If it collapsed...Well, I'm sure you can figure out what would happen."

"!"

—She wouldn't.

Levis ran her fingers down the surface of the quartz. Aiz rushed forward in an attempt to stop her, but it was too late.

The woman clenched her fist and pivoted at the waist, slamming all her strength directly into the base of the column.

The giant crack raced up the weakly glowing red quartz all the way to the ceiling, like the slash of a dragon's claw. The high-pitched shatter echoed throughout the chamber, and the badly damaged support collapsed a moment later.

The ceiling of the pantry began to crumble almost immediately. Large pieces plummeted to the floor.

"......!"

"You'll be buried alive if you stay here. Especially those friends of yours who can't move."

Levis casually glanced at the badly injured members of *Hermes Familia*; then to an exhausted Lefiya, who had pushed her Mind to the absolute limit; and finally to Bete, whose broken leg was in desperate need of attention.

Aiz bit her lip as the first pieces of the ceiling slammed into the floor behind her. Most likely, Levis had this in mind when she absorbed the final blow and made sure she wound up close to the pillar as a result.

More fragments began to fall.

The adventurers started to retreat in a panic.

"Assist the injured! Leave everything behind, escape takes priority!"

Whipping into action, Asfi called out to her allies and directed the movements of *Hermes Familia*.

"I ain't some pathetic mutt! Like hell I need your help!"

"Damn, you're such a pain! This is exactly why I hate dealing with werewolves!"

The chienthrope begrudgingly lent her shoulder to Bete in spite of his complaints.

Exchanging insults, the two raced for the exit.

"Viridis!"

Meanwhile, Filvis was reaching out to help up Lefiya, who had collapsed due to Mind Down.

However—her outstretched arms had stopped, trembling in place.

It was as though she was hesitant to touch her kin with her soiled arms, and her pride as an elf prevented her from moving forward.

Lefiya reached up and took the outstretched hand herself.

"…!"

"Do not…worry…"

The young elf's gaze was cloudy, a weak smile on her face. Filvis's eyes widened.

The elder elf drew her younger kin into a heartfelt embrace before lifting Lefiya off the floor.

Holding her delicate body tight against her own, Filvis raced toward the exit.

"……!"

Aiz watched the adventurers assist one another as they fell back, and she made up her mind to join them.

Her desire to help her injured allies took priority over the woman in front of her.

ON THE SIDE: SWORD ORATORIA, VOL. 3   **229**

"Aria, go to the fifty-ninth floor."

It was just before she turned her back to leave.

Aiz looked over her shoulder when she heard the red-haired woman's voice.

"Things are getting interesting right now. Should answer a lot of your questions."

"...What do you mean?"

"Surely you have some idea? If the rumors about you are true, the blood in your veins will tell you."

"......"

"It'd be a lot easier if you went there on your own," said Levis, hinting that taking her there by force was more trouble than it was worth.

She fixed Aiz with a narrow gaze.

"There are those on the surface trying to use us...but two can play that game."

Levis muttered as if talking to herself. Falling silent, all she did was stand in place.

"Hey, Sword Princess!"

"Aiz, move it!"

Only when Lulune's and Bete's voices had cut through the din of falling boulders did Aiz break contact with the woman's green eyes.

She then took off at full speed for the only unobstructed exit, where the other adventurers had gathered.

Aiz checked over her shoulder one last time just before leaving the cavern for good.

The red-haired woman hadn't moved from her spot at the other end. She was just staring in her direction, green eyes unblinking until she disappeared behind a pile of falling rocks.

Turning away, Aiz helped the last of the wounded to safety.

The twenty-fourth floor's north pantry collapsed that day.

The party of adventurers managed to escape before it was too late.

After surviving a series of fierce battles that would remain largely unknown, Lefiya and the adventurers made a brief stop in Rivira before returning to the surface later that day.

A worried Loki was quick to punish Aiz in her own way once the members of *Loki Familia* returned home, but they had all made it back in one piece. Bete's badly injured leg made a full recovery thanks to *Dian Cecht Familia*'s healers, and Lefiya recuperated from Mind Down after sleeping for an entire day.

Filvis didn't say much when she headed home to *Dionysus Familia*, sharing only a quick smile with her fellow elf. She did feel that the distance between them had drastically reduced and wanted another opportunity to talk about many things with Lefiya in the near future. According to Loki, her god, Dionysus, had a difficult time dealing with this incident and apparently "spent the day bawlin' his eyes out."

Unfortunately, several members of *Hermes Familia* didn't make it out alive. Lefiya didn't know what to say, but Lulune and Asfi softly smiled and only asked her to please put flowers on their graves. They also reassured the elf by saying that each of them willingly became adventurers and were fully aware of the risks involved. The girls knew their allies were prepared to die. Lulune, the one who had accepted this quest in the first place, was clearly grieved…but Lefiya was not in a position to ask.

This incident had left considerable scars on each familia, but slowly and surely, they all returned to life as usual.

"So much has happened…"
On the second day since their return…
Lefiya, feeling much more like herself, lay on her bed in her room with nothing to do, blankly staring off into space. She shared the

room with several other female members of the familia, but the spacious quarters felt exceptionally empty without their company.

"Aria, huh…?"

The orb with the feminine fetus. The Evils' Remnants. The creatures.

Her head was still spinning from all the shocking discoveries, and so many questions were unanswered. However, that name was at the top of the list.

That was what Olivas had called Aiz in the middle of the cavern.

The same thing had happened during the attack on Rivira. The red-haired woman—Levis—called her Aria as well. It sounded like they were searching for someone by that name.

Not knowing the connection between her idol and these mysterious beings got under her skin, so she went to Aiz to ask for an answer. Unfortunately, it didn't help. Aiz didn't tell her anything about what happened in the cavern, what Levis told her, or who this "Aria" was.

An apologetic "Sorry" was all the blond girl offered. Her voice unsteady, Aiz likely didn't understand the situation herself.

"Uwahh…I know it is wrong to press for answers, but…" She groaned.

Plop. She rolled over in bed.

Her golden hair fanned out beneath her as she stared up at the ceiling.

"Lefiya, you all right in there?"

"…Miss Tiona?"

Hearing a muffled voice on the other side of the door, Lefiya stood up.

She went over and opened it to find not only Tiona but Tione as well.

"Are you really okay? That had to have been rough! Should you even be standing?"

"I-I have recovered, as you can see…"

Tiona bounded through the doorframe, asking one question after another. Lefiya retreated a few steps.

Smack! Tione hit her sister across the back of her head to make her cut it out. The younger Amazon's apologetic smile let Lefiya know the sisters were worried about her and had come to see how she was doing.

The headaches and fatigue from suffering Mind Down had been so horrible the day before that Lefiya had stayed cooped up in her room.

"I only heard bits and pieces from Aiz and Bete, so what really happened is beyond me."

"No, you idiot. You're just too dense to figure it out."

"Ah-ha-ha...I just remembered. The two of you were part of the group that went into the sewer systems, yes? Did you find anything?"

The Amazonian twins had accompanied Finn to investigate the old sewer network beneath the city at the same time Lefiya had been fighting on the twenty-fourth floor.

"Found a few of those flower monsters, but nothing I would call useful. Going back in was a waste of time."

Tione shrugged.

Lefiya paused for a moment, deep in thought...Seeing the cages of monsters ready for transport in the pantry meant the Evils were the ones who had brought them to the surface.

But there was a different question on her mind.

"Um, Miss Tiona, Miss Tione...Does the name 'Aria' mean anything to you?"

Lefiya felt horrible for asking around behind Aiz's back, but the thought of forever remaining in the dark on this matter wouldn't let her remain silent.

Tiona and Tione had known Aiz long before Lefiya met her. Thinking there was a possibility they might know something, she decided to take a chance and ask.

"Aria? Never heard that name before..." said Tione as she tilted her head.

"Aria? Oh! I know!" Tiona jumped in.

"Eh?! Y-you do?!"

"Yep, I dooo."

In truth, Lefiya hadn't had much hope that the twins could provide any information. So the fact that Tiona of all people had the answer caught her off guard. "P-please tell me everything you know!" said Lefiya with a step forward.

"Sure thing!" answered Tiona without a second thought.

Suddenly, the Amazon started walking toward the door.

"M-Miss Tiona? Where are you going?"

"Oh, the archives!"

"What? Why would you want to go there?"

Lefiya and Tione gazed at her with confused suspicion, but Tiona didn't care. "'Cause it's faster than me trying to explain!" she said as she made her way through the narrow hallways with a bit of pep in her step.

The three arrived at the archives, open for familia members to use anytime, a few minutes later.

With the scent of wood hanging in the air, the three girls approached rows of bookshelves in the middle of the room. The shelves were packed with books on the Dungeon, strategies for magic users and other styles of combat, as well as incredibly old books that Loki collected on a whim—all the resources of *Loki Familia*. The three girls found used grimoires stuffed into the shelves every so often.

"I saw that name all the time when I was a kid...Now then..."

Tiona dug through her memories as she weaved her way between shelves, hunting for a specific one.

Lefiya and Tione watched as Tiona doubled back more than a few times.

"I know it's around here somewhere...Ah, there you are!"

Tiona's voice turned giddy as she reached high above her head to pull a book off the top shelf.

Surprisingly thick, the volume's cover showed a great deal of wear and tear built up over many years.

Tiona flipped through random pages until she found what she was looking for. "Yep!" she exclaimed with glee and held it out. Lefiya, more confused than ever, took the book from her.

The Amazonian twins looked over her left and right shoulders while the elf read the page.

"Isn't this...a tale of heroes?"

The book was open to a picture of a hero and a woman with long hair standing close at his side.

The black-and-white picture depicted her in an angelic robe.

The name written beneath her was...

"...The fairy Aria."

Together with the fairy, the hero joined forces with a high elf, dwarves, animal people, prums, Amazons...a large group of brave warriors in order to slay a monster.

"She's a little different each time, but Aria shows up in a lot of stories."

"I almost forgot. Back when we were little, you always had your nose buried in books about myths and legends, didn't you..."

"Sure did, hee-hee!"

Lefiya ignored the conversation occurring overhead and focused entirely on the illustration.

...Did this woman...resemble Aiz?

No, this black-and-white picture didn't provide enough details to be sure.

The story itself was based on events that took place in the Ancient Times...a story that unfolded over one thousand years ago.

Fairies...

Children favored by the gods. They were practically deities themselves. While not completely immortal, their lives could span many centuries.

Like elves, they shared an affinity with magic. However, the fairies exceeded elves as magic users, possessing superior magic and the ability to perform miracles.

—*Aiz's "wind"?*

Impossible. Lefiya smiled to herself as she discarded her conclusion.

Anyone could immediately recognize a fairy for what they were, the same way they could identify a deity. Aiz was certainly aloof and had a mysterious air about her, but she lacked the divine presence.

Fairies shared another similarity with deities in that they couldn't bear children. Lefiya dismissed all her silly theories right away.

She had to admit that Aiz's elegant beauty was on par with deities—*But that is simply her hidden potential!* Lefiya's heart declared for the person she adored.

She smiled with a bit of disappointment, realizing it was just a case of mistaken identity.

Lefiya slowly closed the book.

The title engraved on its cover read *Dungeon Oratoria*.

© Kiyotaka Haimura

Catching the White Rabbit

Гэта казка іншага сям°і.

Апынуўшыся белых трусоў

On the morning three days after the events on the twenty-fourth floor…

Aiz walked down Northwest Main Street.

The street was lined with a vast array of shops that adventurers frequented, including an accessory shop constructed from bricks, a small stone fortress that was actually an item shop, a particularly powerful familia's weapon shop—a red billboard marking its location—and many others. Aiz joined her fellow adventurers flowing past the series of buildings that naturally blended together.

Brushing shoulders with humans and demi-humans alike, Aiz reflected on the past few days.

The red-haired woman—Levis.

A human-monster hybrid, creature, enhanced species…She looked into all these terms after the battle and still had difficulty believing what she saw. Aiz had stumbled onto an Irregular that humanity—or even the gods—had yet to identify.

"Destroying Orario."

The city around her appeared peaceful on the surface, but learning what this mysterious enemy intended to do cast a dark, ominous shadow over it.

What's happening? What's going to happen? She wanted to know everything.

Her mind was filled with questions about Levis as well as the things Aiz and her allies had discussed.

That person in the black robe might be looking for answers as well…

Apparently, the one who had given her the quest in the first place, Black Robe, visited Lulune after they all returned.

Receiving a full report on the incident from her and remaining silent for several moments, the mysterious figure gave Lulune two keys before disappearing once again.

Aiz clearly remembered Lulune's confused face when the girl arrived to give her one of the two keys in person. "I'm not sure, but I think they open gnome storage units." With that, the two girls had traveled to the Eastern Ward to test Lulune's theory. As it turned out, the numbers on the keys had matched boxes among the many different containers within the safety vault.

Numbers 687 and 688. The two girls had inserted their keys and opened the boxes to find…the vaults stuffed full of piles of red, blue, green, and purple jewels; gold and silver rings; decorative unicorn horns; as well as several grimoires ready for use. Aiz and Lulune had stared numbly at the sparkling treasure inside.

They could only guess at the contents' value. It was mind-boggling. Aiz had decided to contribute all of it to her familia's preparation for the next expedition, as their funds were starting to run low. The largest amount of money Aiz had ever possessed until now had been obtained when she sold the Udaeus's Black Sword drop item to pay for a broken rapier's cost. The thought of having so many valuable items at once frightened her.

A new question bubbled to the surface of her mind. Just who was this shadowy robed person who could prepare this many rare items as a quest reward?

At the very least, she didn't think this person was an enemy.

The next expedition is set…

After she, Bete, and Lefiya had explained to their superiors everything that happened on the twenty-fourth floor, Aiz had stayed behind to recount everything that Levis told her.

She finished her statement by expressing her desire to go to the fifty-ninth floor.

Finn had considered the proposal for several moments before breaking the silence with "All right, it's settled" and agreed to go. *Loki Familia* officially began preparations for the next expedition.

She had no hope of reaching that floor on her own. Thoughts of new discoveries waiting for her filled her mind as Aiz quietly bided her time until their departure.

"...Such nice weather."

Returning to the present, she whispered to herself as she looked up at the clear blue sky above.

She said nothing else even as she turned from the bright sun shining in her eyes. Making her way through the main street at a brisk pace, Aiz finally arrived at her destination: Guild Headquarters.

She came to a stop halfway through the front garden and glanced down at the parcel she held carefully in her arms: a vambrace.

The one she had picked up on the tenth floor, a piece of armor that belonged to the white rabbit, Bell Cranell. Aiz came here today to return it to the boy's Guild adviser.

She nodded to herself as she summoned up her courage while adventurers around her recognized her and gawked as she walked by.

The top-class adventurer's spirit was alight—determined to return the vambrace and apologize once and for all.

Aiz's inner child rooted for her, cheering as she took her first step into the Guild lobby.

"...Ms. Wallenstein?"

"Good...morning."

She found who she was looking for right away.

The half-elf receptionist behind the counter—Eina Tulle. Aiz walked directly toward her.

Eina wasn't sure what to make of her unexpected visitor at first, but Aiz explained the events surrounding the vambrace in her arms.

"Okay, I understand," Eina answered with a smile.

"I will talk to Bell...Bell Cranell and give him the vambrace myself. Rest assured, I will pass on all the information at that time."

Aiz couldn't help but feel a bit nervous as she tried to find the words to tell Eina, who smiled warmly back at her, what she wanted to do.

"I, um…"

"?"

"…*I* want to be the one to give it to him."

Aiz knew she was making this more complicated than necessary as she spoke.

The boy was an adventurer. Surely he wanted the vambrace back as soon as possible, and her actions would delay the process. But even so, as selfish as it was, Aiz wanted to be the one to return it to him.

Then she could apologize for all the mental and physical anguish he'd gone through because of her.

This time…she wouldn't let him run.

Aiz maintained contact with Eina's emerald eyes while expressing her wishes. Despite mumbling and pausing more than a few times, the half-elf donned a more serious expression and nodded.

"Understood. I would like to offer my assistance."

"?"

"I will create a situation that he will not, cannot, escape from. You will have a chance to speak with him face-to-face." She spoke like a parent, or perhaps a protective older sister, as she proposed her plan. "The nerve of him!" Her voice grew louder as though she were scolding the boy at the same time.

Aiz smiled gently without realizing. The two young women then began to discuss the specifics of their plan like two hunters trying to lure a rabbit from its den with a carrot.

Their discussion took place at the reception counter. Many adventurers came and went, each hoping to acquire information about delving into the Dungeon, only to witness a conversation between a beautiful half-elf and a blond, golden-eyed knight.

Their plan began to take shape. Eina would call Bell into the consultation box before *Loki Familia*'s expedition, and Aiz would corner him once he was inside. They were discussing the specifics for the timing when...

Suddenly—Eina happened to catch a glimpse of someone walking straight toward her and reacted with shock.

Tilting her head in confusion, Aiz followed her gaze and turned around.

—*Huh?*

Hair as white as virgin snow framed rubellite eyes.

He must not have planned to enter the Dungeon today because the boy wasn't wearing any armor over his street clothes.

Aiz was startled at seeing the boy—just a boy—when her shoulders turned to face the new arrival.

...It's...him.

The three were so stunned staring at one another, they forgot to speak. They stood like statues.

" "
...
" "
...
" "
...

The adviser trembled in the face of this aboveground Irregular.

Aiz wasn't prepared, and her mind went blank when their gazes connected.

The boy stiffly turned away.

"Huh?"

Aiz made a tiny surprised gasp just as the white rabbit took off at full speed.

"B-Bell! Wait!"

The boy didn't heed his adviser's words as he tore through the lobby.

*Not again...*Aiz slumped as dismay hit her like a ton of bricks, but the adviser wasn't about to give up.

"After him, Ms. Wallenstein!!"

Eina yelled that they couldn't let him escape, and Aiz came to.

That's right. The blond girl tightened her grip on the item in her hands.

She clearly saw him the moment the white rabbit dashed out the Guild exit.

I—I won't let him!

Aiz raced after him.

She held nothing back.

Passing through the lobby in the blink of an eye, she was out the door and directly behind the white rabbit.

Riding the wind at full speed, she passed him.

"—Gahh!"

She came to an abrupt halt in the boy's path. He couldn't stop in time and plowed right into her.

Arms open, she caught him with ease.

Finally, they were face-to-face.

The boy stood in front of Aiz, appearing to be on the verge of a nervous breakdown.

Eina arrived and explained the situation, but that did little to alleviate the boy's stress. Leaving the two of them to talk it out, the half-elf returned to the Guild lobby. The boy watched her go like a small animal abandoned by its owner, trembling.

The turbulent swishing of his snow-white hair perfectly reflected his state of mind.

"…Um, here."

"!"

Aiz built up her courage and thrust the vambrace forward as she spoke.

The boy took it from her like a defensive reflex. However, he froze the moment he realized what he'd received.

Aiz watched as the boy's face turned bright red. Seeing his reaction made her even more nervous and sparked a flurry of other emotions before—she made her apology.

"I'm sorry."

"Huh...?"

"It was my fault that Minotaur survived and got away, causing you so much trouble and hurt...I've wanted a chance to apologize since then. I'm very sorry."

Aiz was so remorseful that she couldn't maintain eye contact as the atmosphere grew heavier around them.

When she finally looked up, the boy's trembling was nowhere to be seen, and he offered his own mea culpa in a rapid-fire stream.

"N-no, no! It was my fault for going down to the fifth level in the first place! You've done nothing wrong, Ms. Wallenstein! Actually, you're my savior! I'm the one who should be apologizing, never saying sorry and always giving you the runaround...S-SORRY!"

His apology flooded out like a dam had broken. The sudden reversal caught Aiz off guard.

"So, um, well..." The boy flushed even redder as he desperately searched for the right words. At the same time, a strange feeling welled within Aiz. She didn't know what to say, either.

So this is how...he speaks...

Having heard his voice only a few times up until that moment, it was surprising how much he spoke.

She envisioned him being a lot quieter, more reserved. Struggling to convey his thoughts but then talking anyway might have been a little childish, but it was pleasant.

Aiz couldn't help but feel that a character from the stories she'd read as a child had leaped from the page to stand in front of her now. With that voice, the boy expressed himself in so many ways she had never known he could.

Warmth spread from her heart, and Aiz lost herself for a moment as she basked in it.

The boy was still speaking when he suddenly bowed deeply.

"For all the times you rescued me...THANK YOU SO MUCH!!"

His appreciation reached her ears.

The boy kept his head down for several moments before slowly, cautiously standing up.

Aiz could almost hear the misunderstandings clearing. At the very least, she knew the boy wasn't afraid of her and that he had wanted to tell her how he felt as well.

...Do I feel...happy?

Her eyes opened wider, and her face relaxed.

Now that the confusion had been cleared, comforting happiness bubbled within her as a small smile appeared on her lips.

For whatever reason, the boy focused on her smile and turned an even deeper crimson.

"..."

"..."

What needed to be done was done, and everything had been said. The conversation was over.

Standing an arm's length from each other, Aiz lingered in front of the boy. Only time quietly moved beneath the clear blue sky.

He just stood there as well, jerking back into the moment only when he realized where he was. The two made eye contact for a moment before the boy looked away with a start.

Aiz wanted to keep talking, to learn more about him and hear his voice again. However, she knew her tendency to use as few words as possible was a problem. The two of them wouldn't be able to talk without a common topic. Aiz couldn't chat like Tiona or her other friends.

That's it! She happened upon an idea.

"Are you working hard...in the Dungeon?"

"Y-yes!!"

The boy's response drowned out her voice.

Aiz had found a way to bring up something that had been on her mind for some time now.

"You can make it down to the tenth floor now...That's impressive."

Something had felt off the other day when she agreed to look for him and searched the Dungeon. It piqued her interest.

Aiz wanted to know how a rookie adventurer had grown to the point he could hold his ground on the tenth floor in such a short amount of time.

"No, not at all! I've only gotten that far because I have help! I-I still have a long way to go!! I'm nowhere near my goal yet...!"

Aiz watched the boy desperately try to hide his nervousness with another verbal deluge.

What if this boy has a secret that helps him grow?

As I am now...

Visions of the red-haired woman—her battle with Levis—replayed in the back of her mind.

She thought about the journey to the yet unexplored fifty-ninth floor.

There was no way to know what awaited her, only that she would face a slew of new challenges. It wasn't a hunch but a guarantee.

Most likely, Aiz would have to draw her friends and familia into fierce, steadily escalating battles. She would need to be stronger than ever.

The only thing she didn't want was regret.

She wanted to lose nothing.

And to reach even higher.

Even after achieving Level Six, her experiences on the twenty-fourth floor only reinforced those wishes.

"I mean, when I fight monsters in the Dungeon, I'm just winging it like a total amateur. I don't know how many times I did something stupid and a monster almost got me. I know I have to get stronger, but I'm still so weak and I feel like I'm not getting any better at all. Well, um...?"

That's why she wanted to know—

The secret to his growth.

His potential.

The true strength of this boy who has improved drastically in almost no time at all.

Aiz's train of thought ran wild as she watched the blushing adventurer struggle to stop his blabbering.

She worried, and worried, and worried some more, thoroughly weighing various things on a scale, then reexamining her own feelings.

Eventually, timidly, Aiz decided to make the boy an offer.

"Shall I…teach you how?"

"…Huh?"

"—*How to fight.*"

And so…

Aiz became the boy's teacher.

Tiona · Hyrute

BELONGS TO:	*Loki Familia*		
RACE:	Amazon	JOB:	adventurer
DUNGEON RANGE:	fifty-eighth floor	WEAPON:	Urga
CURRENT WORTH:	-89,000,000 valis		

Status   Lv.5

STRENGTH:	A 889	DEFENSE:	A 867
DEXTERITY:	B 778	AGILITY:	A 801
MAGIC:	I 0	PUMMEL:	G
DRIVE:	G	IMMUNITY:	H
FRACTURE:	I		

MAGIC:	None	
SKILLS:	Berserker	• Strength increases after taking damage
SKILLS:	Intense Heat	• Increases all abilities when near death

EQUIPMENT: Urga

- Oversize double-bladed sword. Superior-grade weapon.
- Forged by *Goibniu Familia* for 120,000,000 valis
- Created using the highest quality adamantite mined from the Deep Levels of the Dungeon. Top class in terms of strength, durability, and weight.
- Order made for Tiona. Second version.

TIONA HYRUTE

Afterword

This book, spin-off number three, was written concurrently with book six of the main story and released within two months of it.

Since the story stayed completely aboveground in book six, this story was written primarily in the Dungeon. Every day, I live in fear of someone pointing out that I may or may not have lost track of which series is the main and which is the spin-off.

In the fantasy genre, I have the same affinity for elves as I do for dwarves. I'm naturally drawn to the elegant race of men and women with long, pointed ears. Out of the five races of demi-humans in my writing, I feel that elves are the most developed and explored race (as of right now at least). Since elves tend to stand out on their own in terms of personality, they're very easy to use when setting up a story. I must admit that they've become my "security blanket" of sorts. *When in doubt, an elf will sort it out!* Or something like that.

The elves as a race in the series have been shaped by my own personal bias as well as by how I want them to be seen.

Immense pride in themselves and one another, maintaining cleanliness to a fault, letting only those they trust touch their skin, living extraordinarily long life spans, and possessing hidden magic potential...etc., etc. I feel that I've added my own details about elves not expressed in other fantasy stories. I also believe that because they desire to be more beautiful in mind and body than those around them, they also experience more pain and suffering than other races when they become "hurt." In this story of a heroine, a flower blooming far out of reach, it was fitting to have her less-experienced counterpart be an elf. Perhaps it was inevitable.

And in this third installment of the spin-off, a new elf has appeared.

While I must apologize to the Amazonian twins for their reduced role on her behalf, the story came together very well because of her involvement.

And now I need to express my gratitude.

This book was also released with a limited-edition version thanks to my editors Mr. Kotaki, Mr. Takahashi, and the cooperation of many talented people. Illustrations for both versions were done by Mr. Kiyotaka Haimura. Each amazing piece of artwork took my breath away the first time I saw it and I did everything in my power to get the special edition illustrations included in both releases. I would also like to thank Mr. Takashi Yagi of Gan Gan Joker (Square Enix Division) for his work in transforming the Gaiden into a series of comic illustrations. They're all very well done. Lastly, I would like to include a thank-you from the bottom of my heart to all the people who read this book.

Please look forward to the next installment. I'll take my leave now.

Fujino Omori